TELANTIS REBORN

The Last Shadow Epic, Book Nine

by

AJ Cooper

GALIOPE

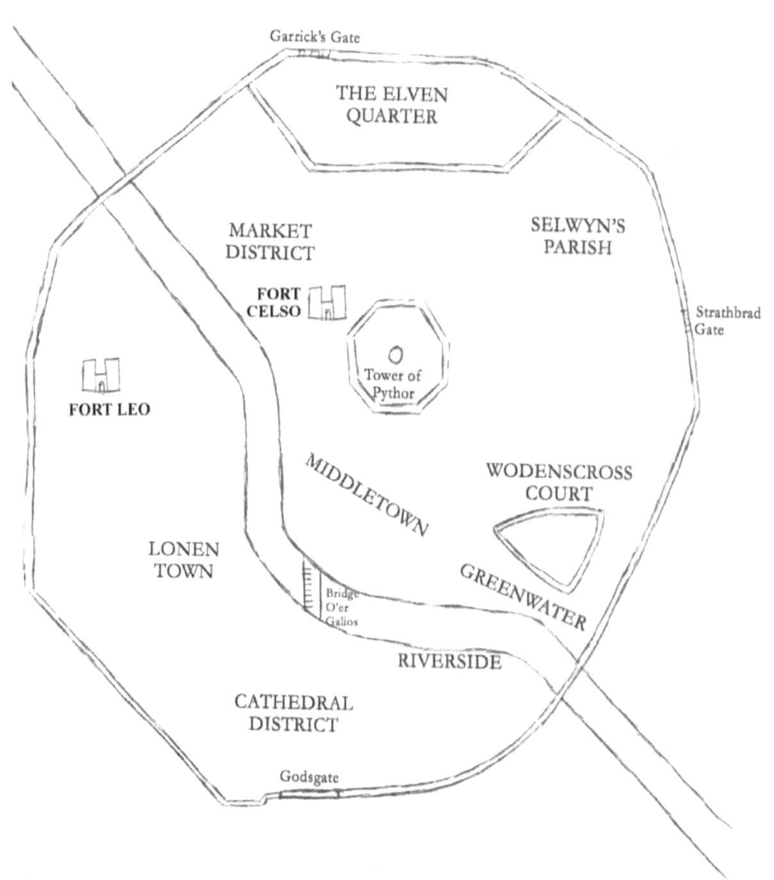

Prologue:
They Ride With Stars

What would become the Dark Land, three-thousand years ago...

"My name is Estendibal. That means 'Star-Child,' " said Star-Child to the elven man she wished to be her lover.

"My name is Gidioms kon Estot," said the man, whose fair hair was red in the waning sunlight. "That means, 'They Ride with Stars.' "

Was that really his name? Star-Child didn't much care. She would call him Gidioms kon Estot if that was what he liked. And Star-Child wished to please him, because she wished to make him her lover.

The sun was setting in view of the land of Baradon. The central tower, colored alabaster, was far away, but its six lesser towers surrounded it along the Narrow Sea, and one was in view of Star-Child and Gidioms kon Estot.

Star-Child did not know which tower it was, in view, but it was near a market square that would become a night market tonight. And at the night market, where wine and all manner of trinkets would be sold, there would be an opportunity for Star-Child to make Gidioms kon Estot her lover. For at the night market, the trinkets sold from all over Varda were hardly the main draw. It was the people — that was why elves went to night markets, and stayed up from dusk until dawn. Some did not even bring coin or silver to buy merchandise, but milled about and talked.

Star-Child could mill about and talk, and she would make Gidioms kon Estot her lover.

"My name is Estendibal. That means 'Star-Child.' I am a rich man's daughter, but I don't have everything I want."

In the distance, her six servants were waiting beside her red palanquin. She rather didn't like the faces they were making. It was hot, but they shouldn't look like they were suffering. They shouldn't be frowning. Didn't they know all they should care about in their lives was making her happy?

"What do you mean, Star-Child?" said Gidioms kon Estot.

"I have a ruby necklace," Star-Child said, "but what I want is a star-gem you can find in the sky. My father says he will build me a ladder so high I can cut a star-gem from the night sky, but I think he is just trying to pamper me."

"It's not pampering you," said Gidioms kon Estot. "If it's what you want, it's what you deserve."

That's what Star-Child thought. She knew it was true.

She crossed her arms bitterly.

"Soon I will not be called Gidioms kon Estot," he said. "I will be called Estenpalori, 'Star-Finder.' "

"You had better be," Star-Child said and whined quietly.

The sun was setting over the land of Baradon's flat plain, and Star-Child was beside herself. Her servants were standing by the palanquin, and they did not know instinctively, by her idle posture, that she wished to get in. She swallowed her fury, and she cleared her throat, loudly… so loudly, then, that the servants stirred, and grabbed the palanquin by the posts, and began to ferry it over to her.

She would tell her father to dock their pay, for the delay.

Night was coming, and merchants were arriving. Would Gidioms kon Estot be called Estenpalori? He had better.

If Star-Child could not have a star-gem on her necklace, she did not know what she would do. Perhaps, she'd grab a whip, and act like the servants, now bearing the palanquin, were the reason why she couldn't have a star-gem necklace.

She hopped into the palanquin with Gidioms kon Estot as darkness settled in, and the night market was in full swing.

~

What did Star-Child want from the night market? She wanted everything.

But Gidioms kon Estot was asking about a ladder. He wanted to buy a ladder tall enough for himself to cut a star-gem from the sky, and fix it to Star-Child's necklace.

He asked about, amid a crowd that was swarming.

Star-Child knew the gods had promised elves like her everything, that they had promised them Varda itself, and that people like her would rule forever. Star-Child knew that the elves could do nothing, think nothing and say nothing, to make the gods not love them best.

Humans were little better than elves' servants, and they would stay that way, she thought, as she saw a lowly human man walking about amid the crowds.

Gidioms kon Estot had found a ladder seller, but the ladders he sold were short, made for reaching high bookshelves.

Star-Child crossed her arms and pouted quietly.

As Gidioms kon Estot looked about, he said in a frustrated voice, "I shall find you a ladder so great, Star-Child, or else my name shall be Iromeres Ié. That means 'He disappoints me.' "

Star-Child harumphed as Gidioms kon Estot walked away through the vendors and stalls, and she lingered a few steps behind.

At one stall there were gold and silver rings, and she bought two, and placed them on her fingers.

At another stall there were bells, and she bought three, and fixed them to her toes.

They had scoured the night market, then, when they reached another ladder seller, and these were tall, tall enough to reach a high wall, but not the stars.

Oh, whatever would Star-Child do? Why were things always so

difficult for her?

But Gidioms kon Estot looked about, and there was a mischievous gleam in her eye. "My lady Star-Child," he said, "I have an idea, and I know just how you will cut the star-gem from the sky."

The stars were now out, amid the black expanse, ripe for the plucking. The moon, a waning crescent, she could cut from the sky later.

"But first I shall change my name to Té Guni. That means 'He is Clever.' And I shall have a kiss on my lips."

Oh, what would she not do for a star-gem about her neck? She kissed the elf who now called himself Té Guni, and watched as he purchased one, then two, then three ladders.

With the aid of Star-Child and her servants, they had pulled and pushed the ladders out into the grassland beyond the night market.

Beyond, there was a fire burning in the tower. The tower watchman was home.

Star-Child harumphed and complained quietly as the man who now called himself Té Guni set up a ladder, then, climbing to the top, set a ladder on top of it. Star-Child's servants handed him the third ladder, and he fixed it, and it was now higher than the tower.

But Star-Child wouldn't congratulate him, or be happy, unless Té Guni's three ladders were high enough for her to pluck a star-gem from the sky.

Té Guni descended.

"No longer am I called Té Guni," he said. "Now you will call me Beveres Kon Hot Aion. That means 'She Kisses Him with Love.' "

Star-Child would not call Té Guni that unless she had a star-gem about her neck, tonight. As Té Guni stood by, she began to ascend the ladder's rungs, one after the other, until she was sweating and trembling.

She feared the sight of Té Guni like a child's toy, the night market a distant dot of light. Her heart trembled as she took the last steps.

She reached for the star-gems in the sky, but they were as out of reach as they had been on the ground.

"I will not call you Beveres Kon Hot Aion," said Star-Child. "I will call you Malios Thó Kon Harairtavi. That means 'She Curses You with Hate.'"

She realized she no longer wished him to be her lover.

She was feeling dizzy, and the contraption of ladders was leaning this way and that, being so high.

But she could see something in the distance. A figure was riding in on a cock-horse.

When she saw the sackcloth robe, she knew it was the soothsayer Varisti. He claimed to be a messenger from the gods. He was riding toward the night market.

~

"Varisti is coming! Varisti is coming!" Star-Child howled.

She could not wait for his message, about how elves such as she were owed everything, yea, the world, yea Varda.

The crowds were dispersing as Varisti arrived, dressed in a sackcloth robe. At once he began to speak.

"Gathered elves of Baradon," Varisti said.

He was a soothsayer, truly, and the King of the Elves had acknowledged that he was an emissary of the gods.

"A race of humans has arrived from the north beyond north," Varisti said, "garbed in loin cloths, their bodies colored with lightning marks. A message from the gods — surrender your kingdoms to them, and let them rule. Honor them, for the gods love them best. They are the Telantines."

Star-Child wailed with wordless fury. At last words came pouring out. "Kill Varisti! Kill Varisti, and take his inheritance."

The elves in the square of Baradon reached for their swords and knives.

Chapter One:
The Dark Land

Beyond ash and dark black rock, Reev stepped through the mountain pass, and Wrinn was a step behind. They had been led by their friend Arn Steelforge to the mountain pass into *Naron Da*, and Arn Steelforge was far behind them.

Naron Da, the Dark Land, was where prophecies claimed Reev would tread Seymus under his feet, but the prophecies had not told him how.

How would he do it? He did not know. The prophecies said he would crush the Dark One underfoot when he got there.

And he saw he had arrived as the rock walls fell away behind him, baring a valley of dark black rock.

The valley stretched into the horizon before them, before disappearing into the distance.

"We're here," Reev said. "We've made it."

Reev saw to his right, a narrow path of land that abutted the raging sea — a sea of towering waves and storms. A pass through the sea, narrow... a way in they could have traveled — and standing in the pass, preventing all entry, an army of countless number, richly arrayed.

Reev could spy, from so high a perch, that they were carrying the green sun-and-tree standards of the elves.

An army of elves was blocking the pass, forbidding the Dark One from receiving reinforcements.

Reev was tired, and he thought he would catch his breath.

But one thing he was certain of, an unshakeable truth.

"Wrinn," he said, "you have been *adari*, my helper. But now I am in the Dark Land. Your task is done. Go be with your people, and live in joy and peace all your days."

Wrinn turned to Reev, eyes glistening with tears. He was sorrowful to leave. "I love you, Reev," he said.

"I love you, Wrinn," Reev said.

But he sensed that Wrinn knew what he knew, that his task was over, and he — an elf, once a slave — would now join his people forever.

"Goodbye," Reev said, and met Wrinn in an embrace.

Tearfully, Wrinn departed, climbing down rocky ridges, amid ash, and a sky that, though dark and blackish, did not seem to have the contours of clouds.

~

Reev then was alone. He stood amid the dark ground, the black ridges and black rocky outcrops — black boulders strewn on dark earth. And he thought he heard a constant sound of distant thunder which never quite ceased, and he saw, having crossed the paths through the mountains, that his body was soiled with black ash.

He staggered then, and then he ran, through the sweltering air, and began to cough as he kicked up ash.

He stopped his descent, wondering what his plans were.

He was totally alone.

Or so he thought.

A figure was standing under the dark sky, clothed in a fine gold raiment. Her hair was a burnt gold, and her green eyes sparkled. She was an elf. She was the Lady of Danyen.

Reev was sure it was just a vision, that if he touched her body her hand would pass through her. Yet he approached her just the same, and he saw she was standing on ash-laden ground, beside a rocky cliff.

Beside her was what appeared to be a glowing sphere of light, peeking out of the dirt.

Reev was just inches from her when she stooped down and picked up the glowing sphere.

It was about the size of a small rock.

"Here," said the Lady of Danyen. "Eat this star."

Reev took the star in his hands and ate it. He felt a fire go down his stomach, and then fill his entire body with warmth.

Then, he felt cold.

"I must crush the Dark One underfoot," Reev said to the Lady of Danyen. "How?"

"You are attired like a warrior of Telantis," said the Lady of Danyen. "You must stride forth as one. You must act in the moment. You must charge into the fray. Charge — into the night — and make war on the Dark One and his minions. How you defeat the Dark One and the serpent's children is up to you. You must find a way. For all rests on this…"

He had eaten the star. He peered into the horizon.

When he looked back, the Lady of Danyen was gone.

And he climbed down the rocky ridge, toward the valley. It seemed he was alone, but Reev knew he was not alone.

~

The ash-strewn country continued, and Reev in his loin cloth, with the Telantine necklace about his neck, was standing unprotected from a cloud-covered yet oppressive sun.

He was standing unprotected when his necklace began to flash.

He took from his pouch his spyglass and peered far into the horizon. The ash-covered ground was into the interminable distance, but far away the rocky ridges and cliffs gave way to deep canyons and rifts.

And then there was a hiss and a growl.

Reev swiped his spyglass back into his pouch, and saw amid the ashen waste an anguiped with pointy green ears and yellow eyes, behind him a band of rokahn and kobolds. They had noticed him, and they were gaining on him.

Reev leapt over the cliffs, over the rocks and ridges. He sprinted, and he sprinted with all he had in him.

A rokahn blew a horn. Before long, the rokahn mounted on black wolves would be following him, and then it would all be over for him.

He was sprinting, looking back, and he could see the rokahn getting closer. They were crude and dull witted, but they were stronger sprinters than humans.

Reev cried out and invoked the gods. He was growing closer to the raging sea that surrounded the Dark Land. He was getting close to a tall tower that dominated the horizon.

He had reached the walls of the tower. He looked back, and the rokahn chasing him were so close they had pitched back their swords and axes, to strike.

But a white light blinded him, the form of something like a rope or a chain, and Reev was drawn upward as if by a sieve, speeding along the tall tower's sides, and at last the tower's summit.

He was at the top of the tower. The tower, he saw, had no rooms or interiors, but was little more than a flat-topped obelisk.

He was not alone.

He was standing now on a high lookout, an inestimably large horizon.

Beside him were men he knew. They were Spymaster Marius, with his tawny hair and blue eyes, now wearing a red and black vest — and Agent Numerio, with hair a dark black and eyes a bright blue.

Reev had met them before, in a different part of Varda. During his sojourn in the Imperial Palace, he had uncovered a clandestine network of spies called the Oculus, one who claimed to have been in operation since before the Empire's founding.

"Greetings, Sage," said Marius. "It is good to see you again."

He had so many questions. There was so much he did not understand, that he had not uncovered.

"Agent Secunda is still recovering from the corrupted bracelet," Spymaster Marius said. "She's in detoxification."

The third agent of the Oculus Reev had met, Agent Secunda, had crossed paths with him thousands of miles south of here, amid the ruins of a cursed city called Qadirra. She had taken a magic bracelet from the arms of a statue, and donned it, and become possessed by its dark power.

"And what was that rope?" said Reev. "The white silken strand, that pulled me up here?"

"After Heaven's Spear was launched, and the anguipeds scattered," said Spymaster Marius, "the spirits of Telantis wage war. You will find the spirits of your kindred here, waging war, the final conquest promised to them… the anguipeds' final defeat, and their final victory."

"It was some sort of rope," Reev said.

"The Dark Tower is claimed by the Dark One. Six towers surround it, forming a hexagon around the Dark Land. Some have been purified, others corrupted. Some have yet to be conquered by the Telantine spirits, but here — a Telantine spirit drew you to safety."

"And what do we do now?" Reev said.

"We were waiting for you," said Agent Marius. "We believed you would enter through that pass, for it was overlooked, and the others are crawling with rokahn and anguipeds."

"What do we do now?" Reev repeated.

"We wage war," said Agent Marius. "But we are outnumbered. We must be careful. We must be cautious."

So far away, on the roof of the world, Reev felt with his spyglass he could see all. But was he really safe?

They had spoken of a Dark Tower. The anguipeds were on the move. The Dark One was watching.

He could sense the Dark One, watching him now.

12

~

The Dark One sensed his enemy enter the land.

He could sense something else… his Hand, drawing near.

A Hand of his own, to wield the Dark One's power, and the Sage's defeat would be complete.

He sent a stirring in the heart of the Dark One's Hand. He called his favored near.

Chapter Two:
Federati

Barcho, Marshal of the Imperial Guard, watched amid the stinging sands of the Desert of Sinn, the Dragon Emperor of Cathay approach Verrus and his entourage, garbed in a red silk robe and a black headdress, before falling before him in an obsequious kowtow.

The Dragon Emperor now acknowledged Verrus as Cathay's ultimate sovereign, and so the Empire's conquest of Varda was complete.

Behind him, the eunuchs of the Dragon Emperor's party had a displeased look.

But Barcho knew that the conquest of Cathay and its possessions was not something Emperor Verrus was focused on. Indeed, completing the Empire's conquests was something Verrus had done at the coaxing of an Imperial Council he hated. His quest, his life's goal, was the extinction of the Telantines from Varda, that they wholly disappear. And so he had gone through familial registries to uncover the identity of every Telantine who lived, that at Verrus's order, they be killed.

Yet seeing the Dragon Emperor kowtow to Verrus, Barcho could not help but feel that Verrus had completed what the Empire had as its goal, the conquest of Varda in its entirety. And now, if any wished to give safe haven to the Telantines during their impending extinction, there were none who could.

There was a wind stirring through the desert, and beyond them was a port, and the shore of the Gemstone Sea.

There was a wind stirring, and junks floating in the harbor that had borne the Dragon Emperor to this place. Having met Verrus in a kowtow and acknowledged his sovereignty, he and his eunuchs turned, to board those junks.

Verrus's warships, too large for the port, lingered in the distance, having dropped anchor. Smaller boats lingered at he docks.

Barcho knew Verrus well. Verrus seemed unhappy.

"I have now completed the conquest of Varda," said Verrus, "and yet… my goals have not been fulfilled."

But overhearing him, the Dragon Emperor turned.

"You have not conquered all of Varda," said the Dragon Emperor in stilted Imperial. "A land remains out of your grip. I lost my wife to *Naron Da*.

"The Dark Land and its Dark City, its dark promises, she loved more than me."

"There is a land out of our control?" Barcho said.

"Where fire erupted, and consumed a city," said the Dragon Emperor, "and destroyed a land… south of the crater is *Naron Da*."

"Fire? A city? A land?" Verrus said, and began to question.

And Barcho sensed nervousness in the one to whom he had dedicated his life, and he saw the traces of cold sweat appear on his arms and neck.

"You haven't heard?" said the Dragon Emperor. "A spear of fire exploded in Ash-Land. Its capital city was turned to a crater. There were no survivors, but in the land, some fled to *Naron Da*, and there they have received safe haven."

"Ash-Land," Verrus said, "destroyed."

And Barcho recalled — Ash-Land, what Verrus's mother, now dead, had called she and Verrus's ancestral home.

"I must investigate this," Verrus said.

The Dragon Emperor gave him a suspicious look, then turned and boarded one of the junks.

"I must investigate this," Verrus said — and then he cried out, as of one haunted by a ghost, "Oh, mother… I'll do it for you."

Verrus had committed matricide, his mother dead by assassins sent from him. Yet the Imperial Council was so weak they could not unseat him, or oppose him in any way.

A matricide, hated by the people… but the Dragon Emperor had met him in a kowtow.

~

They took a ship back to Covered Camp, a military installation on the periphery of the Desert of Sinn, south of the Heavenly Mountains. It was here the Empire had managed its far eastern frontier, a frontier that had now vanished. Cathay and its bejeweled cities that dotted the Sea of Stars were now the Empire's possessions.

And as soon as they reached Covered Camp, Verrus fell apart. Whether he ate, or talked with legates or legionaries, all he spoke of was Ash-Land and the fire that had consumed it.

"I must go there," he said, "I must see…"

And Barcho knew Verrus well, now… Verrus would not rest when he had something in his head. He was crafty and deceitful, and his supreme craftiness and supreme deceit were why he was emperor, but he had a flaw — when he had something in his head, he could not let it go.

"I don't think it's something you should bother with," said the legate of the Ninth Megaran Legion, as they dined with legionaries under the cool of a canvas tent.

"Don't tell me what to do," Verrus said. "Ash-Land… my people…"

And then he wailed, as of one possessed by a ghost again, "My mother!"

The legate's eyes said, "You killed your mother, you fool."

But Verrus did not seem to understand the language of eyes. "I will have a legion come with me to defend Ash-Land. We will destroy and kill whoever sent the fiery arrow, whoever was responsible for such death, such devastation…"

"A legion is far too large for an investigation," the legate said. "An expeditionary force must be sent, in such a circumstance."

"The best of the best," said Verrus.

"Veteran troops," the legate said.

"No," Verrus answered, "the federati."

Barcho looked about and it seemed the camp grew quiet, at the utterance of the name.

The federati were the most feared Imperial troops, a group of hardened killers that had defeated armies much more numerous than themselves. Originally of barbarian origin, now the federati were composed of mostly Imperials who passed a series of stringent physical and mental tests, not least tests that challenged their willingness to carry out morally questionable orders.

"The federati are only appointed to the most urgent tasks," the legate said.

"Urgent tasks," Verrus said. "Is the devastation of my kind not urgent?"

The legate's eyes spoke again, saying "No."

But Verrus had made up his mind, and that day he ordered a band of a hundred federati to accompany he and Barcho to the devastated Ash-Land.

Chapter Three: Invitation Extended

You are invited to the wedding of Fortunato of Ríva and Ambrass Saida

On the 26th of Candlebright, at the parish church of St. Sigmund's in Galiope

Casual attire will be welcomed, with a feast and reception to follow at the Dragonpaw Inn

Ambrass looked at the wedding invitation she had copied with woodblock prints, and didn't think she'd change a thing.

In a guest room of the Dragonpaw Inn that had been turned into her wedding workroom, Glenda looked over her shoulder and mewed her approval.

"Good work, Ambrass," Glenda said. "I can't wait to send them out."

Ambrass had thought she and Fortunato would be wed at a minor chapel, but then there had been an outcry throughout the city, that Ambrass and the Gallians' hero Fortunato of Ríva would not be accorded great honor.

St. Sigmund's it was, then.

She would drop the invitations off at the doorstep of every would-be wedding guest.

Some minor quibbles remained. Who would be best man? Who would be maid of honor? Who would be ringbearer, and who would cast the flowers before Ambrass when she walked down the aisle?

It was a time of excitement, a time of excitement bursting at the seams, the start of a life together — Fortunato and Ambrass, husband and wife, until death did them part.

The wedding would take place shortly after Yule, before the New Year? And where would they live, and what would they do after the wedding?

In Galiope, they would abide.

~

Fortunato was back in Galiope after his long journey, back at his favorite tavern, the Green Girdle. Ambrass's cousin Julian was with him, and both had tall ales. As they clinked them together and drank heartily, his mind was caught up in thoughts of the wedding, between Yule and New Year's, as the year 1156 turned to 1157.

"Julian," he said, "I'd like you to be best man."

Fortunato had realized he had few close friends in Galiope. After Spyke had betrayed them and died, after Nocturne had passed on, the choice of who would serve what role in the wedding was a dilemma.

But truly, all he wanted was now here, he and Ambrass, together — until death did them part.

"I'm honored," Julian said. "And I accept, of course. Ambrass will be so happy to see me standing there, with you."

The wedding date had been set. The invitations would be dropped at every doorstep.

"The entire city is happy, in fact," Julian said. "I can overhear them — it's all they talk about, the wedding of Ambrass and Fortunato."

~

What food would they serve, Ambrass wondered, as she walked down the street with a bundle of invitations? Glenda made a mean mincemeat pie.

And what sort of dress would she ask the tailor to fashion? White — surely — a veil.

The folk of Gallia were looking at her as she passed them by on the street, excitedly. She was like Father Yule, passing over houses with gifts.

All that mattered, she knew, was the wedding date approaching, the marriage of she and her love.

Fortunato of Ríva and Ambrass Saida would be wed, on the 26th of Candlebright, at the parish church of St. Sigmund's, and she and he, and they who were invited, would rejoice.

~

"Your child," Julian said. "What shall you name him?"

Fortunato looked at him quizzically. "I won't get ahead of myself," said Fortunato. "When a child arrives, he or she will be a blessing."

"My other cousin," Julian said, "not Ambrass, took a palm reading of her hands. She said that Ambrass will have a son with you, Fortunato."

Fortunato struggled to trust methods of divination, whether it be palm reading or the cards of *tabbac*.

But the *tabbac* card had told of he and Ambrass's destiny. Could a palm reading also portend the truth?

"What shall we name him?" Fortunato said. "I'll think."

~

Ambrass dropped an invitation off at the doorstep of Ramona Nax, at Sunstone Manor. In the light of the glittering mansions and homes of Wodenscross Court, she could feel her boundless joy rising, joy she was sure would never end.

Boundless joy, from now on — forever. She and Fortunato,

wed.

On the 26th day of Candlebright, at the parish church of St. Sigmund's, Ambrass Saida and Fortunato of Ríva would be wed.

Invitation extended.

Chapter Four:
The Haunted Forest

Before Balor were dark shadows.

All about Balor were dark shadows.

He was deep in the deep dark wood.

He gripped his wand in his hand, his wand that now seemed too short and impotent.

It seemed too powerless to do battle against the forces Balor fought.

His guides, the three hags, had pushed Balor into the Haunted Forest, and he realized he had been betrayed. They did not care for him or for his good. They wished to meld him into their pawn.

The Haunted Forest — where Balor's ancestors had offered sacrifices to the Dark One.

And now, Balor, was deep in a deep, dark wood.

Much time had passed… a day? A night? A year, or two?

He did not know, but there was the shape of dark pines, and there were dark shadows fleeing from him and circling overhead. There was a long trill of some ghostly siren he could not place, echoing amid the deep darkness, the pine trees Balor looked upon now — boughs, a flashing image, dripping with blood.

Whose blood had he seen? Whose blood had been spilled on that pine bough, which time had cleared away?

He stepped beyond the pine boughs, and as he felt a terrible dark presence, Balor came to a realization.

He would stop accepting the power of the one who called himself the lord of this wood. He would fight against it.

He would start fighting.

There was a flash of something, like a whirring of wind, a blur of greater darkness against the great darkness, touching Balor's forearm.

"I will fight," Balor said, now aloud. "I'm not afraid of you! I will fight!"

He shouted, "I'm not afraid of you! I will fight!"

And clutching his wand in his hand, he cast up a ball of purple vampiric energy to light his path.

It was not a bright light, like lightbearers could create. It could not illuminate much, like a pyromancer or electromancer could conjure. But it was a light in the darkness, and it gave light to Balor's feet.

It hovered above his hands, which to him seemed changed.

He had been a boy when he entered this wood, and it seemed just like yesterday. But his hands were much larger than he remembered, and his fingernails were so long as to resemble claws.

How long had he been in the Haunted Forest, ever since he stepped in?

How long?

Had it been an age?

~

He saw motion as he crossed through the needle-covered ground, and he followed the motion through patches of snow, at first at a walk, and then at a sprint.

He caught sight of something dangling, a deeper darkness amid great darkness.

And then the Giant Spider was upon him.

Its back was marked with a crimson red spot. It pierced Balor to the ground, and pinned him there as its mandible twitched, as it made primordial calculations in its head of how to eat him.

Balor's wand had fallen from his grip.

One its legs pierced at Balor, but Balor pushed it aside with a swipe of his arms. Another pierced at him, and he dove away, to the side. There was a storm of bladed legs, then, before Balor summoned up magic power, wild and uncontrolled without his wand, and emptied his reserves, a purple blast of necromantic energy that burned a hole through the Giant Spider and caused the rest of it to wither and drift to the ground like gossamer.

Balor stood up, but he could no longer see his wand.

His wand was gone — his magical energy had largely been expended. He would have to catch his breath an hour, two hours — a dayless day, another night. But the Giant Spider was dead.

How long had Balor been in the Haunted Forest? He did not know.

But he had resolved not to let it control him anymore. He decided to stop listening to the voice of its master. He would fight… he would fight what ailed this wood, and no longer accept its control.

The Haunted Forest would be his.

~

Balor had left his wand behind. He heard a ghostly sound, trilling in the distance, like a ghost's wail but louder and longer. It was disappearing into the distance, and yet he followed it, through the pine needle-covered ground, past patches of snow that had not melted from this year's winter.

Why had he come to the Haunted Forest? The three hags who had beguiled him had told him a reason.

But a hag's word could not be trusted, least of all the hags that had led him here.

He had lived — where?

Galiope.

His father was — who?

Nocturne.

And his mother had been a poor woman. Her name…

Lucy Cotter.

Balor was half human, half vampire.

He had been taken north to a land of snow and perpetual winter, where in the summer a day lasted months and in the winter there were weeks of night.

Yet it was always so cold. Scarcely ever could Balor manage to catch his breath.

A fire would do nicely, but he followed the sound of the ghostly siren.

He had declared he wanted the Haunted Forest to be his. He supposed he would do as he had declared. He would not leave until he owned every square of territory, and nothing was left for its master.

Who was its master?

~

He had come to a path of wood and iron, what Balor recognized as a track, like what horses pulled against.

But these weren't tracks for carts pulled by horses. They were tracks for carts pulled by something else, something mightier and stronger.

He could hear a distant rumble, and another siren, now almost deafening.

Through the fog and the darkness of the Haunted Forest, there was a bright spot of light, and the bright spot of light was approaching.

When the iron horse came rattling down the tracks, the siren call was deafening. A beacon was shining from its frontmost carriage, and a man was clinging to it, or what appeared to be a man.

His face seemed melted, like it was dripping against his skull. His eyes too seemed to be dripping, more liquid than solid. He wore a pair of overalls stained with blood. His fingers were scarred, and on the tips of his fingers, bones were visible.

He was the conductor, Balor realized, of the haunted iron horse in the Haunted Forest. Balor had said he would conquer the Haunted Forest, and leave nothing within it that did not belong to him.

Would he then flinch, or quiver, or dare to show fear at the conductor of the haunted iron horse? As the iron horse sped by him, he saw one of the carriages had a door hanging open. He grasped the door by the handle and allowed the shutting door to sweep him in.

He was in the carriage, then, a carriage with windows that had been smashed and shattered glass lying on the seats, whose cushions had been removed.

Where was the haunted iron horse taking him?

Wherever it took him, Balor would conquer that, too.

Chapter Five:
The Light's Firstborn

Wrinn was among his people.

He was among the elves.

Elves were about him, elves all around him, and they had come to the pass that led into the Dark Land to do battle, for war.

They were doing it for Reev and the Telantines.

He was pushing through the ranks of the elves. Amid the ranks of warriors were many tents, and there was a great tent in the center of the army, colored blue. That, Wrinn guessed, was where the king slept and ruled, where he gave his orders. And if he were to fully join his people, he supposed he would have to start with a petition of the elvenking.

~

Outside the tent were two figures, standing in the hazy sunlight.

There was a tall figure, and there was a very short one.

The tall figure was one Wrinn had seen before, the elvenking with long brown hair and bright brown eyes, a breastplate of steel and a helmet fixed with a crown, shining silver in the daylight.

The small figure was a child, the most beautiful child Wrinn had ever seen. His dark hair seemed bright in the hazy sunlight. His bright blue eyes were bright indeed. His ears came to the slightest of points. He looked sort of like Fortunato, and sort of like Nenré.

He was Alondir.

And the elvenking seemed to have noticed Wrinn staring at his grandchild with wonder.

"Alondir stuns even the most cold-hearted," the elvenking said. "Not even a rokahn could bear to harm him."

Where was Fortunato? Wrinn thought, the last time he had seen him was in the midst of the desert.

Where was Nenré?

"Where is Nenré?" Wrinn said.

"Alondir's mother," the elvenking said with eyes of sadness, "died of dysentery somewhere in the Smoking Desert. But you can see, before me, her legacy lives on."

Wrinn didn't know what to say, how to comfort him.

Nenré — gone. And Wrinn didn't have any good news about Fortunato.

"Wrinn," the elvenking said. "You were not unaccompanied. The Sage was with you."

"The Sage said my task was done, that I should leave him and be with my people," Wrinn said.

"And with your people you are," said the elvenking. "You have proven yourself, Wrinn. And you should know, I have made a decree, abolishing the distinction between elf and *dra'datsi*. All elves, like you, whether born in the human world or not, are welcome to their birthright. We consider you and those like you a full elf."

But Wrinn thought the greatest birthright belonged to the Telantines.

"Other former *dra'datsi* are here with us, having joined the battle," the elvenking said.

Tens of thousands of elves were guarding the pass, of all tribes besides the Lonen. Even vampires were fighting Seymus, now.

"Other former *dra'datsi*," said the elvenking. "One, who has not ceased asking about you, day or night. Her heart trembles when she speaks your name."

"Who is she?" Wrinn said.

~

When the elvenking led Wrinn to Rosalie, Wrinn didn't know

what to say.

All he knew was that Rosalie was beautiful.

"Rosalie!" Wrinn said to the elven maiden, wrapped in a pink shawl, her hair fair and her brilliant eyes bright even in the Dark Land sun.

"Rosalie," he said, softer, "it's you…"

"Shomré," the elven maiden said. "And I think you should change your name, too. A slaver gave you that name."

But Wrinn didn't think he'd ever change his name. And he would have a hard time calling her Shomré.

But he would try.

Shomré reached into her pocket, and pulled out a wilted flower. "You made a promise to me, Wrinn."

"I did," Wrinn said. "What say tonight, Shomré?"

~

Wrinn and Shomré were wed in the Dark Land, with the elvenking officiating.

The elven warriors looked on as Wrinn took Shomré's hands in his, and kissed her.

They made love in a tent, and fell asleep to whispered words. At such a time as this, they were married.

At such a time as this… battle coming.

A great war was yet to come.

Chapter Six:
To a Land of Ashes

The warships had sped through the Gemstone Sea, and Barcho knew that Verrus, quietly, was in a panic. The news, that fire had devastated Ash-Land, had consumed his every thought, for his mother had made sure he knew where their familial line was from — from Ash-Land, a land hardly thought of, impoverished and far from any sea or body of water.

The news — fire leveling a city, and scattering a people, suggested the work of gods that Verrus did not heed, that he had no regard for. But Barcho also did not think it was the work of the gods, but something else Verrus had little heed of — the wonders of the ancients.

The Telantines had been advanced. Could the Telantines be in the process of rebirth?

Barcho knew if he suggested it, Verrus would take his wrath out on him. So he remained silent as the warships passed along the shore, as the sands of the Desert of Sinn gave way to rice paddies and tea plantations. They drew near the Sea of Stars.

~

They would restock their supplies.

Quintus, the chief of the hundred federati, was striding across the deck.

He had, like the other federati, a breastplate of iron strips that maximized mobility, a watered sword of Getan style, a curved Khazidean dagger, a mental toughness proven through strenuous tests, and a willingness to perform morally questionable tasks that was second to none.

Quintus had the look of a federati, a killer, with a scar running lengthwise across his face, hair cut so short as to not be pulled, and bulging muscles that threatened to spill out of the breastplate he wore. "Your Worship," he said to Verrus. "We must restock on food and water. The journey to Ash-Land is going to be long."

"I delegate it to you," Verrus said. "After all, you know the way."

"Now that Cathay and its possessions are in our control," Quintus said, "I'll have the king of Cauli restock our supplies."

"Take care of it, then," Verrus said.

~

A day later, they were hugging the shore. In the distance was a gleaming city along a natural bay, a city dominated by three hills, each hill crowned by a pagoda.

Barcho knew it as the capital of Cauli, Geong.

The warships lingered, and Barcho watched and waited. There were junks in the bay, but the warships transporting Verrus and his federati were too large to dock.

So they would wait.

An hour later, they were not alone. From the bay, turtle ships powered by rowers were emerging from the bay of Geong, turtle ships with prows carved in the shape of dragons. At the head of the turtle ships was a warrior of Cauli garbed in armored plates of steel, bearing a spear and a bow at his back.

The warrior of Cauli had a taunting look to his eyes, and when the turtle ship, powered by rowers, was close enough to reveal the whites of those eyes, it stopped, lingering in the waters.

"The King of Cauli will only heed the commands of a true Imperial," said the warrior, "not one of the serpent's children."

Inestimable wrath appeared in Verrus's eyes, and he reached for his sword — as if he could strike from afar.

"The King of Cauli gives no shelter or aid to the serpent emperor," the warrior continued.

"Kill them!" Verrus shouted, but Quintus barked orders, and commanded the warships to move on.

They left the turtle ships and the port of Cauli behind. They had enough supplies to get to Cathay proper, to the capital city beside the northern Plain of Song.

As the turtle ships disappeared into the distance, and Cauli had vanished from view, Verrus continued to grumble that they had rejected him.

~

Along the edge of Cauli they traveled, through the Eastern Ocean, and the warships three in number skipped along the waters. For days they benefited from good winds.

One night, as the autumn deepened, and there was a chill wind, they were in view of the Sea of Stars, and Verrus's grumbling was seeming to reach an apogee.

Quintus, leader of the federati, was focused solely on the mission at hand, and had ignored Verrus's constant complaints.

"How shall we get there?" Verrus said. "How shall we get there, again?"

"Ash-Land is difficult to get to," Quintus said. "But south of the eddies and the maelstrom, there is a harbor deep enough for our ships to lay anchor… a trail through desert to the capital of Ash-Land."

Barcho knew that Verrus was accustomed to being carried in a litter through the streets of Imperial City, but Barcho thought the hardened federati would not abide that, not even for the emperor. Verrus would have to put aside creature comforts and luxury if he wished to embark upon this investigation he had sought after.

"Difficult to get to," Verrus said. "But I will make sacrifices for the folk of Ash-Land."

"Oh, mother," Verrus howled, taken again with something, regret and sorrow for the one he killed.

He had rushed to the edge of the deck and was clutching the railing, as above the Sea of Stars a cloak of stars glittered in the night sky.

The stars now glittered in the Sea of Stars, as the winds began to change, and there was lightning, and there was thunder.

Days later, or was it a week? Or a month?

There was blowing wind, a scourge of rain and keeping control of the ship was a battle, as the warships and the federati broached the northern regions of Cathay.

The capital city on the Plain of Song appeared on the horizon, buildings stretching into the distance beyond the shore, cloaked in smog and the sand constantly blowing in from the Plain of Song. Verrus idled with his ships, and Barcho watched, as junks sailed in, and men of Cathay handed them bags of rice and kegs filled with water. Quickly, they would speed on their way, and Verrus thanked them and the Dragon Emperor, as they fixed their sails, and continued on a northward passage.

With the bad weather behind them, they traversed a northern route, along the eastern edge of the known world. Past the land of the Dweorg they ventured, and Barcho did not know what month it was, only that it was cold and growing colder, that the nights were growing longer, and it was growing darker. North of the Dweorg, they were in a part of the world that was scarcely inhabited.

Indeed, it seemed no one lived here amid black earth and black rock, a dry cold desert lacking rain. Yet Quintus, leader of the federati, began to bark orders, and the warships drew to shore.

There were no people, but there was deep water, and there they dropped anchor.

Verrus took a small boat to the shore. Quintus and the hundred federati swam, even with their swords and armor. Barcho questioned what he should do, but after a bit of indecision decided he — as representative of the Imperial Guard — would follow his liege in all respects.

He took a small boat to the blackened shore and that night, Verrus, Barcho, Quintus and his hundred federati, took their first steps down a desert road toward Ash-Land.

Chapter Seven:
Hieros Gamos

The purified tower overlooked the Dark Land.

The purified tower, conquered by Telantine spirits, was Reev's refuge.

It was also the Oculus's base of operations.

Reev had learned, in the weeks following his arrival, that Spymaster Marius and Agent Numerio were not the only agents of the Oculus operating in the Dark Land. No, occasionally agents would arrive, scaling the walls of the tower — never pulled by a spiritual rope, like Reev — and give Marius reports of this or that section of the Dark Land.

Reev would use his spyglass, and note the movements of rokahn, kobolds and anguipeds, but the conquest of the Dark Land, and the crushing of Seymus underfoot, he was approaching with caution and shrewdness.

He knew he was badly outnumbered. He knew he had to act with wisdom, and that each step had to be carefully considered.

He wondered where the Oculus was getting their supplies. Every few weeks, an Oculus agent would arrive with bags of road-bread and canisters of water.

"Are we safe here?" Reev said one cool morning as a hazy sun rose over the Dark Land.

Spymaster Marius strode to the edge of the tower. "The Telantine spirits have purified this tower," he said. "Here, we are safe, and the anguipeds cannot hurt us. But, Reev, you and I know well, a war cannot be won in fortresses and fastnesses. Wars must be won through attack. We must press ahead."

"And how will we attack?" Reev said. "How will we conquer?"

"Our ears and eyes are throughout the northern portion of the

Dark Land," said Spymaster Marius, "agents trained to understand the rokahn and anguiped tongue. We have learned that the anguipeds are protecting something very important in one of their dark-holds, something they do not name explicitly, but which they have given a nickname to: *Hieros Gamos*."

"They are guarding it," Reev said. "That must mean they're desperate to stop us from letting it fall into their hands."

"Indeed," Spymaster Marius said. "A hundred rokahn stand guard over it, and an anguiped leads them. They dare not say what they are guarding in their dark-hold explicitly, and that tells us that they fear even us knowing what they are in possession of."

"That means, all the more, that we must take this *Hieros Gamos* from them," Reev said. "So why don't we?"

"We don't have the numbers," Spymaster Marius said. "The hundred rokahn are the roughest of the rough. And there are more nearby, for them to summon. What's more, it's not a normal dark-hold, but finely made, and the doors are sealed by magic."

"Where is this dark-hold?" Reev said.

He drew his spyglass out of his pouch.

The sunlight glistened on the Bracelet of Might he wore, with its bright orange gem, the Bracelet of Might that gave him supernal strength.

"It's hidden in a canyon," Spymaster Marius said. "Five miles away, as the crow flies. You wouldn't find it unless you were looking for it."

Reev fixed his eye to the spyglass, and peered at the canyon-covered earth, any one of which could hide the dark-hold in which the *Hieros Gamos* was being hidden.

As Reev stirred in the hot air, and saw the hazy sun, the smoky sky that let in little light, he realized he was of a different disposition than Spymaster Marius. "If we are to defeat the Dark One and his children," said Reev, "how can we expect to achieve victory if we are unwilling to take risks? Perhaps, we don't have the numbers.

But you have wonders — forgetfulness powder, disguises… what else?"

"Don't tell me how to run the Oculus, Reev," Spymaster Marius growled. "I won't put my men in harm's way if there's no hope of victory."

Don't tell Reev how to run the Oculus, Spymaster Marius had insisted. But Reev was his own man. The Oculus couldn't tell him what to do.

"You said it's in a canyon," Reev said. "Which canyon?"

And Spymaster Marius pointed him to a canyon far in the distance, on the periphery of the horizon.

Spymaster Marius had decided to play the coward. Reev would play the hero.

He took a step off the tower and light swirled about him, light transporting him from the highest heights to the rocky ground below. His shoes hit the rocky earth, and the Telantine spirits had ferried him down, just as they had ferried him up.

Spymaster Marius had said the dark-hold hiding *Hieros Gamos* was impregnable, but Reev didn't believe the enemy they faced was invincible. He believed the enemy they faced was condemned.

He strode, then, through the ash-covered rock, amid bleakness and barrenness, past gray boulders and black pebbles. All about him was a constant pealing of thunder, spilling above-head and in the distance, forming an unending rumble. But there was no lightning, just a sun veiled in a hazy dark sky. The Dark Land was without life and without rain. Nothing survived except that which hated life and goodness.

Nothing, except those who wished to conquer it.

A rokahn patrol was passing him by, riding on black wolves,

and Reev ducked behind a boulder, allowing them to pass. He saw them as they rode by, about a dozen in number, led by a green-skinned kehrad with a curved saber at his side.

What was *Hieros Gamos?* Was it possible for Reev to know?

He knew he was taking a great risk, charging boldly ahead, going where Spymaster Marius dared not, but he thought he was doing as his ancestors had, the warriors of Telantis. Against terrible odds, they had waged war on the anguipeds and won. Surely, Reev would follow in their footsteps.

He pushed past the boulder, over rock-strewn ground, under the hazy sky, through the hot air that though dry was uncomfortable. The air, too, was difficult to breathe, choked with ash and stinging particles, made worse by the soil that Reev disturbed with each step.

He was at the threshold of the canyon that held what rokahn had codenamed *Hieros Gamos.* He was at a high perch, and had removed his spyglass from his pouch.

He fixed the spyglass on the canyon and saw the situation was far worse than even Spymaster Marius had described.

There were more than a hundred rokahn standing in the vast canyon, guarding a pair of double doors. There were two-hundred rokahn and kobolds, and dozens of anguipeds, and something that was much fiercer.

A two-headed giant stood at the double doors, which led into the canyon itself.

Not a dark-hold, but a fortress carved into rock.

Not just a hundred rokahn, but two-hundred.

And a two-headed giant with eyes that gleamed red, a tongue lolling out of knife-like fangs.

A giant that looked of Hell itself.

Yet Reev vowed to enter in.

Reev vowed to conquer the fortress, and take *Hieros Gamos* from his enemy.

Chapter Eight:
Taking Charge

The ghostly siren of the haunted iron horse echoed in Balor's ears, and in his mind. He could feel the breadth of the iron horse shaking as it rattled down the tracks, as it rattled through the Haunted Forest.

Balor had lost track of time, and he didn't know if a day had passed or an hour, a week or a month or a year, since he boarded the haunted iron horse.

But he knew that time in the Haunted Forest did not pass like normal time. He had grown older — his hands were larger. He feared what would happen if he found the crystal clear waters of a pond, and dared to look at his reflection. He feared to see the reflection staring back at him, at himself — having changed… now, in the midst of a Haunted Forest and its dark master.

Here, where ancients sacrificed the innocent to the Dark One, evil intent and evil memory lingered.

Hadn't Balor hoped to conquer it? Hadn't Balor hoped to deal the master of the Haunted Forest his defeat?

Hadn't Balor hoped to take control of the Haunted Forest, and make him its master, rather than the one who currently ruled it?

What now could he do?

He realized, he couldn't just sit on the cushionless seats of this iron horse carriage, and expect things to change. He had to change it himself.

He had to take charge of the haunted iron horse.

~

He pushed through doors, through the carriages of the iron

horse, amid its ghostly trill. He realized he was alone, but in the Haunted Forest being alone was an illusion, for darkness was all about, and darkness whispered in one's ear. The master of the Haunted Forest reigned, and his minions were all about any who walked under the boughs of its trees, tempting the entrants to despair.

Balor pushed on, past an empty carriage — through an iron door, to a carriage that had no roof, bare to the elements.

Balor realized that the iron horse that haunted the Haunted Forest was going in a circular path, which it did not divert from. Yet he recalled the iron horse had a conductor who was driving its movements, and causing it to never cease its path.

He pushed past the empty carriage, his wand long gone from his grip. He peered outside, and saw through the shattered window of another carriage, they were on a lonely stretch of track, underneath black-boughed pines, as from the clouds was falling a constant rain.

He was at the front of the iron horse, then, on a railing open to the air.

The conductor of the iron horse turned to Balor with his melted face, his soupy eyes, his fingers which bones were peeking out of.

And when the conductor looked upon Balor, and saw no fear, he in turn was terrified.

The conductor took a step back, and his jaw dropped, baring sticky gums. He realized, as Balor looked at him coolly, that he could do nothing — he could do nothing, now, that Balor was not afraid.

Balor summoned up the magical energy within him uncontrolled though it was, without his wand. A blast of purple necromantic energy erupted, glancing off the walls of the iron horse, and the haunted conductor exploded in a burst of flesh that withered in the air, turning to shriveled strands before it hit the ground by the power of necromancy that Balor had summoned.

The siren of the iron horse wailed in return, as the iron horse picked up speed to rattle down the tracks.

Balor looked on, and saw, as the iron horse sped down the track that bordered the Haunted Forest, that there was a fork in the tracks, one left, one right.

The iron horse, Balor realized, had not been turning in all this time, as the conductor — now destroyed — directed the iron horse. It had been circling down the leftward route, not right.

Balor looked about him, and saw there was a wheel of wood on the railing.

He seized the wheel by his hands, which again stunned him by their size.

He'd grown old.

He yanked the wheel to the right as they approached the fork in the tracks, and the iron horse echoed a ghostly wail, louder than before — in protest — as if it itself was sentient and at last turned with a roar down the rightward track.

~

The iron horse gained speed as it rattled down the track. The rattling of the wheels itself were becoming a deafening thunder. The beacon, fixed to the front most carriage was burning through the fog and darkness of the Haunted Forest like a copycat sun.

And then, Balor saw, up ahead, an immovable obstacle.

There was a barrier up ahead, a barrier of rock. Balor scrambled as the sirens of the iron horse were like a panicked scream. He scrambled, and tried to vault off the railing, as the iron horse made impact.

The explosion sent Balor flying through the cold air, to the cold ground, amid fog and mist — and now wreckage spilling out in every direction.

The front carriage of the iron horse had disintegrated to flaming shrapnel, and the other carriages were in varying degrees of shrapnel and flame.

An inferno now lit up the foggy Haunted Forest, but Balor, lying on the ground, saw the iron horse had done damage of its own. The rocky mound it had crashed into had been sundered apart, baring something glittering in the light of the burning iron horse carriages.

The iron horse had rent the rocky mound, baring what lay beneath the granite shell... sparkling white crystal.

And it was then that Balor remembered why the three guilesome hags had brought him to the Haunted Forest.

They had brought Balor here so that, from wood and crystal, he could fashion a mage's staff.

He had crystal — and now, there was wood, all about him.

How could he fashion his own staff?

As he stood in the cold brisk wind, he had an idea.

Chapter Nine:
Amir Alfajr

Barcho and Verrus, the hundred federati, and the federati's captain Quintus had marched for days under a hot sun that was growing hotter, that threatened — by Barcho's estimation — to spell their end.

The federati had called the path they were taking a road, but it was not clearly marked and though the captain of the federati, Quintus, had traveled this route before, they were having to conserve water and food so as not to run out before each stop.

There was precious little water, but a day or two days' journey between stops, there was a spring or the waters of a babbling creek. All around them was a blackened, ash-covered landscape, air that was smoky and growing smokier, a sun that increasingly appeared to be wreathed in haze.

And Barcho knew, if Verrus's mother was to be believed, it was here his ancestors originated from, amid this rocky waste, this ash-covered soil, this sun that blazed down with such severity. How could a people live in such a place, Barcho wondered?

His ancestors, in Kheroe, were considered to live a hardscrabble life in an arid place that lacked water, but the world about him now was so severe as to seem unearthly.

Five days or ten days, or was it twenty, or thirty — after they had disembarked from their ships, Barcho peered ahead, through the blazing sun, and saw Quintus making a signal with his hands.

Had they at last arrived in Ash-Land?

Or were they hopelessly lost?

Barcho realized that at Quintus's signal, the hundred federati were not hastening their steps toward their destination, but instead stopping the march altogether. They were drawing their weapons.

Quintus drew his watered steel sword, amid blazing sunlight and blackened rock.

There were dark shapes approaching, swiftly distinguishingly themselves amid a rising cloud of ash. They were speeding through the air, under the hazy sun, and as soon as they drew within yards, Barcho distinguished the shape of wings.

He had seen wings, and then he was on the ground, pulled overhead of Verrus to serve as a human shield. Barcho drew his sword in the burning sun, as the winged shapes descended — what looked like legless humanoids, wreathed in cruel mockeries of wings that were little better than skin flaps. The winged monsters were screeching as they tore at the hundred federati with mockeries of claws that were little better than exposed bone, as Verrus did not relinquish Barcho but instead pulled him tighter, now not a shield but a second layer of skin to save him from this fate.

The winged monsters did not seem to be attacking Barcho or Verrus though. They were solely focused — it seemed, as time went on — on the hundred federati.

And the hundred federati were winning.

The winged creatures attacked in a swarm, a wild flapping of wings that could quickly overwhelm men without control of their emotions. But the federati were built of sterner stuff.

Calmly yet forcefully, they tore the winged creatures from their bodies and dispatched them with lengths of watered steel. They spewed black blood when they were riven open, and their organs spilled out of the wounds like garbage emptied from a pail.

One by one, the federati were cutting them down, and as they did battle, Barcho watched as he willingly served as Verrus's shield.

The winged creatures seemed to have faces, wretched faces like corpses twisted in grimaces of agony. The faces moved little even as their wings flapped and the bone claws struck.

Quintus swept his watered steel sword with a controlled wildness, cutting a winged creature in half and beheading another.

In time, the winged creatures began to drop to the rocky ground, lying still in pools of black blood and rotted organs.

Barcho thought it was at last safe to remove himself from Verrus, and pushed himself free from Verrus's grip.

Verrus was then lying on the rocky ground, a coward.

Quintus was approaching, his face spattered with black blood. He sheathed his watered steel blade.

"I heard talk," Quintus said, "that when the folk of Ash-Land die, if they are not buried deep within the ground, their bodies can be given a twisted sense of animation, that they burst through the dust and fly, tormenting any in their path for a few weeks…"

Was Verrus truly descended from such folk?

"They are called ash-wings," Quintus said.

"Did you have to slash them so violently?" Verrus said from the corners of the bloody battlefield.

Quintus did not look at Verrus with contempt. He was a man on a mission. All he cared about was his duty, and the words of others he did not pay any mind.

"A day to Ash-Land," Quintus said, "we're close."

~

When they crossed a river through black earth and black rock, there was a city lying abandoned. Buildings hewn of black rock lay around a city square, and carts lay unattended at street corners. Yet the city's abandonment seemed to be recent, for the carts had produce — sheaves of wheat left to rot in the sun, and pomegranates that though rotting were fresh enough to be recognized as pomegranates.

"Who did this?" Verrus said, at first a shout and then a howl. "Who did this?"

And Barcho sensed that Verrus knew, the fire and ash were why the city had been abandoned. But where had the fire struck? Where had the greatest damage been dealt?

Under a sunny sky, under gray clouds, they pushed past the ghost town, down a road that was also abandoned, which charted a path through untended wheat fields — gold heads of wheat ready for the harvester's scythe, now untended to.

~

An abandoned street turned to an abandoned road, when they came to the crater.

"The capital of Ash-Land was here," said Quintus on the edge of the crater, stretching into the distance — a crater so large as to disappear into the horizon, so deep Barcho feared taking a step off the edge.

Verrus wailed, and then he stooped over. Vile liquid dripped from his mouth. "I think I'm going to be ill," he said.

Barcho, stunned and staggered by the devastation, was trying to imitate the federati and put on a bold face.

"Who did this?" Verrus screamed. "Who did this?"

The crater was staggering in size, the devastation too complete for Barcho's mind to contemplate. And Verrus's wailing and terror was spreading to him.

Barcho aspired to be like the calm, collected federati, but realized he couldn't.

"Who did this?" Verrus screamed. He howled, "I will kill him, Mother! Do you hear me, Mother? I will kill him!"

Him — Verrus had attributed it to one person.

An arrow of fire, sent from a far place, had destroyed the Ash-Land capital.

As Verrus fell to his knees and altered between wails of despair and oaths to kill who did this, as the hundred federati stirred in the light of the hazy orange sun, Barcho saw they were not alone.

~

Figures were approaching from the sides of the crater, figures garbed in black cloaks.

In the light of the orange sun, their faces appeared to have a greenish hue. Yellow gleams were in their eyes. There were about a dozen, and the chief of them, walking ahead, had a cloak that was more gray than black, and a scimitar at his side.

"Hail!" said the man in the grayish cloak as he and his party approached.

Verrus stood up from his crouching position and fixed his eyes on him.

"You are men of Ash-Land…" Verrus could hardly speak.

Barcho saw that tears were in Verrus's eyes.

"We are men of Ash-Land," said the man in the grayish cloak. "True *qizim*, we are. And we have heard of you, Emperor Verrus, and have expected your coming. We know, you are a *qizim* too, and we believe you are the one who will rebuild the House of the Tannin. We believe you are *Amir Alfajr*, the one who will extinguish the Telantines forever."

"Who did this?" Verrus howled, and the animalistic fury building up within him could not help but be released. "Who did this? I vow on the Candles of the Tannin, on my grandmother's grave… I will kill him! I will kill him!"

"The one who destroyed our city is south of here," said the man in the grayish cloak. "South, across a stormy sea. But an army of elves has moved in to through the Steaming Gates, to block all entry.

"But if you are *Amir Alfajr*, you will find a way… you will enter into the Dark Land, and you will slay the one who destroyed your people's city."

"I will!" howled Verrus, "I vow… on the Candles of the Tannin… on my grandmother's grave… I will kill him! I will!"

Verrus turned south.

"I will kill him!" Verrus screamed.

Chapter Ten:
Bachelor and Bachelorette

Outside the city of Galiope, and along its streets, the trees had set aside their green wardrobe and had changed to ruby red and flame orange and fiery yellow. All about, the air was cold, and when Fortunato, striding to the next bar in the company of gypsies, walked down the street, his breath turned to fog in the night.

He'd drunk deeply all night, this night that Julian had insisted upon. It was an Imperial custom for a man's friends to take him out for a night of wild drinking sometime before his wedding, but he learned now it was a gypsy, and a Galiopean custom, too.

But where were his friends, now? Gastreel had died. Wrinn was gone — presumably, to the Dark Land, if he and Reev had somehow survived. Spyke had betrayed him and met an end fitting for a traitor. So he was left to borrow friends from the woman who would be his wife, her relatives and those she loved dearly — among whom was Julian.

Julian was leading them now, from the Green Girdle to a bar he knew better, one in Selwyn's Parish where the gypsies now lived. They had departed from Galiope, and now, he learned, they had been spirited back on the wings of a genie's wish. And if the gypsies ever wondered again whether they belonged in Galiope, now there was no room for doubt.

"Come on!" Julian said, "We'll leave the Green Girdle behind. You'll never want to go back there again."

But the Green Girdle was Fortunato's favorite bar, and he didn't think that would ever change.

~

When they reached the townhomes and sprawling astrologias of Selwyn's Parish, Fortunato saw that the wagons that had once lain idle on street corners are long gone.

"What happened to your wagons?" Fortunato said.

"When the genie took us here," Julian began, "he didn't send our wagons with us. I guess he wanted to send us a message, that we belong here and we'll never go anywhere else…"

That seemed the most likely explanation of the genie's actions to Fortunato.

"Here! Up ahead!" Julian shouted.

Julian, the director of the party, had taken pains to drink the least of the group, but he was still staggering slightly as they pushed through a colorful avenue, in the light of streetlamps, to a bar marked with a sign:

The Silver Spoon

At a high table, sitting in stools, Fortunato had yet another tall ale.

The patrons in the Silver Spoon were mostly gypsies, but there were a few non-gypsies too, what gypsies called kallowen.

As liquid gold and blood-red wine washed away all anxiety and hesitancy, Julian was beginning to speak more boldly.

"Ambrass's father and mother are long gone," Julian said. "She confided in me quietly, she hopes your father walks her down the aisle."

Petro and Alessa, Fortunato's parents, still lived in Ríva, as far as he knew. But he did not know what had become of them.

Dare he invite them to his wedding, after all the trouble he'd put them through?

Dare he send for them?

Would they want to come?

~

In the Dragonpaw Inn, Glenda had decorated the main hall with pink ribbons and pink flowers, and had announced to all prospective patrons that the inn was closed for the night.

So now, it was just Ambrass and Glenda, Rose and a few of Ambrass's female cousins, on a cold autumn night heavy with expectation. The wedding was now just weeks away. When the trees shed their leaves, and snow was falling from the sky, the wedding would be imminent.

Glenda had made cherry pies, and had poured herself and Ambrass a cup of wine. Surrounded by friends, they had peppered her with questions about the upcoming wedding and nuptials.

"At St. Sigmund's Church," said a female cousin, sitting in the booth next over. "You're so lucky. Do you feel lucky?"

"I feel like I'm the luckiest woman in the world," Ambrass said.

Glenda was sitting in the booth across from her, and Rose was sitting by her side.

"I hope this party is all you wanted," Glenda said. "I spent a few weeks planning it."

"It's perfect, Glenda," Ambrass said.

She wouldn't have wanted suggestive cakes or illicit entertainments like some women did. She wanted the company of friends, all female, while her love gallivanted with his friends on the other side of town.

But Fortunato, having lost so many over the years, had borrowed friends from her.

"Tell us about how you met Fortunato," Rose said.

"I met him here," Ambrass said, "taking care of him after he suffered a wound… a wound that no one could survive, or so we thought."

"Perhaps, a Telantine can survive such a wound," Glenda said.

"Perhaps, that's why," Ambrass said.

"Your father and mother must be so excited," Rose said.

Ambrass thought Rose was a seer, that her blindness had given her a sight beyond the reach of many, but she could not see all. She could not read everything, it seemed.

"My parents passed away not long after I was born," Ambrass said.

"I'm sorry," Rose said. She paused, and touched Ambrass's hand, laying hold of her forearm. "I sense, though, someone special will walk you down the aisle at St. Sigmund's. I can't wait to witness it."

If Rose couldn't sense that Ambrass's father and mother were dead, what else was she wrong about?

And yet she wouldn't let Rose's comment spoil such a special party, such a special night.

She would enjoy all these friendships for as long as she had them. Her future, she knew, lay somewhere, probably inebriated, on the other side of town.

"Someone special," Rose said. "Some people, very special. Some very special people are coming to your wedding, Ambrass. This, I am sure of."

Ambrass squeezed Rose's hand and then she let go.

And despite Rose's words that had threatened to reopen old wounds, she realized something in the flickering light of the hearth.

"Glenda," Ambrass said, "will you be maid of honor?"

"I was hoping you'd ask," Glenda said. "Of course…."

Chapter Eleven:
A Wife's Word

The armies of the elves were massing in the pass called the Steaming Gates.

Wrinn, the husband of Shomré, like the other elves, was here for battle.

He was here — to assist the Telantines in their final victory, to ensure that nothing could stand against them. And the same day as scattered reports came in from the north of a possible incursion from Ash-Land, a rokahn army appeared from the south, intending to dislodge the elven armies from the Steaming Gates.

But all the strength of the elves, of their treaty-allies the Viegs, even the vampires, would face them.

The rokahn stretched into the horizon, from one edge of it to the other — rokahn and kobolds alike, some mounted on black wolves and others on foot, garbed in black armor. A vast host, inestimable, would be met by another vast host, inestimable, a force of light against a force of darkness.

And where were the Telantines?

Wrinn knew of one Telantine behind enemy lines.

Were there others?

Wrinn drew his quarterstaff, thinking of Shomré in their tent. He was not just fighting for Reev, now, but also for her. Her — whom he had pledged to marry countless years ago, in the land of Almania not far from Gallia. Their matrimony had at last become reality.

He uttered her names under his breath as the mighty host approached. "Shomré... Rosalie..."

And he saw from amid the gathered ranks of rokahn one approaching, a man of harsh features and a green visage, pointed ears that were like a mockery of elvenkind. It was an anguiped, but Wrinn didn't know if the elves had encountered anguipeds before.

The anguiped strode forth, and as he did, the elvenking galloped to the front of the lines on his Elvish horse. His Elvish horse was glittering with steel barding.

The anguiped shouted to the elves, "The Lord of this Dark Tower and this Dark Land, our father, obliges you to cease your blockade and help his children in the fashioning of the House of the Tannin. He obliges that you bring him offerings and supplications in accordance to the regulations of the Tannin, and cease your fighting at once…"

The elvenking drew his *estirion* blade. It sparkled blue and cerulean in the sunlight.

"The Lord of this Dark Tower and this Dark Land, our father," the anguiped said, "obliges that you do the will of the Tannin, and finally destroy the Telantines. You do not have to fight against him."

"We honor the gods, not your Tannin," said the elvenking, "and the Telantines we fight for, that they may rule. You shall not dissuade us from our task, you Son of Nachash."

"I believe in time, you will learn from your mistake," the anguiped answered, "and when the Telantines are all gone, you shall bring offerings to the House of the Tannin. For you should know, *Amir Alfajr* is coming, and you will not be able to stop his arrival. The pass of the Steaming Gates will be cleared, whether you try to resist him or not."

The rokahn, countless in number, began to hoot and howl war cries. But when the anguiped walked back into their ranks, they did not cross the battle plain. Horns began to blow, and then the rokahn withdrew.

What ever would become of the army? Wrinn knew, though the elves had brought the fullness of their strength, that the elves were less numerous than the Dark One's armies.

But all this talk of Tannin and a rebuilt house and *Amir Alfajr* befuddled him.

For now, the anguipeds, the Dark One, and the rokahn, would leave them be beside the Steaming Gates, the pass through the Sea of Ghosts that the elves guarded.

For now, the elves would be left alone, for the anguipeds were for now attempting a strategy of temptation and deceit.

Yet once it was clear the elves would not succumb, the Dark One's fury would be sudden and unending.

Wrinn, Shomré, and their people, would stand fast in their support of the Telantines. And then all the powers of evil would be fixed on them, on the Steaming Gates.

~

The rokahn could not have gone far. But the elves, having stood firm, had built campfires amid the tents, and were resting in shifts. Under a sky too hazy to reveal the stars, Wrinn had found Shomré outside their tent, and had begun to relay to her all that had transpired.

"A House of a Tannin," Shomré said, "a lord of a tower, and a Dark Land… oh, explain it to me Wrinn."

"They're trying deceit," Wrinn said. "They're trying to stop us from fighting the Dark One and his servants. They're trying to stop us from giving aid and comfort to the Telantines…"

"And we won't," Shomré insisted.

"Neither you or I will," Wrinn said, "that's for certain."

Other things that the anguiped had said troubled Wrinn.

He had insisted the blockade would be removed, and he said it with confidence. He had said something of *Amir Alfajr,* and to Wrinn's ears that smacked of a title rather than a name.

"Reev," Shomré said, "the Sage… where is he?"

"I do not know," Wrinn said. "But the gods said he would crush

Seymus under his feet, and that's good enough proof to me that he is doing well."

Shomré's eyes were peering beyond the lights of the campfires, past the dark shapes moving in the distance. "Wrinn," she said, "I hope the elvenking knows not to take an anguiped's word. He is probably readying a counterattack, some deceptive trick. There are likely rokahn moving from the north and south, ready to dislodge our positions."

Yet Wrinn was more concerned about the north, about what the anguiped had called *Amir Alfajr*. Wrinn had learned in the time since his arrival that the anguipeds' homeland lay due north of the pass that the elves were guarding. Almost the whole population had fled into the Dark Land, but perhaps some of them had remained behind.

Chapter Twelve: Courage

So high on a tower, on the roof of the world, Reev at last told Spymaster Marius, the chief of the Oculus, what he had seen.

Under a night that was indeed dark in the Dark Land, with no stars or moon visible, he explained all. "There was a two-headed giant guarding the fortress and what the rokahn codenamed *Hieros Gamos*," Reev said.

Spymaster Marius had a grim look, then. "A two-headed giant," Marius said, "a creature of darkest hell. What the learned would term a jotunn, a being under the power of the Dark One himself."

"A jotunn," Reev repeated.

"Yes," Spymaster Marius said. "A creature, dangerous indeed. In fact, so dangerous and deadly, I recommend you do not speak even the name of its kind aloud, like I just did. I fear, by speaking it, you will alert it.

"And we shall dispense with any goal of retrieving the *Hieros Gamos,* if a jotunn guards it," Spymaster Marius said. "Not even all the agents of the Oculus together could kill a jotunn."

Reev was disappointed.

"Don't be so sour," said Spymaster Marius. "The Oculus is still at work. When Agent Numerio returns from his patrol tonight, I've assigned a mission for you. You and Agent Numerio will descend the tower tonight to lay an ambush. For an anguiped courier is tonight on his way to deliver a cache of weapons to the Dark Tower."

Reev was itching for a fight, itching for battle. But he supposed a jotunn was too mighty a foe for him to hope to defeat.

He supposed the anguipeds would keep in their possession whatever they had called *Hieros Gamos.*

~

It was late, though whether it was midnight or the witching hour or later, it was impossible to tell — for there were no stars and only the vaguest hint of a moon amid the constant haze of the Dark Land.

It was late, but Agent Numerio was scaling the walls of the tower with his pitons.

Agent Numerio was then standing in the deep darkness of the Dark Land night. His bright blue eyes, though, seemed to glisten, and offer a bit of light, as he pulled himself onto the tower's flat roof.

Reev could see he was armed with a dagger that dangled from his belt.

"Agent Numerio," said Spymaster Marius. "Are you ready?"

"I am," he replied.

And Reev had a thought, one he couldn't quiet. "Agent Numerio," he said, "let's try something…"

Instead of having Agent Numerio climb with his pitons back down to the ground of the Dark Land, Reev thought that Agent Numerio might hitch a ride.

At his urging, Agent Numerio laid a hold of Reev by the shoulders, and then Reev took a step off the tower.

The Telantine spirits swirled about him, a brilliant white light, and Agent Numerio whimpered softly as Reev dropped toward the ground.

But when he and Numerio were on the ground level, Numerio was in one piece — ready, even more eager to do battle in the wake of the Telantine spirits' help.

Reev followed Agent Numerio through the darkness, through black rock that seemed darker because of the dark sky, and as Agent Numerio drew his dagger, Reev drew Doomblade.

What were they doing, and where would they go? They would lay ambushes, but it didn't seem to Reev that they were doing any real damage to the Dark One or the anguipeds. They were lurking in the tower, keeping apprised of the anguipeds' movements. But what hope was there, really, that Reev and the Oculus could conquer the Dark Land?

Amid darkness, there was faint illumination — Reev retrieved his spyglass from his pouch, and fixed it to his eyes, and saw that it was an anguiped carrying a lantern, and that behind him were dark shapes. "An anguiped," Reev said softly.

"The courier," Reev said softly.

Agent Numerio nodded, and then he gulped.

Was Agent Numerio nervous?

Reev placed the spyglass back in his pouch. The haze-veiled outline of the moon glittered on the Bracelet of Might he wore. He wondered if he'd ever use the Bracelet of Might again.

Agent Numerio rushed through the night, and Reev followed after him a step behind.

The warm air of the day had not at all left, and Reev was breathing in ash-filled air, when Agent Numerio struck. He threw a pouch of bane powder at the anguiped carrying the lantern. His aim was slightly off, and the pouch exploded at the dark shapes behind the anguiped.

There was a fit of coughing, as Numerio charged, and as he and Reev drew near, Reev saw that he and Agent Numerio were badly outnumbered, that there were ten more anguipeds behind the anguiped who had been carrying the lantern.

Anguipeds drew swords and daggers, and charged Agent Numerio, as the bane powder cleared from the air.

There was the sound of shredding fabric as an anguiped's dagger cut through Agent Numerio's tunic, and blood spurted in the light of the moon.

Reev shouted, as Agent Numerio turned and fled, sprinting away as fast as his legs could carry him, leaving Reev behind.

Reev felt something swell within him. He saw a face, ten thousand faces looking down on him from above, in his mind's eye.

He charged the anguiped with the lantern, and pitching back Doomblade, pierced him straight through the heart.

The anguiped dropped the lantern, and the lantern burst into fire, casting all its light about the black ground, baring Reev in his Telantine loin cloth and his Telantine attributes.

The anguipeds before Reev wailed in terror and fled in every direction.

Reev's eyes scoured the landscape for Agent Numerio.

Agent Numerio had been frightened, and fled.

~

Reev was standing alone. There was no tranche of weapons.

Then he turned, and he was not alone.

A woman was approaching, garbed in a gold raiment, carrying a lantern Reev thought he had seen before. When he saw the karsé, the white veil she was wearing, Reev knew it was an elf. When she removed the karsé, Reev knew he was seeing a vision, and that it was the Lady of Danyen.

The Lady of Danyen was standing before him, her green eyes sparkling in the light of the lantern she bore.

"Do you now see, now, Reev?" the Lady of Danyen said. "Do you now see the terror you inspire in the anguipeds just at the sight of you? Do you now see that all hope rests in the gods, and in your kind?

"You made quick work of them, when they saw just who you were. And so I will not abide any talk, that a jotunn stands in your way. Are the gods not more powerful than a jotunn? Are those the gods favor not more powerful than an anguiped?"

"So you're saying — " Reev said.

"I am saying," the Lady of Danyen said, "you know the anguipeds are hiding something they call *Hieros Gamos,* something they dare not even speak by its name. Will you stride forth boldly, Reev, as your ancestors did, against odds that seemed impossible? The odds are not impossible for those the gods favor."

Against impossible odds?

The odds were not impossible.

Chapter Thirteen: The Whisper

Balor stooped down and picked the tree branch from the ground.

It had fallen from one of the towering pines, and after much searching, Balor thought he found a branch thick enough and tall enough for a staff. It would need a little cutting. And the crystals which he had bundled in his arm would need to be fitted to it.

Balor recalled something, a memory from the days or months or years or hours he had spent in the Haunted Forest… that long ago, a carpenter had set up shop here, and he had left behind his tools. His tools would then be available to him, his tools and his open air workshop. There, Balor would be able to complete his work.

And yet Balor had more questions. The guilesome hags who had brought him here had brought him here to fashion a staff.

But why had they wanted him to fashion a staff, and why had they wanted him to become a mighty wizard?

For now, all Balor thought about was conquering the Haunted Forest. He wanted ownership of the Haunted Forest to be transferred from its current master to him.

Balor thought, in that endeavor, a staff would help.

A staff was a mage's greatest tool.

~

A harsh wind blew as he approached the carpenter's workshop. The harsh wind had a whisper of anguish and plague on its edge.

As he took a few steps closer, the whisper became words — "You… it is you…"

Balor turned around in the face of the wind, buffeted by a frosty breeze, as pine boughs above-head bent in the face of the hissing whispered words.

"You… it is you… you are the Hand of the master of this wood…"

Balor spit back curses at the wind, at the words and he who sent them. He saw dark shambling shapes approaching, what looked like corpses given animation, pale, with jaws hanging loose.

Balor realized in a split second that these were his undead minions, from before he had entered into the wood, now commandeered by the master of the wood and sent to harm him.

But amid the darkness and vile words, there was another presence, as Balor's back pressed up against the carpenter's bench.

A thought…

Put them to the test…

He stepped nearer to the undead minions, and allowed them to get close. They were inches from him, then, and Balor could feel their cold breath on his face like they were wild animals. But he did not move or resist, and when they had gotten close enough to strike him, they dared not touch him.

Balor brushed further against the carpenter's bench.

See? The creatures of this forest cannot truly hurt you.

Balor turned, then, ignoring them, and the specters of his undead minions shrieked in fear, as he turned to the carpenter's bench, to the hand-drill and the whittling knife.

He set to work, as the specters of his undead minions fled in fear.

With the whittling knife he carved the branches from the pine bough, one after another, and they fell to the ground. Then, with the hand drill, he began to drill a hole from the top of the wooden stick.

He heard a howl in the distance.

A woman lurked, twice Balor's side, by the edge of a tree, with purple bags under her soupy yellow eyes, tangled teeth, and drool escaping her lips.

The creatures of the forest couldn't hurt Balor. Ultimately, they would be easy to conquer.

He continued to drill into the stick, as there were wild yelps and shouts, a blood-curdling scream, and as the light of the moon cast the shadows of creatures standing just behind Balor.

But Balor ignored them.

He fixed the crystals into the hole he drilled.

Then he infused the staff with magic.

It burst into life, blazing white and when Balor felt the staff in his grip, he was filled with focus and control. Each jet of necromantic energy he shot would be shot in a perfect arc. Nothing would spill over.

But as he lingered at the carpenter's workshop, he heard another voice.

Will you decorate it?

With the whittling knife, he turned — in view of abominations and aberrations in the distance trying in vain to scare him — and carved the form of a skull into the tip of the staff.

The walking corpses, the Giant Spiders, stood in the distance helplessly.

Balor fixed his eyes on them, and, dropping the whittling knife, strode forth.

~

He blasted the Giant Spider with a spear of necromantic energy; the perfect spear cut a hole straight through its bulbous body, and what did not disintegrate into wisps slumped dead to the ground.

"Do not do it to us!" said one of the abominations, taking the form of a dead woman. "Please, Balor! Do as your ancestors did, and make an offering."

Balor shot a disc of bright purple necromantic energy, and it beheaded her.

"Careful!" howled an abomination, taking the form of a stack of corpses, legs and torsos and arms stitched together, with a sallow head on top. "You will summon the master of this wood, and he shall not treat you kindly."

At the threat, Balor fixed his eyes on the abomination, and flexed his arms. Now full of energy and focus and control, the magic responded perfectly. Torsos, arms, and legs wilted and withered until the stitching fell apart.

The head continued to talk. "You will pay for this, Balor! You will never be king!"

King... Balor recalled, a memory half-buried in fear. The guilesome hags had fashioned him a crown out of wood.

He reached for his head and touched it.

It had been on his head so long, he no longer felt it.

Did they wish him to be a king?

The master of the wood did not want him to be a king. That made him think Balor being a king would be a good thing.

But what would he be king of?

Chapter Fourteen: Let Me Through

In the sunlight the armies stirred, and as the armies stirred, Wrinn left the tent where Shomré was still sleeping, into the hazy orange sun of the Dark Land.

His quarterstaff was at his side, and he was ready, as always, for battle.

It seemed like the anguipeds were desperate to break the elves' hold on the pass called the Steaming Gates. But they had tried trickery and failed. What next did they have, up their sleeves?

Wrinn knew, now stirring in the Dark Land's oppressive heat, that the elves were outnumbered, but they were in a strategic position to be envied. For from the violent sea, which no one could cross, to the mountains and the sulfurous springs that gave the Steaming Gates their namesake, elves covered every bit of navigable ground. None could enter and none could leave the Dark Land, for east of the mountains was the Dwarf Kingdom, and surrounding the Dark Land were the towering waves of the Sea of Ghosts.

Wrinn amid the gathered warriors, the elven men and the elven women, tried to determine where the disturbance had been coming from, whether there was an incursion from the north or from the south.

Wrinn truly did not know.

But following his gut, he pressed north. He could see warriors drawing swords and shields and hurrying in that direction. He hurried, and then he ran, in the poor air, under the hazy sun, until he had reached the front lines.

~

There, facing them, were hundreds of anguipeds, but these were not dressed for war. They were civilians, garbed in the black cloaks Wrinn had seen anguipeds wear, the most heavily armed having a knife or a large dagger. "We entreat you, a word with your king," one was shouting.

There was an elf, the Field Marshal, one whom Reev knew as Sintari. Sintari, second only to the king in the wake of Crown Prince Velérion and Nenré's death, wore a steel breastplate and a green cape. His pointy ears poked out of his long blond hair. In his hand was a sword of iron, and he was hugging a shield to his breast.

"Who do you think you are," said Sintari, "you son of Nachash, that the elvenking would deign to speak with you? None may enter the Dark Land. That is his command."

"Ask him," said the anguiped. "Ask him to hear our petition."

"I will not," said Sintari.

"Why?" the anguiped said. "Do you not trust him, that he would not heed the word of a Son of Nachash? Why don't you ask him, and prove it to yourself?"

Sintari grumbled something. Wrinn watched him walk away and depart.

The warriors stirred in the light of the sun. Wrinn feared what would happen. He feared the anguipeds looking at him and wanted to charge forth and cut them down.

Sintari had listened to the anguipeds, their command to test the elvenking.

Wrinn had stirred, and when he heard noise, he turned to look, and his heart dropped when he saw the elvenking riding behind Sintari on his horse.

The anguipeds had demanded an audience with the elvenking, and the elvenking had granted it. The anguipeds' words had worked on him, and that was a mark against the elven armies blocking the

Steaming Gates.

The anguiped who had requested the elvenking had a look of supreme delight now that his desires had been fulfilled. "Your Majesty the Elvenking," he said as the elvenking clopped into hearing range. "We are men of Ash-Land, fleeing our destroyed city. We are not warriors, but farmers who had not left our fields behind in time. The bulk of us have already fled into the Dark Land, but we did not speed south with the haste of our neighbors.

"The Telantines' weapon of domination leveled our capital and our shrines of the Tannin… we are now separated from our families beyond the Steaming Gates. You should know, we consider the Telantines supreme *mugush*-folk, but we believe elves such as yourself can be reclaimed for the Tannin, with proper cleansing and rule and regulation, and the foreswearing of certain foods.

"In fact, we invite you to destroy the Telantines along with us, and live forever in victory. After all, we have observed all the rules and regulations of the Tannin and have worked so hard to vanquish our ancient foe…"

"Farmers," the elvenking repeated dully. He seemed taken with something in the hazy orange light.

His eyes radiated grief.

Wrinn knew, he had lost much — Velérion. Nenré.

"Our cause is not against farmers and civilians," the elvenking said, "nor would we wish you to be separated from your families."

Was the elvenking really going to let them pass?

Wrinn prayed under his breath, that it was not so.

"We have heard of the weapon destroying your city," said the elvenking. "And there were no survivors. But the Telantines wished it to happen, and so I suppose… I suppose we must help them."

Wrinn looked at him in horror. He was not the strong leader Wrinn remembered.

But then Wrinn recalled his behavior in the city of Danarion, how he had almost abandoned it to the rokahn and kobolds.

Wrinn prayed the elvenking would be given strength.

"I'm sorry," the elvenking mumbled. "We will help them. We will help — must help! The Telantines. And we shall.

"But our cause is not against farmers or civilians. We will only block an army. You aren't carrying any weapons, are you?"

"Only the weapons at our sides," said the anguiped.

"We shall let you pass," said the elvenking.

Sintari looked like he was fighting disgust.

As the anguiped approached, followed by the others, he said, "I think you shall follow the rule and regulation of the Tannin in time, Your Majesty.

"But I think you should know — there is an army on its way from the north, intending to dislodge you from the pass. Our father, who lives in the Dark Tower, would not wish you to know. But you have been so kind to us, I will inform you."

"An army," the elvenking repeated softly, at a whisper, "from the north…"

The rumor spread from warrior to warrior, and from warrior's wife to warrior's wife. How big was the army? Wrinn did not know.

"But anguipeds cannot be trusted," said Shomré that night after Wrinn had retreated to their tent.

"No, they cannot," Wrinn said. "They told us, and whatever reason why they told us, it was for our ill. But sometimes they can modify a truth with a lie, and there's still a truthful core behind one of their statements."

"An army," Shomré said. "Who knows how large or how fierce it is?"

And was it rokahn? Wrinn did not know. North of the Dark Land was a region so vast and unexplored as to be uncharted. The army, coming from the north, could be of any people group, rokahn or no.

Wrinn did not want to trouble Shomré, his wife, with the elvenking's weakness or wavering. He did not want to further fill her with fear, a warrior's wife at the end of the world, at the end of Varda.

It was the end of Varda, Wrinn knew, but it was also a beginning.

Chapter Fifteen:
Father of the Bride

Ambrass and Fortunato — wed. Each day filled Ambrass's heart with expectation, a welling feeling of joy close to bursting. As she stared out into City Square from the Dragonpaw Inn's main hall, she could see snowflakes gently falling down from the heavens. Outside, it was winter, and the wintry air was cold. It was the month of Candlebright, and her wedding was at the door.

The wedding… her future.

As she lingered in the corner of the Dragonpaw Inn's main hall, she reflected on how she and Fortunato's story began, a warrior who had suffered a wound that everyone had thought he would succumb to.

Dark iron… a terrible wound. But in the end, it could not overcome a Telantine. What else could a Telantine do? Now, Ambrass knew, a Telantine could forge a northward path to Galiope from the desert that no one else had before.

A Telantine could also win her heart, and never let go of it. What else could a Telantine do?

Fortunato was all she thought about, and she would be together with him soon. Forever, in matrimonial union, she the bride, he the bridegroom.

She knew when the wedding happened, her life would change forever. She would try her best to treasure these moments of expectation. Could the reality be greater than what her imagination had created?

How could it be?

But Ambrass thought it would be.

Glenda was approaching from the corners of the Dragonpaw Inn, beaming.

Ambrass had a strange feeling that Ambrass and Fortunato, husband and wife, was a life goal of Glenda's, too. After all, she had assigned Ambrass to take care of a wounded Fortunato, and had there been a cunning gleam in her eye?

"Are you ready?" Glenda said.

"I don't think I'll ever be quite ready," Ambrass said. "I'll just rush in."

The tailor had fashioned her a white dress with a white veil. It was being held in storage.

She had picked out the flowers with Glenda's advice, blue and white. She had picked out a flower girl. The ringbearer — Ambrass's toddling cousin.

Ambrass would have picked Bala, but no one seemed to know where Bala was. So many of the people she knew from the time when she had met Fortunato were gone.

Gastreel — dead. Bala — vanished. Nocturne — passed away.

Ambrass had survived, and Glenda had survived. Reev and Wrinn were on a mission.

"Ready," Ambrass breathed, "as ready as I'll ever be."

As snowflakes whirled outside, and on streets were wreaths and holly, and all about the city was the joyful expectation of Yule, to that added the joyful expectation of Ambrass and Fortunato's wedding, Ambrass tried to catch her breath.

But as the doors to the Dragonpaw Inn opened, she realized that in an inn so busy as the Dragonpaw, there was little chance of that.

The doors had opened, and two figures were standing in the light of the hearth.

When Ambrass saw them, she thought they were like two figures from a dream.

They were both dressed in thick winter cloaks, and they were a man and a woman. The man had salt and pepper hair that was more gray than black. He was on the verge of elderly, with light brown eyes that Ambrass thought radiated the height of kindness and warmth.

As for the woman, her hair was blond, and her eyes were blue, and to kindness and warmth was added a strength and motherliness. Ambrass felt she knew who the woman was even before her husband announced it.

"I'm Petro," said the man. "I think you may have heard of us, Glenda. This is my wife, Alessa… we are Fortunato's parents."

Glenda made some wordless exclamation.

Ambrass felt timid, as if she were in the presence of greats.

And then Glenda went from wordless wonder to frenzied host. "The best room in the house for you," Glenda said, "and it shall be free."

"I will pay," Petro said, "I will insist."

Petro's eyes fixed on Ambrass, Ambrass with the shuddering heart. She wanted so badly to impress him.

"You are Ambrass," Petro said. "When my son told me he was marrying the most beautiful woman in the world, I wasn't sure I believed him, but now I do. Well, the most beautiful save Alessa."

Words to flatter her — but Ambrass curtsied and smiled.

"He wasn't sure I'd be able to make it," Petro said. "I wouldn't miss it for the world. My son's wedding… and I hear, you'd like me to walk you down the aisle."

"Would you?" Ambrass said.

Her heart trembled.

"I'd be honored," Petro said.

Ambrass thought she'd be getting to know Petro and Alessa in the coming years, though they lived in Ríva, so far away. For now, she'd bask in their presence as the wedding date approached. It was now not just weeks away, but days.

Her heart trembled — the fulfillment of all her hopes, her love with Fortunato at last fulfilled.

As Petro and Alessa got settled into their rooms, Ambrass felt wonderstruck that she had at last met Fortunato's parents. And she had so many questions, though there was precious little time to get to know them before the big event.

~

Late at night, she was in the Dragonpaw Inn main hall, all alone. She had a cup of wine she had ferried from the Dragonpaw Inn's cellar, and was reflecting on all those they had lost.

Gastreel had died, and Nocturne was gone… Reev and Wrinn, vanished from view, now engaged in a war against the Dark One.

But Ambrass had gained the world. Fortunato and she would soon be wed, and though she had lost her parents, now she had gained a new father and a new mother. Petro and Alessa would be her parents now, at least in a sense.

She took a sip of her wine, and tried to think of what she had gained, rather than what she had lost.

Chapter Sixteen: Might

"Will you send your agents with me," Reev said, "if I fight the jotunn?"

Standing at the top of the purified tower, he knew what Spymaster Marius would say. He knew it before he opened his mouth.

"The jotunn cannot be defeated," Spymaster Marius growled. "It is invincible.

"And so we will not waste our men's lives on a fruitless endeavor."

"Then I will defeat the jotunn and take the *Hieros Gamos* alone," Reev said.

"If you wish to die," Spymaster Marius said, "I will not stop you from throwing your life away."

But Reev knew, and the Lady of Danyen had said, they would need to attack rather than just defend. And sitting idly by, and never charging forth into the fray, was no way to conduct a war.

But charging forth armed with nothing but reckless bravery didn't seem like much of a strategy, either.

Reev was among cowards who would not risk their lives.

What had the Lady of Danyen said?

Stride forward.

Charge — into the night.

Pluck the *Hieros Gamos* from the fortress himself.

Reev looked upon Spymaster Marius with condemnation at his cowardice. Then he drew Doomblade, and stepped off the tower, and allowed the brilliant Telantine spirits to guide his feet to the ground.

With Doomblade at the ready, he charged across the rocky

ground.

~

Reev knew the canyon, and the door. He had witnessed the jotunn face to face.

He knew what he was up against.

To the rational man, the Lady of Danyen's words were so foolish, it would appear she wished him harm.

But the Lady of Danyen did not wish him harm.

What would he do, then?

He would follow her words, the ones Reev trusted because he trusted the Lady of Danyen.

Wielding Doomblade in his hand, he ventured along the rocky earth, praying ceaselessly under his breath that he would find a way where Spymaster Marius had said there was no way.

The air was sweltering. The sun was a hazy orange.

And the situation was far worse than Reev remembered.

There were now more than two hundred rokahn and kobolds gathered in the valley. And the jotunn was now armed with a spear fit for a giant.

The Lady of Danyen had told him to stride forth as a warrior of Telantis, to charge in amid odds that seemed insurmountable, because the odds were not insurmountable for those the gods favored. But to Reev, it seemed so reckless as to be suicidal.

Yet what would he do, and what could he do, when he was charged with the crushing of Seymus underfoot? Could he show any reluctance or fear? Could he hesitate?

No, he knew he could not. Against an army of hundreds of rokahn, and a jotunn, a creature under the control of the Dark One himself, could a single Telantine prevail?

He would charge forth and make war on the Dark One.

He sprinted up to the edge of the cliff, to the rift where rokahn were gathered far below. He allowed the sun to bathe him as he brandished his sword, standing unafraid in their sight.

And remembering the Lady of Danyen's words, that the odds were not impossible, he leapt from the cliff, down into the hosts of the rokahn below.

Wild panic consumed the anguipeds and the rokahn, and where he dropped they scattered.

Yet the jotunn's eyes fixed on him with a Hellish gleam, and it drew its spear as it looked upon Reev with a boundless hate that overcame its fear.

Reev chased the fleeing rokahn and pierced a kehrad through to the armor.

But he thought, once the initial terror passed, they would return to fight him.

So where did that leave Reev?

The jotunn struck with his spear and the earth seemed to quake; he missed Reev by an inch, but a crack had opened up in the dark earth and rock.

Reev barreled away, and dove, as the jotunn gave wordless cries, as Reev rolled to the ground — and some rokahn ceased their flight, having realized Reev's seemingly hopeless situation.

Reev staggered backward, knowing the jotunn could easily catch up to him with just one or two strides.

And he saw — overwhelmed by the battle — the sight of a jagged black boulder lying inert on the ground nearby.

The Bracelet of Might flashed in the sun.

Dare he?

Dare he try what no one had ever tried before?

He rushed ahead, as the jotunn charged, running under the

jotunn's massive legs. The jotunn speared the ground and the ground quaked.

Reev rushed across the dark ground to the boulder and seized his arms about it. The jotunn turned and fixed its Hellish red eyes again on Reev, as Reev flexed his muscles and saw the orange gem of the Bracelet of Might begin to burn like fire. He flexed, and heard a crack as the rock was dislodged from its earthen tomb. He strained with all his might, and felt the rock give way, and Reev was heaving a boulder above his head that was ten times larger than himself.

The jotunn rushed forward, as Reev threw the boulder.

The boulder struck the jotunn and the jotunn uttered a hopeless cry, as legs and arms bent and were crushed, and dirt was kicked up. There was a deafening crack as the boulder flattened the jotunn, and then burst through the doors of the fortress, baring the room beyond.

The rokahn and anguipeds who had lingered uttered wild screams of panic and fled into the heat of the day.

The jotunn was now a tangled mass of flesh, crushed by the boulder. The fortress doors were crumbled rubble. *Hieros Gamos* was now there for the taking, whatever it was. Reev would now uncover what the anguipeds had feared to even speak by its name. And it would be his.

The impossible odds had been overcome. The jotunn, the Dark One's Hellish servant, had been killed.

And the odds were not impossible for one the gods favored.

Chapter Seventeen: Not Afraid

Balor had his staff.

Now, he had a mission. He would conquer the Haunted Forest. He would become its master.

But who was the master of the Haunted Forest?

Balor knew his minions had assayed to stop him. But now Balor had a staff. Now, all the powers of magic and the arcane were at his fingertips, and they were focused.

About him were ghostly pines, amid cold air, a winter that never ended so far north. Snow was drifting from the sky as he stepped through the dark wood, a darkness threatening to grow darker, made darker by the whispers on the wind.

"Shall you be my Hand?" said a voice, echoing like an icy dagger to the heart, carried by a ghost on a wind.

"I already have a Hand," said the voice. "Shall I have two?"

Balor turned around as the icy wind kicked about him, stirring the pine needles at his feet.

The powers of the arcane were in him and within him, but he wondered if a different power was required to defeat the master of this wood.

He turned about.

There was another voice — another voice, telling him to go east, in the direction of the sun.

The denizens of the Haunted Forest were nowhere to be seen. The corpses hopping about with hungry faces were gone, leaving only black pine boughs laden with snow. They knew Balor knew they could not harm him.

But could the master of the Haunted Forest harm Balor?

Eastward he stepped, carefully, as snow swirled about him. The sunlight glittered on his hands. The sunlight — he realized — was breaking through where it had not before. Was the sunlight coming in because he was not afraid?

"I am not afraid of you!" Balor shouted. "You will not long be the master of this wood!"

There was a howling wind, a frenzy rattling by Balor's ear.

The master of this wood had said Balor could be his Hand. But Balor would not be his Hand. He would take his staff, and spear the master in the heart.

Through the winds, on which were whispers, he pressed, as snowflakes gently fell from the sky. Who was the master of this dark wood? Who ruled the Haunted Forest?

He wondered…

"Seymus…" the word carried on the wind.

Was Seymus the master of the dark wood? Was the Dark One the master of the Haunted Forest?

Balor's heart shuddered and he fought against fear. The Dark One was a mighty foe, wasn't he?

But he steeled his heart. He remembered the voice he had heard at the carpenter's workshop. He remembered, nothing in this Haunted Forest could truly harm him. Did that include the master of the wood?

He pressed on, and the snow crunched against his boots. The air was an icy chill on his lungs. Winter never ended so far north, but now the wintry part of winter was at its fullness.

The wintry part of winter. Balor continued on. He continued eastward, step by step. He saw, the sun.

And then he saw something else.

Before a vista of the sea was an altar chiseled with skulls. Its stone table was black with ancient blood. As he stood before the altar, he realized what had occurred here, the sacrifice of innocents, of humans and of elves alike, for the dark master of this dark wood.

And a face was shimmering into view, ghostly in the light of the sun — a green face, red eyes, and the forms of horns bulging from its head.

"Balor," said the figure, whose form it seemed was struggling to appear in the light of the sun, "I will give you the world, if you give me your soul."

There was no reward worth that price. "No," Balor said. "Never."

The figure screamed, as if it had been struck, and then all was sunlight...

All was sunlight... and there were no whispers on the wind. There was no dark feeling. There was nothing, then, just one forest among many. The Haunted Forest was no more. Just a forest of pine remained.

~

Balor strode out beyond the forest, and he saw an army of undead waiting.

It was an army he had created many years ago. They had been waiting all this time, and he realized years had passed, years in what once had been the Haunted Forest.

The Haunted Forest had been purified. There was no such thing as the Haunted Forest, anymore.

Years had passed... that meant, Balor had changed.

Was there a name he had used to call himself? He thought there was, but it escaped him.

How old was he now? He no longer felt a child. He wondered if more years had passed in the yearless wood, than years had passed in the real world.

But Balor sensed that world was real, too, in some sense, even if it were not material. He had witnessed terrors and he had changed. His body had developed and grown bigger. He had new wants, new desires.

And he knew now that the guilesome hags had wished to make him a king. He did not want to be a king, but for the fact that the master of the Haunted Forest did not wish him to be one. If the master of what had been the Haunted Forest did not wish him to be a king, then he thought he wanted a throne.

After all, he had a crown.

Where did kings rule? They ruled in the elven capital, Danarion. Balor thought he would claim the elven kingdoms for his own. He was but one man, but he was a necromancer, and over time, a necromancer could build an army from the dead. Thousands of walking corpses stretched before him, and they served as his soldiers.

Beside the forest were the waters of a river. Balor walked up to the edge.

When he saw his changed face, he swallowed terror. There were dark bags under his eyes. His skin was pale, and he looked a young man in the flower of his youth, but for his morbid appearance.

And the wooden crown on his head had petrified.

Chapter Eighteen: The Command

The gates into the fortress were open; they had been destroyed. A boulder, and the tangled arms and legs, the bloodied mess that was the body of the jotun, lay amid the vast space.

The anguipeds and the rokahn had long scattered, and whatever they had been hiding in there, what they had codenamed *Hieros Gamos,* was there for Reev's taking.

Reev brandished Doomblade and plunged into the darkness with a shout.

And he was inside the darkness of the earth.

~

There were pillars, he saw, and a simple walkway carved in the midst of them. The darkness seemed total, but for a vanishingly faint light far up ahead. This Reev charged after, first running and then sprinting with all his might. His legs, his arms, worked like a machine, in concert, speeding him ever faster to his goal.

And then, beyond an open portal, was *Hieros Gamos.*

A red-faced figure was fleeing from Reev as he approached the waters of a pool. There was a man, garbed in a loin-piece, lying in the waters of the pool, which had a faint red glow. He was covered in suction cups attached to wires amid the stone surface of the pool and he seemed to be in pain.

He was grumbling softly, whining, until he turned his steely gray eyes to Reev, and recognition dawned in them.

The man looked like Reev, with a head of dark hair and a fair complexion, an aquiline nose that conquerors were said to have. Reev felt he had seen the man before in a dream, but he knew who the man was long before he announced it.

"Father," Reev said.

Simeon Nax — he was sure.

He had not been dead; he had been kept prisoner all this time.

Reev rushed to his father and began to remove the suction cups from his body, and with each removal of each suction cup his father whined softly in pain.

"Reev," he said, "you've rescued me…"

Reev's father was alive, though his state had not been good.

"What have they been doing to you, Father?" Reev said.

"You scared off my tormentor, Gibboroth," Simeon Nax said. "The Dark One's messor has fixed my body to wires, and has been using my life's energy to give power to him and allow him to manifest in the mortal world."

"They won't be using you that way, anymore," Reev said, as he removed the last of the suction cups with a loud pop.

He looked into this Father's gray eyes, as emotion swelled within him and threatened to overtake him. "Father… I thought you were dead. Well, really, I didn't know what to make of your disappearance. You know, Cobalt found me."

"Cobalt," Simeon Nax said, and there was a light in his steely gray eyes, a light of recognition and remembered love. "Cobalt — have you taken good care of him, son?"

"The best," Reev said. "I sent him away from us when we reached the dunes of the Desert of Hamma. He's probably back in the Elf Lands already."

"Frolicking in the fields," Simeon Nax said, "having done his life's duties…"

Reev looked about in the dark chamber, fearing that Gibboroth would come back. Reev had only seen a glimpse of him, a red face and something hanging from that red face. Gibboroth, a messor for the Dark One, had duties that were different from a messor of a manorial lord, surely.

"Come," Reev said, "I'll help you up, Father. Let's get out of here…"

"I think," Simeon Nax said, "my time's about up, son. I'm not sure I'll be able to walk."

"Then I'll carry you," Reev said.

With the Bracelet of Might flashing on his left arm, Reev grasped hold of his father's body and heaved him up. He was much lighter than the massive boulder that had destroyed the jotunn.

"Oh, Reev," Simeon Nax said, "when I held you in my arms for the last time, and said goodbye, it was the hardest thing I'd ever had to do. But I knew Gastreel had made the right decision, spiriting you away to Norwood to keep you safe from the Dark One. And here you are, all this time later, rescuing me from my tormentor. Gastreel was right…"

But as Reev recalled, Simeon Nax had disappeared before Reev's birth. Was Father misremembering?

It did not matter. Reev rushed ahead, through the darkness of the corridor, beside the pillars, and then into the open air of the Dark Land, under a hazy sun now waning in strength.

~

He was carrying his father in his hands, what the rokahn had been to frightened to call by his name, not *Hieros Gamos*, but Simeon Nax. The Dark One had used his body's energy to allow his servant Gibboroth to manifest, and now Simeon Nax had been rescued from the grave danger he had been in.

Reev rushed across the black rock and the ash-strewn landscape, as Simeon Nax's eyes were winking shut and threatening not to reopen, as Reev feared his father was about dead.

But as the purified tower appeared in the distance, Simeon Nax opened his mouth and seemed to gargle slightly, to give a sign of life. "Reev," he said. "Reev."

He wanted to say something.

But Reev's father was dying.

~

Reev was pulled up the sides of the tower by a spiritual rope, and a spiritual rope also carried Simeon Nax along with them. They were on the surface of the tower, then, the roof of the world, with Spymaster Marius looking on — and a look of wonder in Spymaster Marius's eyes.

"Reev," said Spymaster Marius. "You did it. You slew the jotunn. You brought us *Hieros Gamos.*"

"Not you," Reev said. He set Simeon Nax down on the surface of the tower, as a light appeared in Simeon Nax's eyes.

He opened his mouth to speak, and Reev had a feeling these would be his last words.

"Reev," said Simeon, "the armies are gathered before the Dark Tower. The serpent's child is about here, and you must draw him out. Go to the Dark Tower, and drive the armies gathered about it before you. Then the serpent's child will show his face…"

Simeon then shut his eyes and exhaled. He took pained, labored breaths, as pain and discomfort seemed to swell about him. Then he was still.

There was stillness, and then there was light, a shining form up above head and a sound like a thousand chariots echoing in the air. Light bathed Reev and Simeon, and then Simeon was gone.

"Where did he go?" Reev said.

"He has gone where Telantines go," Spymaster Marius said. "And do not pity him, but be glad for him, for now he is in a better place than us…"

There was a bright shining form floating away, before

disappearing into the sky. The sound of the thousand chariots grew fainter and then at last vanished.

"What now?" said Spymaster Marius. "*Hieros Gamos* did not help us."

"Quiet," Reev snapped. "It helped us indeed. My father, freed from his prison, has died in peace. And he told me what to do. I must draw the serpent's child from his lair — the Dark One's Hand. He said I should drive the armies gathered about the Dark Tower before me."

"You slew a jotunn," Spymaster Marius said. "But if you are telling me you will drive the armies of the Dark Tower before you, by yourself, it seems you are claiming to be a demigod."

"I am not," Reev said. "But I know what I must do. And I know the Oculus can help me no more.

"But perhaps, you can tell me the way."

Chapter Nineteen: Metamorphosis

The sun was hazy. The ground was dark. And when the alarm had sounded, Wrinn knew that the promised army had arrived. It was arriving from the north.

As Wrinn kissed Shomré, once called Rosalie, goodbye, and fled northward through warriors as they drew sword and spear and rushed into formation, he feared it was the last time he would see his wife. And under a burning sun, and heat, he prayed it was not the case, that he would return to Shomré, and that he would return to Shomré in one piece.

They were not rokahn.

No, the armies gathered to do battle were elves. Their standards were waving in the wind, black flags with two red stripes. The soldiers were more heavily armored than any elven army Wrinn knew, and were covered head to toe in breastplates or chainmail. In the back of them were crossbowmen with bolts at the ready.

They were elves, but in the hazy sunlight of the Dark Land, it seemed they were in the midst of a metamorphosis. Their pallid skin had a greenish hue and they seemed to be changing into a form similar to anguipeds. How was that possible, Wrinn wondered?

"The Dark Elves!" howled an Umen Elf wildsaber with his sabers drawn. "The Dark Elves have come to fight for their master. Now we know who their true master is!"

There was a storm, the thunderous sound of galloping hooves, and the ranks of the elves seemed to part. The elvenking had come riding on his Elvish horse, and had drawn his shimmering blue *estirion* blade.

"Look at you, children of Loni," said the elvenking. "You claim to be the children of Loni, but now it is clear you have another master."

The black-and-red standards wafted in the wind.

And as the armies of the Lonen Elves, called Dark Elves, brandished their swords and spears, another form was appearing besides metal and blade. There was a beast in flight, swiftly approaching, if a dragon the most abominable of dragons, with scale-less skin that was colored a cadaver white, and eyes deeply inset into a reptilian head. It was flapping monstrous wings, and gnashing monstrous white teeth, and waving monstrous claws. On its back rode an elf garbed in armor, with a crown forged into his helmet. That elf, the King of the Lonen, was carrying a greatsword in both hands as he guided the white drake with his stirrups.

"Servants of the Dark One!" howled the elvenking.

"We have no time for your superstitions!" the Lonen king shouted. "The gods or Seymus are nothing to us!"

"You say the Dark One is nothing," said the elvenking, "but look — you come to his land, and your every action serves him."

"You will not stop us from entering the Dark Land, O lord of superstition and misrule. You will be defeated, and none shall sing of you." The Lonen king lifted his elbow, and bolts flew from the Lonen crossbows, piercing scores.

Wrinn gripped his quarterstaff and charged into the Lonen front lines, as other elven warriors — Lamen, Umen, and Nurnen — did battle with the Dark Elves. Far in the distance, the elves' treaty allies, the Viegs, howled war cries and charged as well, before sicking their brown wolves on the Lonen.

Wrinn struck with his quarterstaff and disarmed a Lonen warrior, sending his saber ringing to the ground, before drawing his longknife and slashing his throat. Down went the Lonen warrior, as more bolts flew and as the fullness of the true elves did battle against the fullness of the Dark Elves.

Wrinn spied out of the corner of his eye, the vampire troops, pale and black haired, shredding Lonen with animalistic frenzy with their swords before leaping upon them and latching onto them with their fangs, drinking them dry — making use of their curse, and turning it into an advantage.

But as the armies swirled, and two unstoppable forces met, there seemed to be a show on display for all gathered there. For the elvenking and the Lonen king were in the midst of a battle, greatsword against *estirion* sword, and Elvish horse versus white drake.

The white drake dove from its high perch and bit with its rancid fangs at the Elvish horse, but the Elvish horse bucked and dove, then hoofed its way to the other side of the battlefield. Then it charged and speared the white drake with its hoof before piercing its neck with its horns. The elvenking struck with his *estirion* sword as the Lonen king gripped the stirrups and guided the white drake away, narrowly avoiding the elvenking's blow.

A storm of bites and claws followed, and the Elvish horse scrambled. It did not escape without a bleeding wound, claw marks and blood dripping down its side. But the elvenking hammered repeatedly with his *estirion* sword until the Lonen king fumbled and fell backward.

Estirion met tempered steel; the elvenking's *estirion* burst the Lonen king's greatsword and it was riven in two pieces. The elvenking clucked and went galloping, and as the white drake writhed, the elvenking's sword beheaded the white drake in one smooth motion.

The white drake's head rolled to the ground, as its body writhed about in its death throes, before falling still. The elvenking charged after the helpless Lonen king and the Elvish horse's hooves battered him twice, crushing his skull, before the elvenking pierced the Lonen king's heart.

Both white drake and rider lay bleeding on the floor.

Buoyed by the elvenking's victory, the elven armies began to drive Lonen armies back.

The sun was setting when Lonen trumpets blew and the Lonen armies, called the Dark Elves, scattered and fled in every direction.

91

Chapter Twenty: The Wedding of Ambrass and Fortunato

Wedding bells were ringing in St. Sigmund's. Ambrass was struggling to catch her breath. She had donned her white gown and her white veil, and Petro of Ríva, Fortunato's father, was holding her hand in the narthex of the cathedral. Much of Galiope, most any of note and many not of much note, had filled St. Sigmund's pews, this morning, the twenty-sixth day of Candlebright.

A veil covered Ambrass's face, as she waited with bated breath, as the orchestra began to play, and the strumming of the viols started — a sign she should begin to make her way down the aisle.

She walked slowly, as she had rehearsed, as the people gathered in the cathedral stood up and turned — as they turned to look at her. She could see them, Anthanlas and Ramona Nax, Ramona Nax's husband Nicollo, her son Ash... there was her cousin Charlotte and her cousin Chloe, her great aunt Clementine and her uncle Hostus. They were all looking at her with eyes gleaming, radiant with expectation, at so happy a day.

And then she saw him, the bridegroom, Fortunato, dressed all in black, waiting for her at the altar, next to Jiovan the priest. As the orchestra continued to play its tune, she drew nearer step by step, with Petro of Ríva's arm in her own. She was at the altar, then, and Petro took his seat, and as the priest began his homily, she looked into Fortunato's eyes and saw in his her own soul.

~

Ambrass's cousin Julian walked up to the lectern. "Today's

reading," he said, and placed the priest's book on the desk. He opened to a page of the massive tome.

He began to read:

The dawn will not come until
The Fertile Queen is married
The Lovers are one
The doomed city is destroyed in flames
The serpent's children are crushed underfoot
And Balor sits on Solendir's throne

Beside Ambrass, Glenda, maid of honor, stirred, and her eyes sparkled.

As the priest again fixed his eyes on the prospective couple, Fortunato fixed her wedding ring to Ambrass's left finger.

The priest eyed Ambrass and then he eyed Fortunato. "Fortunato of Ríva, do you take Ambrass Saida as your lawfully wedded wife?"

"I do," Fortunato replied.

The priest turned to Ambrass and said, "Ambrass Saida, do you take Fortunato of Ríva as your lawfully wedded husband?"

"I do," Ambrass said.

"You may now kiss the bride," the priest said.

Fortunato met Ambrass in a passionate kiss, to cheers from the gathered wedding crowd. And Ambrass was complete in that moment, and she realized, she had all she ever wanted.

The wedding crowd was standing as they cheered, as wedding bells began to ring anew, and the orchestra started to play. Fortunato grabbed Ambrass's arm with gusto, and then together, man and wife, they began to walk down the aisle to adoring faces.

~

In the booths and tables of the Dragonpaw Inn, the wedding guests gathered. Glenda served pies made from fairy morels and endless cups of wine, and indeed the cellar of the Dragonpaw Inn was opened, and free to guests. Ambrass had her fill of wine and ale, and Fortunato too, but all was expectation — all, burning desire.

In a room of the Dragonpaw Inn, Ambrass and Fortunato made love.

And the Lovers were one.

Chapter Twenty-One: Only Two

The federati had led Barcho and Verrus to the shore of a sea.

In the light of dawn, Barcho could see the raging waves, so towering as to terrify, which no boat could possibly cross without certain death or grave injury.

"There must be a pass," Verrus said, "another way in."

"An army is blocking the only pass into the region," said Quintus, leader of the federati. "We federati have dispatched armies far greater than ourselves, but if the Elf Lands have emptied all their people into the war effort. We won't be able to defeat so many."

Verrus grumbled inordinate curses.

Yet Barcho knew, and surely Quintus, that failure was not an option, that whether they had to risk the violent waves and howling winds, or cut a path through the elven armies, Verrus and his party would not be returning with their tail between their legs. Verrus heard the one responsible for the ruin of his people was beyond these shores, and the Empire he ruled was of little concern to him.

Verrus was striding to the rocky shores. Something was glittering in the sand. It had a look of gold, but it was not a coin — it was too long and thin. Barcho strode up to it, and saw it was a quill.

It was a quill, like that used for writing, but it was not a feather. It was metal.

Verrus took it in his hands and when he took it, he seemed changed, his gait different in the light of the dawn. He waved the quill about, and then he struck it in the sand.

What was he doing?

Barcho watched as something appeared in the distance, the ghostly form of some object in the sand which quickly faded to nothing.

But Verrus had taken notice of the ghostly object. He took the quill and struck the ground, and then he struck again, all the harder. The object reappeared, by the shore, and it was a book with gold pages, lying amid the grayish-black dust.

Verrus rose and walked up to the book. He took it in his hands. He said, "What's this?"

"Be careful," said Quintus. "Be careful, for I think there is a dark magic in this land."

Barcho walked up to Verrus as Verrus set the book down and got onto the ground. He opened the book, and the pages of the book were blank.

"Whatever it is," Verrus said, "it's no ordinary book. It's a wonder."

"We should be careful with wonders," said Quintus.

"Careful," Verrus grumbled. "I'm sure a *mugush*-folk would like me to be careful."

With the quill in his hands, Verrus pressed its edge to the gold pages. It made a blood-red mark when he made a stroke.

Verrus wrote:

The sea.

The raging waters of the sea seemed to bubble and boil in response to Verrus's writing, as if nature itself and the elements responded to the writing of the book.

Verrus wrote again:

The sea was stilled.

There was a howl from the sea, the waves reaching a maximum crest, and then plummeting. The sea which once raged was now silent and as flat as glass.

Verrus cackled at what he had done.

Enough ships for the federati.

Three warships appeared by the shore, their decks lined with metal plates, their prows carved into the shape of serpents.

Verrus pressed the pen again to gold paper, and more red writing appeared.

Experts to pilot them.

The shapes of red-faced creatures appeared, red-faced beings with beards that ended in tentacles. They were at the ships' wheels.

And then Verrus seemed overcome with something, and began to wail quietly, wails which softened into a moan. He looked down at the gold pages.

My mother, back from the grave.

A woman appeared, one who had the look of Verrus's mother. Her hair was wild and tangled, and she wore the fine purple dress that Barcho remembered Valeria Verra wearing. But her eyes, when she looked at Verrus, were gold and black like a cobra's. She seemed ready to gnash her fangs.

"Oh, Verrus," and the woman's voice was just like Valeria Verra's, "why did you let it happen? The destruction of Altalac, our capital? If you had applied the ingenuity that mama monster had instilled in you, you wouldn't have let it happen. I told you to keep a watchful eye on the Telantines. I told you to manage every part of the *mugush* Empire with exactness, until the last of the Telantines were killed!"

"Quiet!" Verrus growled.

"I told you, and now Altalac is gone!" said the woman with the cobra-eyes. "Altalac, our capital, where our forefathers lit candles for the Tannin. And now it's disappeared, because you didn't listen to mama monster."

"Quiet!" Verrus howled.

"I told you, Verrus! I told you!" the woman's voice was now cutting. "You are not half of your ancestor Thuban. He would not allow Altalac to be destroyed."

Verrus pressed gold pen to gold paper, and left red ink behind.

She was eaten by wild dogs.

Dogs appeared, vicious dogs of Hell, with eyes burning like flames. Claw by claw, and tooth by tooth, they devoured the woman with the cobra-eyes until she was a puddle of blood and flesh on the ground.

The dogs were killed.

Invisible blades cut the dogs to ribbons.

Verrus had a dark gleam in his eye. He looked to Barcho, then to Quintus and his federati. "This is cheating. I will earn my victory."

He pressed, again, gold quill to gold paper.

In blood-red ink, he wrote his command:

The magic book and the magic quill became my sword.

The gold twisted and melded, and stretched to great lengths as it took a new shape, and then — in the light of the morning — a new color. It was no longer gold, but green, a massive bastard sword with a serrated edge.

"Serpentax," Verrus said as he held it in his hands.

Barcho saw there was writing on the edge in a language he could not read.

Verrus heaved Serpentax in his hands. "We will test it," Verrus said, "on the weakest link."

Before Barcho could turn and flee, Verrus had pitched back his sword.

Barcho saw the fires of Hell as the blade pierced him through the chest, and the blackened wound did not bleed, but burn. He wailed, at his life's choices, his life's choices to follow the serpent's child to the land where serpents ruled.

Chapter Twenty-Two: Fearing and Hoping

In places the Dark Land seemed empty, but Reev knew it was not empty.

There were pits where the rokahn were spawned, and there were rokahn, and there were ghosts.

The ghosts he did not see as he walked down the road, the road that Spymaster Marius told him would take him to the heart of the Dark Land, and the Dark Tower.

Reev felt bold, walking down the road in his loin cloth, bearing Doomblade at his side — a coin necklace of Telantis about his neck, and his neck tattooed with Telantine lightning marks. He did not hide who he was as he strode — to what? His destiny.

To drive the armies before the Dark Tower by himself was indeed something that seemed impossible. But he had charged into the fray with boldness, heeding no fear, and found a way to kill a jotunn. His very appearance drove anguipeds and rokahns into terror.

They remembered Telantis. They remembered the Telantines.

Eating road-bread and drinking from springs and pools, he passed the first day without seeing any sign of the enemy. But on the second day, he began to see fortifications in the distance, black castles built on high hills, lookouts that surveyed the ashen earth. The land was beginning to rise, and also descend, bearing rifts and canyons, his hills and deep valleys, growing unnavigable.

Reev knew boldness had its place, but on the third day since departing the tower, he saw an army of countless number approaching in the distance. Peering at them, from afar, with his spyglass, he could see the multitude marching down the road with an anguiped on an anguiped horse leading them. Amid the forms of anguiped warriors in splint mail armor and sabers, rokahn and kehrad and black wolves, kobolds and kobold mages, there were jotunns marching amidst their midst.

There were jotunns, and there were no boulders handy.

Boldness had its place, charging into the fray against wild odds was what a warrior of Telantis did, but shrewdness and caution had to be the default. Reev hurried off road, into the depths of a canyon, and hid as the thunder of the army's feet passed him by, the infernal cries of the jotunns and the cruel shouted orders of the anguipeds.

He waited them out that day, and he wondered what the army intended to do, whom the Dark One had selected as the target of his fury. Reev waited, and he slept that night, and when he arose in the morning, he could still hear their marching feet.

~

Reev followed the road, but he did not walk upon it. In canyons and in rifts in the ground, he made his way in a circuitous route that followed the road. He knew there were lookouts and towers throughout the Dark Land to keep an eye on intruders. He knew the enemy's eye was on him, as he attempted to draw near the Dark Tower.

Another day passed, and he made slow progress. More days passed, as the rocky hills and canyons were giving way to an ascent. There were makeshift towns, now, in the ashen earth, in the poor, hot air — buildings built of cinderblock and dried grass, and anguipeds walking among them. Reev knew that after Heaven's Spear had been launched from the doomed city of Qadirra, it had struck the anguiped homeland and the anguipeds had fled into the Dark Land. Here, they were building a new life for themselves — at least, that was what the survivors were doing. But the poison earth did not seem good for agriculture, and whatever tangled trees managed to lay roots in the ashen soil were stunted. Somehow, they were managing to survive, however, and regather.

Yet Reev felt that their project was doomed. Whatever crops they managed to grow would lack nutrients. And the Dark One who ruled this land could not mend this poison earth.

Reev pushed on, as days became a week, a week two weeks, and his cautious but purposeful gait at last bore the fruit he had been seeking.

~

Here, at the height of the Dark Land, was a valley. And before that valley was a monument that dominated everything in its wake.

A massive tower stretched from the ground toward the heavens, a towering work that seemed crafted by a twisted mind. Its sides rose up in unhallowed symmetry, the bricks of its walls seeming to suck all color and light around it into a black void. No ornament did the tower have, only an effect on the mind — to despair. It stretched and dominated the bleak ashen valley, and as Reev craned his neck from the bottom to the top, he saw the top of it, too, was unornamented. A monolith it was, without beauty, only deadly symmetry. And Reev could not bear to imagine the twisted mind who had designed it, or how many lives had been lost in its making. Reev had a sense — it had stood for millennia. It had to be at least a thousand feet tall, and Reev wondered that, if there were stairs, how it was possible from one to ascend to the high heights and survive.

He fought a temptation of despair at the sight of the tower. But when he looked to the bottom, there was fear. For the valley the Dark Tower dominated was vast, and every inch of it was covered in rokahn camps. That an army so numerous could exist befuddled the mind, at how so many mouths could be fed. Were they thirty thousand? Fifty thousand? A million?

They were without count, and they and the valley that surrounded the Dark Tower stretched into the horizon.

Reev's father, a Telantine, had told him to drive the armies of the Dark Tower before him. And now the doubting words of Spymaster Marius seemed reasonable.

Reasonable… but for the prophecies, that Reev would crush the Dark One under his foot. And he would have to draw the Dark One's Hand, what his father had called the serpent's child, from his hiding place. He would have to draw the enemy out, and then he would have to strike.

Duty demanded no less. But how could he possibly drive so many rokahn before him?

Reev knew, seeing the Dark Tower and its deadly symmetry, that it would take more than striding forth in the garb of Telantis.

Chapter Twenty-Three: To Love and to Cherish

Wrinn had witnessed the Lonen Elves fleeing in defeat, but he thought they hadn't seen the last of them.

They hadn't seen the last of them, maybe, but Wrinn had seen something else, elves in a state of metamorphosis. Though they had claimed not to heed the Dark One or heed his existence, they had functionally chosen to serve him when they had refused to go to war. And now their skin had changed to a greenish hue, and they had begun to look more anguiped than elf.

The sight of it terrified Wrinn, the sight of it happening to someone else, the fear it could happen to him. But Wrinn was not the Dark One's child, nor would he ever be. He would never turn into an anguiped like the Lonen Elves. And the Lonen Elves, Wrinn thought, had earned their moniker, the Dark Elves.

Their king, now, was dead. Their armies had scattered. But as a dark wind blew across a scorching hot plain, and the air shimmered in Wrinn's sight, there was something, the sound of pealing trumpets.

All the strength of the elves had been brought to the Dark Land, to fight a war that had begun more than a thousand years ago. Would they expect not to face an enemy just as fierce as before, or fiercer, even though the strength of the elves was faint, and a shadow of what it had been?

Through the camp, the Field Marshal, Sintari, was riding on an Elvish horse, shouting, "Draw arms! Draw arms!" as he sped through the gathered warriors, some sleeping and some in a state of alert.

Wrinn's tent flap opened and Shomré appeared, Shomré who not long ago was called Rosalie. "Going to battle, my husband?"

Shomré said. "I will say a prayer for you."

"Say a prayer for me," Wrinn said. "In fact, let's pray together."

Shomré met him in an embrace, and she led a prayer, and then he did.

When Wrinn finished the prayer, he asked, "Let me never turn into an anguiped. Let me never be the Dark One's child."

And Shomré looked at him, and where he was afraid at what he had seen, Shomré's confidence washed over him. The gods loved Shomré and Wrinn, and Reev, and they always would.

~

The army had been sent from the Dark Tower, and it intended to dislodge the armies of the elves from their place, guarding the Steaming Gates. They were rokahn, they were kobolds, and there was something else — giants walking among them.

They were like elves the size of towers, with eyes of a fiery red and tangled masses of teeth. Some wore spears as large as towers, or clubs cut whole from a tree. As they burst through the elven lines, some elves wailed as they drew swords and spears, as they braced shields against their chests.

Wrinn heard a cry, "Jotunn!" as the giants stormed past the elven front lines, and with sweeps of the club and spear, killed scores with each stroke.

But as elves did battle with rokahn and kobolds, and as lightbearers faced off with kobold blood mages — spears of light against distortions of the blood — the jotunns now making quick work of the elven lines were facing a foe they had not before, one they had not faced during the First Shadow War, which now they faced in the second.

As the jotunns struck and killed scores, a nimble foe as speedy as a jungle cat were shimmying up their legs and massive torsos — vampires with all the speed of the creatures of the night, and as they reached the jotunn's chests, buffeting them with a frenzy of dagger blows and knife blows.

The jotunns wailed as the vampires struck them, death by a thousand cuts, and as they began to drip vile acidic blood from their bodies, the strikes of their spears and their tree clubs was growing weaker.

Wrinn watched as a jotunn fell, killing elves in the wake of the cloud of dust he kicked up. Dust swirled over the elven armies, as one by one the jotunns died.

The sight of the dying jotunn seemed to threaten the confidence of the rokahn, and to the extent that the rokahn could show fear on their mottled faces, they showed it.

Wrinn charged and buffeted a kobold mage with a frenzy of blows, dislodging his staff from his hands and then pummeling him, at first to the ground, and then to his death.

Some rokahn began to retreat in a frenzy. But anguipeds on anguiped horses gave orders, and the gathered armies then began to make an ordered retreat.

Countless elves had died. But the armies of the elves had stood firm, and it seemed there was strength in the elves yet.

~

When he returned to camp, Shomré was waiting for him.

Wrinn did not know what name he liked better, Rosalie or Shomré. Shomré, Wrinn knew, was a crude translation of the human name. But whether he liked the name or not, he knew he loved the one who bore it.

"Victory," said Shomré, "and you are in one piece."

"Victory," said Wrinn, "but the armies of our enemy are vast. And they have giants of darkest Hell in their employ."

"All the armies of the Dark One," said Shomré, "all the armies of darkest hell, will not be able to stop the coming of the dawn."

But Wrinn knew that the dawn would come from elsewhere, not from the elves standing guard over the Steaming Gates. It was Reev's task to crush the Dark One underfoot, and Wrinn knew, it was now his task to be the husband of Shomré.

It was Wrinn's task to take care of Shomré, and to cherish her all her days.

The war, and the guarding of the Steaming Gates, was just a way for them to survive. It was the reason the elvenking's men gave Shomré bread and wine each day.

Wrinn kissed Shomré on the lips.

Chapter Twenty-Four: Sir Yes Sir

Balor had walked out of the Haunted Forest to find an army waiting for him.

It was an army he had conjured in his youth.

He had walked at the head of that army to find something else, a land utterly abandoned.

The towns of the vampire kingdom were abandoned, dotting lonely roads now untended to. Now, at the height of winter, wooden markers marked the roads as they wound from one town to another, but all towns were abandoned, and the vampires had left their posts. In fact, not a single vampire seemed to have remained behind, man, woman or child.

Balor feared some terrible fate had befallen them, but he had another thought besides fear, that what had befallen them was good, hope inestimable, bottomless hope.

A people freed from a curse…

That was a thought, spilling out of him, as Balor walked at the head of his undead army.

He had formed a goal, one made because it was what the master of the Haunted Forest did not want. The master of the Haunted Forest did not wish him to be a king, so Balor thought he ought to be one. He knew the elvenking ruled in Danarion, on a throne called Solendir's throne. And Balor did not know the way, except that it was south of here, in a land as blessed as the Vampire Kingdom had been treacherous.

He did not know the way, but he vowed to find it, as much as he could.

~

Balor did not know how to navigate, how to discern the way. But he knew a road that would take him out of the Vampire Kingdom entirely, one that wound its way southwards toward a rough wilderness. He knew the undead servants he hired could only respond with grunts and groans, and that they would be of no assistance in Balor's southward journey.

He had called the hags guilesome, but they would be of great help, now. They had given him a crown, a crown that had turned from wood to stone. They had taken him to the Haunted Forest, a forest now conquered, and then had set him loose. They were of little help now.

~

The road through the snow took him south, days, as he remembered, through the black pines and the snows of the taiga. When he reached the Black River, partially frozen, Balor crossed into the wild lands beyond. There were pines and there were floes of ice. There were bears and there were Snow-Men. But Balor was now possessed of arcane power, arcane power now focused and perfected with a mage's staff as his tool.

He departed in a southward direction. He prayed he would continue in that southward direction, having no guide nor skills. But he had used the undead soldiers as beasts of burden, and had piled in their packs road-bread from the abandoned towns.

They did not eat, but they hungered, and there were thousands at his beck and call.

Balor would fear the freezing wind, but he would not fear the bear or the Snow-Man. He would fear the drifts of snow, the icy gale, but not the armies of the gathered elves, who would only make him stronger. A necromancer was a difficult foe to face, and a skilled necromancer was the king's worst nightmare.

An elvenking sat on the throne, but Balor would take the throne from him, because the master of the Haunted Forest didn't want him to.

It was a child's reasoning, and perhaps Balor was still more child than man. But it was a child's reasoning he would stick to.

~

A day after they disembarked, and the snow drifts were piled to Balor's knees, and sometimes to his waste. Was he going south? As long as he wasn't going north, whether he was straying east or west, he would eventually come to a part of the world that was inhabited.

There were trees about Balor, and icy rivers. There was the howl of the wind, and sometimes the distant cries of Snow-Men that would terrify the cognizant. And the road-bread, he saw, was full of worms, but he ate it still.

He pushed on a day later, and snow began to fall from the heavens. Would he make it south? Would he find his way to a place where there was no snow, where there were elves and towns and farmland? Would he find his way to the city where the elvenking ruled, a land he recalled was a place of perpetual sunlight and plenty?

The snow built to a blizzard that night, as Balor shivered in a tent that he had ordered his undead minions to erect. He did not know how to make a fire, but he was determined to push on. He was determined to push on, because the master of the Haunted Forest did not want him to.

He had a helping of rotted road-bread in his hand, and he picked apart the worms, and then he ate it. There was a wild frenzied cry of a Snow-Man in the distance, a wild terrified screech. Balor thought the Snow-Men would know not to approach an army, but if they were so foolish, they would face an army of the living dead who had forgotten much, but not how to wield the blades they carried.

How long had he managed to travel? How much distance had he managed to put behind him, this day?

Amid the snowy landscape, the rough terrain, Balor thought it couldn't have been much.

~

It couldn't have been much, but they set out again the next day through the snow, through the raging blizzard and storm. The air was icy, and as Balor gave orders, and pushed past drifts of snow, in a landscape where he could hardly see his own legs moving in front of him, he could feel the opposition of the master of the Haunted Forest all about him, and the opposition he felt drove him forward.

Chapter Twenty-Five:
In the Country

Ambrass and Fortunato were husband and wife, and they had made love, and made love again.

They were in a cabin outside Southkirk for their honeymoon, a cabin which overlooked the waters of a frozen pond. Around the frozen pond were trees, some bare of leaves and some with green boughs that never lost their life, whether it was winter or summer, fall or spring. Ambrass thought she liked the green pines best.

"I like the green pines best," she said to her beloved, Fortunato, as she sat at the window, beside the fire, with a cup of Yule tea. "I like them best, because whether it's freezing cold, or whether the weather is kind, they're always green."

"I like the broadleafs best," Fortunato insisted, as he took the tea kettle and poured himself a cup of Yule tea, then sat down next to her. "Because in the summer, their greenness fills the forest, and in the fall, they put on a dazzling show."

Oh, the silly arguments they had, when all their hopes were fulfilled, and they were bound in matrimonial union.

Fortunato had rented the cabin for a week, and the journey had been arduous, amid drifts of snow and the winter they faced. They had spent New Year's at an inn on the road, and said goodbye to the year 1156, and said hello to the year 1157.

Ambrass thought her imagination would not tell the true tale of their joy, and she realized it was true, that now wed, she was happier than she had ever been.

But Ambrass wondered if the greatest joy was up ahead. She wondered if there was something better than a wedding and the bridegroom's kiss.

She stirred in the cold air. She felt she was not adequately warm.

"I'll be back, my love," she said, and took barefooted steps across the wooden floor, to their rented room where they had stowed their belongings.

She found a suit of luggage where she had stowed her clothes, and picked out a pink chemise. She pulled it over her shirt, and felt a bit warmer, but she thought that perhaps she'd feel much warmer in Fortunato's embrace.

As she stepped again, gingerly, over the wood of the floor, she called out to him, and he looked back. She saw his eyes, and they stole her breath.

"How do you like it?" Ambrass said.

"It looks good on you," Fortunato said, "but then again, everything does."

How handsome was he in the sight of the fire, her beloved. They had made love, and then they had made love a second time.

They had rented this cabin, their honeymoon, for such a purpose. This cabin was in the South Country, famed as a place for lovers such as they.

Seeing her beloved, as she strode about him and then sat in his lap, as she hooked her arm around her neck and felt his warmth, she realized what a fool she had been to even think of Gaius and Nocturne, when all she had ever wanted had walked into the Dragonpaw Inn one winter's eve like this, wounded, and gazed into her eyes.

Fortunato, her beloved, was no longer wounded. Hot blood ran through his veins, and he was at the height of life and health.

So, she realized, was she.

"What a fool I was," Ambrass said aloud, "to even think of Nocturne. What an utter fool I was, to dwell on Gaius even a moment."

Would Fortunato say the same of the elven princess he had wooed? He opened his mouth to say something, and then he stopped himself.

Was there something stopping him, or someone? Some legacy he had left behind?

"Oh, you don't have to answer, Fortunato," Ambrass said. She poked him on the nose. "You don't have to say anything back. I know, Nenré was a fine woman."

Fortunato's mouth hung agape even further, but still he refused to repudiate his old love.

Would she come back to haunt Ambrass and Fortunato's wedded bliss? Ambrass had an inexplicable certainty that she would not have to worry, that Fortunato was hers and hers alone, forever.

But Ambrass thought Fortunato was refusing to say something.

He was refusing, and then his mouth hung open fully, his delightful lips perked into position, and he spoke. "Nenré and I had a child," Fortunato said. "And I don't know what's happened to my son. He was with the elves, when I left him."

"With the elves, he is well taken care of," Ambrass said. "With the elves… well taken care of, I'm sure."

And it hurt Ambrass slightly that Nenré's romance had gone so far, but Ambrass only had warm feelings for Fortunato's child. "What was his name?" Ambrass said.

"Alondir," Fortunato replied.

"Alondir," Ambrass said. Something stirred inside her, a feeling, as Fortunato took Ambrass's hands in hers, and then picked her up, and laid her before the light of the fire. As his hand went to her chemise, to remove it and then more, she thought, and was certain — Ambrass and Fortunato would have a child, too.

Another thought — *children.*

~

Oh, how dear was winter, and how gentle were snows, how toothless was a blizzard, in a cabin with your lover in the country.

There, snow was joy and all winter threw at you was bliss. As

Fortunato and Ambrass spent their honeymoon in the cabin, the winter of 1157, the snows and howling winds only made their joys complete, and the wines they sipped together all the more festive.

How happy was winter, and how joyful were snow and gale, how festive was a blizzard in a cabin in the woods, how wondrous the wine huddled by the fire, in the joy with your lover in the country.

The Lovers were one, and Ambrass and Fortunato knew they would be one, for all their days.

Chapter Twenty-Six: The Threshold

The army of rokahn was too large for Reev to face.

And so he withdrew, wondering just how he would obey the words of his father, how he could possibly drive the armies before the Dark Tower and draw out of the serpent's child.

He wondered, and then he thought better of idling in open view, in his Telantine loin cloth, with his necklace and the lightning marks tattooed on his neck. He thought better and he had withdrawn. He had withdrawn, and he found himself on a road, bending southward in view of the Dark Tower and its valley.

The road wound through ash and rock, under the hazy sky and the dim orange sun. Reev followed it openly, his boldness coming from a source he did not know, as a dry and scorching wind blew from the south. As he walked, the air seemed enveloped in smoke and smog, and to sting him as he strode, and the air was worsening in quality, not getting better. Up ahead were cliffs, and a smoky horizon — dim lights up ahead, and a greater light.

It was a woman in a brightly shining gown, a woman with burnt gold hair and bright green eyes, the apparition of the Lady of Danyen. Reev followed her off the road, onto the edge of one of the cliffs, where she turned in her shining white raiment.

"*Velati Sonoren*," she said to him, "you are at the threshold of the Dark City."

"The Dark City?" Reev said.

"There is a Dark One, and a Dark Land, and a Dark Tower," the Lady of Danyen said. "Does it surprise you, therefore, that there is a Dark City, where those who wish to live in lawlessness and disorder go? Where theft and murder are not punished, but rewarded? Where criminals punish the law abiding for minor infractions, but leave the worst offenses unpunished?'

"It sounds like a place I wouldn't like," Reev said.

"You would hate it," the Lady of Danyen said, "but it is the only place where a young man dressed in the attributes of Telantis would not suffer immediate harm. For here some humans live, not only anguipeds and rokahn and kobolds. Indeed, it is where the humans of the Dark Land abide, and not anguipeds and their spawn."

"And shall I go to the Dark City?" Reev said.

"You shall do as your father told you," said the Lady of Danyen. "You shall drive the armies before the Dark Tower, and draw out the serpent's child. For only when the Dark One seems in imminent peril, will his Hand feel urged to act."

"Shall I go to the Dark City?" Reev said again.

"As I said," said the Lady of Danyen, "you will do your father's command. But as for how, it is beyond my knowledge. I do not know how you will drive the armies of the Dark Tower before you."

She wouldn't answer his question.

But as Reev turned, and looked back, and the Lady of Danyen was gone, he did not think there was anywhere else to go besides the Dark City. What else was there to do, when he did not know how to drive the armies of the Dark One from the tower?

~

And so, remembering the Lady of Danyen's statement that he would not be harmed, he began to walk down the road under the dark smoky sky, as the distant pinpricks of light through a smoggy veil became windows lit with candles and hearths. The architecture was harsh and angular, and as the darkness was broken by the lights in the windows, Reev saw arches that came to harsh points, and the distant forms of pinnacles and spires. As he walked through the dark streets, he began to take note that he was not alone, that dark shapes were appearing alongside him in this Dark City, in this Dark Land.

There was a cart full of melons, and a man standing beside it, and he was taking bids.

"A silver!" said a woman gathered beside him.

"Two silvers!" said a man with buck teeth.

"A silver," said a man standing far in the distance, wreathed in the Dark Land's darkness, "and two stabs in the back for your worst enemy…"

Reev passed on, not knowing what he would find, or how the streets of the Dark City would bring him further to his goal — a plan to drive the armies of the Dark Tower before him.

But where else was there in the Dark Land to go?

He was passing through another street, and there was a broad stone square. Lights and lanterns were set up in the corners and at the perimeter, but they barely pierced through the Dark Land's smoky haze, the dark sky and the cloudy haze that blocked out sunlight.

Was it day? Was it night? In the Dark Land, the distinction was blurred.

And Reev was standing in the square alone in his loin cloth and his Telantine necklace, standing uncertain.

But again, he was not alone.

A woman was on a litter, and the doors of a litter were open to reveal her. She was garbed in a flowered red silk gown, and her face was whitened with paint. Her lashes were darkened, and her head of black hair was tied up in a bun. Onlookers, admirers were gathered around her.

"Yes," she said, "come, behold the Lady Jinn, who left her husband, the Dragon Emperor, for hopes that the dark sire of this Dark Land would have her hand in marriage instead…"

It was a dark and dismal place. And there seemed to be no light or love. How could Reev defeat the great darkness of the Dark City, in this Dark Land?

He turned down the street.

Was there an inn to stay at? There were buildings, and there were dark arches. The darkness was so great, the figures walking by him seemed like shadows.

The darkness cloaked him, and perhaps that was good, for Reev was not hiding who he was, a Telantine. He had ventured into the Dark City, in this Dark Land, as boldly as he had gone to fight the jotunn before the fortress.

But what did he have to show for it? Dark shapes — dark figures. A Dark City of inestimable darkness, in the inestimable darkness of the Dark Land.

There was darkness, and then there was a hand grabbing Reev by the shoulder, pulling him into the alley.

"What do you think you're doing?" the man spoke a language that, although Reev intellectually perceived he did not know, he understood every word.

What did that mean, Reev's recognition? Reev thought he understood what that recognition meant, even before the man started a light, and a candle was burning, and he saw, beneath the folds of a cloak, tattoos of lightning marks on his neck.

"What do you think you're doing, walking about openly like that? Are you crazy?" the Telantine man said.

"I'm crazy, I guess," Reev said in the same tongue, in the relative security of the alley. "I killed a jotunn by myself. I guess I was overbold. A little — what's the word — cocky?"

"Cocky," the Telantine said. "Well, I think you had best be more careful in the future."

Even with the bright candle, the darkness of the alleyway had hardly dispersed.

Reev felt something fall about his shoulders, a rough woolen cloak. "There are others of our kind," the Telantine said, "plotting the destruction of the Dark One. And I suppose, you're the one promised to crush the Dark One under his feet. I'm Blarer. Pleased to meet you."

~

In an oiled cloak, as an acid rain began to pour, Reev followed Blarer through the dark streets of the Dark City, and at times lost track of him, because his candle hardly pierced the oppressive smoky darkness. But to be among his kind, and not those who wished to live out their days in the Dark City, was a blessing indeed.

There was light that the Dark One could not squelch, in the shadow of the fearsome tower. There were warriors of light plotting against him, even here. And as Reev tried mightily to follow Blarer and his vanishing candle, he uttered a prayer of thanksgiving, that his boldness in striding through the streets of the Dark City had led him to his kind, and the overflowing love he felt just by being in their presence.

Blarer — or the figure of his candle — turned down a street, and then to stone steps. There was the sound of an opening and shutting door, and then he was inside a house.

There was a stone fireplace and a blazing fire. Lanterns and candles, whitewashed walls, and torches on sconces, conspired to burn away the Dark City's hazy, smoky darkness. And beside Blarer, Reev saw another Telantine standing amid the houses's light.

Blarer, he saw, had brown hair, and the other Telantine was blond, with eyes of hazel. Leaning against the walls of the house were swords in leather scabbards, two in number — probably belonging to Blarer and the other Telantine.

"I'm Reev Nax," he announced to Blarer, and then he turned to the other Telantine. "Who are you?"

"Ajax," he announced. "It is good to be with you."

"Good to be with you," Ajax continued, "a perfect description. We've got to stick together, here, in such a place."

Here, with Ajax and Blarer, behind the doors of the house, he felt safe. But was the eye of the Dark One upon them here? Did he know that three of his greatest enemies had gathered in the Dark City, in the Dark Land?

"Two Telantines live in the Dark City," Reev said.

"Two Telantines dwell here," Ajax said, "as they plot and plan, and get ready for the Great War."

Ajax paused.

"I suppose you're the one who was promised to kill the serpent's child," Ajax said.

"How do you know?" Reev said.

"The coin necklace you're wearing," Ajax said. "Something about you. The fact that you've arrived so suddenly, and I've never seen you before."

Reev nodded.

"But how will you kill the serpent's child?" Ajax said. "And how will you tread the Dark One under your feet?"

"I must drive the armies of the Dark Tower before me," Reev said. "I must draw out the Dark One's Hand from his hiding place, wherever that may be. I thought I would have to drive the Dark One's armies from the tower alone. But now I see, I don't have to be alone."

"It's not good to be alone," Blarer said, "when you're facing such a fearsome enemy."

Reev allowed himself to exhale. He saw, in the fire, there was food cooking in the pot. He realized he hadn't eaten all day, and now, without fear banishing his hunger, his stomach was growling in response.

"Pepper in the pot," Ajax said. "Meat, simmering. The Dark City doesn't have much, but it does have food. And we have dinner cooking."

"How will we drive the armies from the tower?" Reev said.

"We'll find a way," Blarer said. "The gods will show us."

Chapter Twenty-Seven: At the Steaming Gates

The winds were howling in the Dark Land. Wrinn had drawn his quarterstaff, and wasn't sure what the Dark One would throw at the elven armies next. But for now, he would wait, and stand guard outside the tent that Shomré was sleeping in.

Of late, she seemed taken with something, exhaustion and fatigue, a disorientation perhaps caused by the rough climes they had found themselves in. And Wrinn supposed, these were the roughest climes of all, the Dark Land where the Dark One ruled, and where the Dark One's minions held sway.

Wrinn was a part of the light fighting against the darkness. Somewhere, far away, Reev was fighting the Dark One alongside the Telantines, and the elves would follow the Telantines' lead.

The landscape around him was alien, the sun veiled in hazy orange, the black ground poison, refusing to allow anything to grow. The poor air, the heat and the particles stinging his lungs, was getting to him. It was getting to him, and then horns began to blow.

They were blowing from the south, and they were not elven horns.

~

The Dark One had tried something new, to dislodge the elves from the Steaming Gates. Now rokahn did not face them, but anguipeds wearing bronze masks, their bodies covered head to toe in iron-plated armor. They had in their hands two-handed swords, and they seemed to stride forth with unnatural bravery, bravery that Wrinn had never witnessed before in anguipeds.

One anguiped had a mask that was slipping. His eyes were

twitching, and foam was escaping from his mouth. The anguipeds, which Wrinn saw were so numerous as to be uncountable, stretching into the horizon, had been fed some poison that took away their cowardice, and had driven them mad.

Horns began to blow, and the frenzied anguipeds charged with their two-handed swords. Wrinn gripped his quarterstaff in both hands and faced them with as much bravery as they could muster.

The anguipeds' swords flashed as they attempted to cut into the elves front lines, as sword met sword and sword met spear.

The Umen, Wood Elves, had sent their wildsabers to do battle, and the wildsabers slashed with their sabers in a frenzy to match the anguipeds' chaotic style.

The anguipeds, their minds twisted by the poison they consumed, were throwing themselves into the elves heedless of the danger, and as elves fell, one after the other, Wrinn wondered if this was the force that would put an end to the elven armies once and for all.

An anguiped swordsman struck at Wrinn, and Wrinn dodged. He pushed him to the ground with his quarterstaff, then, sliding to the ground, pierced him in the heart with his longknife. Over and over again he pierced, and the anguiped continued to twitch, heedless of all danger. The mask slipped, and there was fear in the anguiped's eyes, as Wrinn dealt the final blow, piercing him in the heart.

The anguipeds had cut swathes through the elven lines, but as Wrinn looked up, he could see the elves had steeled themselves, and were fighting back. And the elves' treaty allies, the Viegs, had sicked their brown wolves on the anguipeds.

The countless brown wolves, much larger than a normal wolf, were laying into the poison-frenzied anguipeds with their fangs and claws, cutting through them with a frenzy that matched them. As Wrinn rose to the ground and battered away another masked anguiped's frenzied blows of the sword, he witnessed Theudo, the human king of the Viegs, charge forth in his winged helmet, riding on a brown wolf, stabbing an anguiped in the heart with his spear, and then another in the stomach.

The anguipeds had done great damage in their reckless charge, and as Wrinn looked about the elvish lines he could see faces of fear.

He saw faces of fear, and then he saw hope, as the elvenking charged forth on his Elvish horse, having drawn his blue sword of *estirion,* now racing ahead of the elves' front lines, and bowling his way ahead, into the anguipeds.

He was slashing furiously with his sword and calling out in a loud voice, naming Elvish heroes of the past: *"Solgaressi! Kanenthas!"*

The masked anguiped swordsmen seemed to lose the fearlessness of the poison they had consumed at the sight of the elvenking, now wreathed in sunlight, hacking and stabbing with a fury that seemed superhuman, as he layed countless low in a short span. His Elvish horse struck with his hooves and horns, impaling and sending many anguipeds to their death.

And Wrinn thought, despite the anguipeds' number, that perhaps there was a hope for victory, perhaps the elves guarding the Steaming Gates would not be thwarted.

Wrinn called out for the gods then, to give him strength, as more anguipeds appeared. He rushed into the front lines and bowled over an anguiped, then another, fearing what would happen, that he would expose his flank, but determined to do damage to the Dark One and his armies. Within moments he had pierced deep into the anguiped lines, and he had gotten far away from the elves. He was deep into the anguiped army, alone.

No, he was not alone — the elvenking on his Elvish horse was deeper into the anguiped ranks, and the anguipeds were staring at him, transfixed, as if he was a messenger of the gods. The elvenking was slashing with his sword like a wild animal, with a frenzied gleam to his eyes, cutting anguipeds dead with a hunger and a bloodthirst that would rival anyone.

Wrinn felt a hotness in his arm, and saw an anguiped had slashed open his forearm. He began to back away, then, as the anguipeds made a counterattack, and Wrinn feared that he and the elvenking would be lost amid the sea of black cloaks and glittering armor, under a hazy hot sun that threatened to undo him.

The elvenking was a signal and a symbol of their hope, riding astride his Elvish horse and cutting down anguiped warriors, one after another.

But as Wrinn made an ordered retreat back to the elven armies, and hopefully, a medic, he saw that the anguipeds were holding aloft something in the air, what appeared to be a tent held up on wooden posts. They were holding the tent aloft, in the blazing sunlight, and the sun was baking down on it.

The elvenking was staring at the tent, transfixed.

And as he stared at the tent transfixed, the anguipeds were leaving him alone.

An anguiped struck at Wrinn, though he was bleeding. He speared with his quarterstaff and then bashed with the blunt edge. He made an ordered retreat, and then he turned in a frenzy.

He vowed to live to fight another day, for Shomré's sake.

As dusk fell that day, the anguipeds began to retreat. The elven armies at the Steaming Gates had stood firm.

Chapter Twenty-Eight: Wormy

Balor did not know if he was making perfect progress. He knew he was walking, and he was trying to walk in a straight line. He knew he would follow his gut in the daytime, and in night, whenever he was so lucky as to see stars, he would push through the drifts of the snow in the direction opposite of the North Star.

But he thought his uncertainty, perhaps, the nagging doubt, was part of the arsenal of the master of what had been the Haunted Forest, the one who desperately wished him not to be a king.

Balor had a crown, but not a throne, he thought, as he pushed through a drift of snow he thought might end him, under a steely gray sky now emptying its reserves of snow onto the ground, as the undead army behind Balor shambled forth.

He peered into the direction he was now facing, through a stand of scraggly black pines, and as he did, a harsh wind blew in its wake. Balor thought he saw a green face, eyes blazing red, a mouth of fangs — a command so harsh, spoken in the wind, *"Stop this!"* he for a moment was tempted to cease his walking.

That face, that command, told him he needed to keep walking. The master of what had been the Haunted Forest was a good compass, to tread wherever he wished Balor not to go. That would lead him directly to a throne he could take, and all the majesty of the elvenkings.

~

As he pressed on, making slow progress, as the snow was building to his waist, he subsisted on moldy wormy road-bread and availed himself of the water of streams. It was amazing how helpless he was traveling through the icy waste, being so poor at making fires that most nights he did not bother. Most nights, huddled in the tent, uttering words to someone — who? – that could hear him, he shivered in a rawhide blanket, his heart and his mind full of simple purpose, to become a king, because it was the opposite of whatever the master of what had been the Haunted Forest wanted him to do.

It was days later, or was it weeks, or months — since he set out, a bright day in a snow-covered tundra, when Balor saw he was not alone.

There was a party of rokahn approaching, garbed head to toe in black iron armor, a countless host from one end of the battlefield to another.

Balor knew in an instant that the master of what had been the Haunted Forest had sent them here, to stop him in his tracks and ensure a kingship would never belong to him.

Balor would show the Dark One's party who owned the snowy waste.

As his undead soldiers charged into the rokahn ranks, Balor summoned columns of necromantic energy, withering twenty rokahn with each blast, shriveling their bodies to gossamer strands and leaving their bodies behind. The noise of battle erupted, sword against spear, as something else lit up the night, a loud screech. There were dozens of flying forms amid the cloudy sky, cadaver-white horrors with red eyes, which Balor knew as wylocks. They were the Dark One's eyes, and they were the Dark One's dread beasts he sent in combat.

They lived in the Dragonteeth Mountains.

Was Balor not far from his goal?

A wylock soared for him, opening its maw of mangled fangs.

Balor shot a jet of purple necromantic fire, but the wylock dodged nimbly.

Balor shot a ball of vampiric energy but missed, and then the wylock was upon him.

The wylock sank its claws into Balor's chest and blood spurted, and Balor almost lost his grip on his staff. He wondered if the Dark One would prevail, and all hope of a kingship vanished, but vowed to fight back, harder than ever, and ensure his own victory.

When the wylock opened its maw of fangs, the sight of it frightened Balor, and magic poured out of him, an explosion of purple fire, decimating the wylock bodies to bits.

The undead soldiers were cutting down the rokahn, one by one. As Balor stirred to his feet, and tried to regain his composure, he set to work, giving unlife to any rokahn that fell, raising up new soldiers, so that his army would grow.

~

In the waning light of day, Balor made an accounting of the dead. Some rokahn had been withered to death, could not be turned to undead thralls. But he saw the Dark One had truly sent a legion to stop him. Thousands of rokahn had been sent to stop him, and of the dozen wylocks, three he had managed to turn to undead thralls at his fingertips.

Balor's army, he saw, had swelled to ten thousand, a mixture of undead vampires and undead rokahn, joined to them the undead forms of three wylocks, barely moving their wings and seeming to hover just barely above the ground.

The Dark One had tried to stop Balor, but had only made him stronger.

Would he learn his lesson?

No, his fury would be swift, his retribution total, as his eyes fixed upon him from the Dark Land. Balor could sense the anger now, the opposition formed from whispers in Balor's mind, the temptation to give up and surrender all he loved, to abandon all hope of kings and kingship.

But Balor already had a crown of stone, petrified on his head. He was making his way to a throne, and the army sent to stop him told him he was moving in the right direction, southward at an ambling direction.

Southward, where there was less snow.

Southward, where there were people.

Chapter Twenty-Nine: Band of Brothers

"He wants to drive the armies of the Dark Tower away," said Blarer to Ajax, repeating Reev's words in the relative safety of their house. "He thinks it will draw out the serpent's child from wherever he is hiding."

As Ajax ladled a bit of soup into bowls one morning, he seemed to ponder it in his mind.

Reev had wandered, openly, in the Dark City in the attire of Telantis, a risky gambit before Blarer and Ajax had rescued him. But if he had not been so bold, he would not have attracted the attention of his own kind.

"Are there more of you?" Reev said.

"There are more of us in the city, yes," Blarer said. "And there is a band of us, abroad, in the Dark Land, waylaying fortresses — one all the forces of the Dark One have not had the ability to squelch. The army is led by a man named Pandarus."

Reev took his bowl of soup and began to eat it quietly. Then, he spoke. "You are attired like I am, and there are other Telantines. But Telantis is long gone… how, then, are there so many of you?"

"Some of us were awakened to our identity," Blarer said. "Others are from remnant states throughout Varda, of which there are many. But I see you found your identity in a way different from all of us."

"I found a coin necklace in my grandfather's house," Reev said, "and a map of an island, New Telantis."

"The Isle of Serpents," Blarer said, "where all the survivors originate from. And you are from tribe Nax. My family is from Tribe Gens."

Reev looked about, and saw that in the Dark City, even the

lanterns and the candles and the fire could not seem to banish the darkness and gloom. But Blarer and Ajax cast a light of their own selves, a light of joy and love — good company, amid such darkness.

"We must drive the armies before the Dark Tower," Reev said. "We must draw out my enemy, the Dark One's Hand. Words from my dying father, and I have an inkling they were given to him from above."

"I think you're right," Blarer said.

"But to drive the army from the Dark Tower, we'll need backup," Ajax said. "A lot of us, in fact."

"You said there was a band of Telantine warriors, marauding across the Dark Land," Reev said. "Perhaps, we can start there."

"Perhaps, Pandarus would be willing," Blarer said. "Perhaps, not. For the army before the Dark Tower is countless, and we're Telantines, but it seems like suicide."

"It seems like suicide," Reev said, "but I've taken it as a command from above."

He had taken it that way, but it didn't mean it was so. To drive so many from the tower and its bleakness seemed utterly impossible. But slaying the jotunn by himself had seemed impossible.

"Do you know where to find Pandarus?" Reev said.

"Last I heard," Blarer said, "he was setting fire to the Dark One's smithies in Abollonia."

"Would you be willing to show me the way?" Reev said.

"We came here to defeat the Dark One," Blarer said, "and if you're the one who will crush Seymus under his feet, we can't help but give you our aid."

They had finished their soup. They clipped their swords to their belts. They draped cloaks over their bodies and then they gave Reev a cloak of his own.

Together, the three Telantines stepped out into the hazy darkness of the Dark City, that though daylight had arrived, darkness was all about.

~

They passed away from the borderlines of the Dark City an hour later, and as they pressed westward, some of the oppressive darkness seemed to fade away. The poor quality of the air was getting to Reev, the particles stinging and tickling the back of his throat, under a hazy sunlight.

They were on ashen earth, and there were tangled thorn-bearing trees growing on the side of a gravelly patch of ground that seemed to aspire to become a road. As they walked, a day and then two days, two and then three, sharing road-bread and camping amid rocks and canyons, the poor quality of the air, the dryness, was being mixed with something else, smoke and bitter fumes that threatened to undo them all. As Reev, Blarer, and Ajax pressed on a week – or was it two? — they came to a high cliff overlooking a deep valley — and there, before them, was all the Dark One's industry.

There were rokahn camps, surrounding pits carved into the ground, and everywhere flashes of fire, smithies forging swords and axes for the Dark One's innumerable host. It was a wonder Pandarus even tried to raid the smithies, but according to Ajax and Blarer, he had been met with some success.

Blarer seemed mortified, Ajax afraid, at the sight of the rokahn camps, the forges crafting innumerable weapons for the innumerable rokahn. Here, the Dark One's armies were armed, as they were sent to pillage and waylay distant lands all over Varda.

And what a victory it would be, Reev thought, if the Dark One's industry could be stopped, if water doused the raging fires, and put an end to them. That, according to Blarer, was what Pandarus had intended to do.

But Pandarus clearly hadn't made much of an incursion, for this region, stretching into the horizon, was at work. The smithies were without number, and rokahn were surrounding the blazing fires, the countless blazing fires delivering the Dark One a constant supply of spears, axes and swords.

"You said Pandarus was here," Reev breathed.

"I said it was where he was last seen," Blarer answered dully.

Reev had been so mortified at the sight, so paralyzed by dark wonder, he had forgotten he was standing in clear view of the rokahn gathered about the smithies and forges.

"Whatever shall we do," Reev said, "and how can we hope to find him?"

"We will look," Blarer said.

"Perhaps, a bit of surveillance in this region is in order," Ajax said.

~

In their cloaks they wandered, along a rocky cliff, as the smell of the toxic fumes threatened to undo Reev and send him into a panic. Occasionally the rocks would crumble underneath his shoes, causing noise that threatened the entire operation.

While Blarer and Ajax kept a careful eye on the rokahn, Reev searched about for Telantines, for men in loin cloths or otherwise, in the midst of a raid on the Dark One's smithies.

But Reev could see no Telantines, nothing — really — save the fires of the smithy and the countless rokahn gathered about them. As the lightless day was pressing into a lightless night, the smoke swirled about Reev, and Reev began to cough.

He coughed, and then it was a hacking fit, loud and deafening noise, as Blarer and Ajax looked at him in a panic, and far away, there were the sounds of rokahn shouting in their guttural tongue.

Blarer, Ajax, and Reev, on a cliff's edge, watched as rokahn began to pour forth, spilling out from their ranks, looking directly at them. "Let's get out of here!" Blarer shouted.

They were sprinting, then, sprinting across the ashen landscape, and as Reev looked back he could see the rokahn gaining on them, sprinting much faster than humans, even Telantines, with their monstrous rokahn legs.

Reev uttered prayers under his breath, fearing that his recklessness had spelled the end of their mission and the Dark One's victory… the ruin of the Telantines.

And if Reev was in any state, any situation, to do so, he would have begged Blarer and Ajax's forgiveness.

Reev felt a slimy hand grip his thigh, and then yank him to the ground. He could hear, face down in the dirt and dry rocks, Ajax and Blarer shouting as they were forced into binds.

Reev at last looked up, and saw the rokahn had caught up to them, and were swarming about the three of them as they struggled in the dry dirt and rocks.

There were about three dozen rokahn, dark shapes in a lightless day that would quickly turn into a pitch black night.

They were rokahn of mixed species, and so they were speaking in the Imperial tongue. "Bind these three Telantines and take them to the Dark Tower. Deliver the one carrying the coin necklace to Mudamir. He will know what to do with him."

They had fastened Reev's hands tight with rope, so hard he worried his wrists would bleed. He eyed Ajax and Blarer, and saw no condemnation for him in their eyes, just a determination to wriggle out of the situation alive.

But what hope was there of that?

They would now be transported, the three of them, hands bound, to the Dark Tower, to "Mudamir." They would surely die, and the Telantines' hopes were gone.

~

The rokahn pushed them through the night, and when Ajax or Blarer or Reev tried to slow their gait, whips cut them in the back. The rokahn had removed their cloaks, baring Reev's loin cloth and Ajax and Blarer's trousers. They were Telantines, full and true, and when they at least ceased their journeying at some unearthly hour, the rokahn eyed their Telantine attributes with hate.

Back to the Dark Tower, they would go, or so the rokahn intended. As they stopped, and Reev was allowed to catch his breath, he prayed silently as the moonless night endured.

He wondered if all hope was lost for the mission, for the treading of the Dark One underfoot.

As he stirred in his binds, trying to sleep on the rocky soil, he thought of Gastreel his mentor, now in Heaven, of his ratling foster parents Skreek and Neek, who had raised him for much of his life. He thought of the people he knew back in his hometown of Norwood, and how they were faring with the Dark One and his armies now on the march.

Bitter tears were welling in his eyes, but perhaps they weren't bitter. Perhaps they were borne of a lack of hope.

Yet he had inexplicable hope as the rokahn's dark shapes circled around him and Ajax and Blarer, amid the dim darkness of the night. He had a hope that was irrational.

How good it would be, though, to see Gastreel's face at at time like this, to see him riding on his horse Ivy and striding into battle — a burst of lightning to strike the captors of him and Ajax and Blarer dead.

But Gastreel had gone on to the grave.

All was darkness. All was stillness.

What would Reev do now? If he got to to the Dark Tower, was it over for him and the Telantines? The Six Servants of Seymus were dead, but Reev had no doubt that the Dark One would have another way to kill him.

What had happened to the Dark One's sword, Serpentax? He remembered a shard — colored green.

Was Serpentax in the hands of someone now? Was it in the hands of the one they called Mudamir?

As he laid down, he peered into the lightless night, amid this lightless land, and his prayers were ceaseless. He prayed for rescue, he prayed somehow that the journey would end here, and he'd be able to crush Seymus under his feet.

He had prayed, and then he looked with his eyes to Ajax and to Blarer. He could see them struggling to sleep in the night. They were in danger, too.

All their kind was in danger from the rokahn, from the Dark One and his servants, from the crushing of the Dark One underfoot the rokahn were now trying to thwart.

He uttered a vow, then, in the darkness of the lightless night, that he would find a way to crush the Dark One underfoot, that Telantis would be reborn.

Chapter Thirty:
Not Always Dark

"I like you."

"I like you, too," Wrinn said to Rosalie, now Shomré, lying in bed. "I love you, in fact."

But when Wrinn turned to Shomré, she was sleeping, fast asleep in her bedroll.

Someone else had said that. Who else could have? Wrinn strained his mind to think.

He was frightened then, for he knew the Dark Land was a place of inestimable darkness, and there were evil whispers on the wind. He did not want the evil masters of this Dark Land to like him.

"It was not always dark," another voice echoed through the night, and then Wrinn realized, it was a tree talking to him.

Wrinn was what elves called a tree-speaker, one who could communicate with plants and the green growing things of the world.

Yet it was a wonder that in such a place as the Dark Land, anything could grow. The land was poison. The rocky soil was poison.

"The rocky soil is poison," said the voice, *"but I've managed to sprout leaves."*

Wrinn climbed out of his bedroll. The trees of the Dark Land demanded his attention, and he would give it to them. He would give it to them, at least for now.

He pushed open the tent flap.

He stepped into the warm, though poor, air, of the Dark Land, and as he stood in the darkness, he wondered if the air was poisoning his body, if by battling the Dark One and his armies here he was trimming ten years off his life.

"No," said the voice, "*the things which move about, which have legs, will recover from the bad air. But we cannot move. We set our roots here, and can never leave.*"

Wrinn followed the voice through the stillness of camp, the tents where warriors and their families were sleeping, amid the relatively flat ground of the Steaming Gates.

He wanted to see what trees grew here, amid such soil, which trees had dared to speak to him. They knew he was a friendly audience, that he was willing to listen to them, to their complaints, their wants and needs, and not carelessly set them aside.

"*The Dark Land was not always dark,*" the tree continued. "*Once, it had good soil to grow.*"

~

Wrinn passed beyond the tents, and was coming to the shore of the sea.

The sea, once raging, was now glasslike and still. Where waves once threatened to destroy any ship that so much as touched the waters, now it was so tranquil it didn't seem there was a wind to so much as rattle the sails.

Yet he had followed the voice in the stillness, and as he continued to follow it, he saw a moon struggling to appear in the darkness of the dark sky, a faint haunting image, like a light cast through a mirror.

And then he saw, by the waters of the now-tranquil sea, a stunted tree struggling to grow.

Its leaves were waxy and green, but some of them were dead, turned to red flakes. The tree was not much taller than Wrinn, and Wrinn thought with a little pull, he could tug it free of its weak roots.

"*The Dark Land was not always dark,*" the tree repeated, and now its voice was clear, not distorted by the ambient noise of the camps.

"The Dark Land was not always dark. Once, trees of paradise grew here, and they bore fruit by the bushel. Trees like me bore so much fruit, the elves could not carry them away in one basket."

"Elves?" Wrinn said.

"The anguipeds were elves," the tree said, *"but they were not good like you. There was a darkness in them, waiting to break free. But I sense there is a goodness and light in you that will never leave, that you will always love the gods and the gods will always love you. In Telantis, when it is born, you will live happily all your days.*

"You will live happily — and someone is with you."

"My wife," Wrinn said, "Shomré."

Wrinn was learning so much from the trees. He tried to picture the Dark Land as it had been, not as it was right now. He tried to picture, instead of ash-strewn rock and boulders, and stunted trees, and a sea he feared to touch, let alone drink, trees in full bloom — grassland and flowers, and probably cities growing up amid the beauty.

He tried to envision it, and yet he found he couldn't, so dark was the dark land.

"I like you, Son of the Forest," the tree said.

"I like you, too," Wrinn said.

Was it true? He supposed it was. And he supposed it was good to know that not every living thing in the Dark Land was under the power of the Dark One.

Here was a tree, remembering the good times now long gone by, reminiscing about how things had been so long ago. They had been so good — or had they? Had there been a darkness threatening to eat away at the Dark Land all along?

But the grass he imagined was only in his imagination, the trees bearing fruit, season after season, were just a vision. Was it possible that the Dark Land could be restored?

Wrinn wondered if, when the dawn arrived, if the dawn would shine on the Dark Land, too.

For now, it was just a dream, just a vision.

But he was glad to know, to have heard the tree's wisdom. He wondered how old the tree was, how it was possible for the tree to know, but he supposed the tree shared roots with older trees, trees that might better remember. And the tree came from the seed of a tree much older. Did trees, with their seeds, share knowledge from generation to generation?

Wrinn did not know.

"The Dark Land was not always dark," Wrinn said. "And perhaps, it can be restored."

Chapter Thirty-One:
A Throne for a Crown

Where Balor was treading now, there were broadleaf trees, and thawing snow now trickling in streams down hills. The broadleaf trees had not regrown their leaves, but the patches of melted snow, and the warming air, indicated that spring had arrived in these northern parts of the world. He was in the southern portion of the Elf Lands, but where were the elves?

As he and his undead army moved through the woods, he at last saw a road, a paved road making its way through hills, going east or west. Where would Balor go? It was anyone's guess.

But he recalled, as he beheld the road, that the elvenking's throne was on the western sea. And so he turned west down the road, in the direction that the sun was going.

~

He was in the Elf Lands, full and true, but where were the elves?

He did not see them passing down the road as he walked at the head of his army, amid the spring wood, the gloomy carpet of fallen leaves, the gloomy trickles of melted snow, the broadleafs that though beautiful had refused to bud. It was not lost on Balor how far he had come, how far he had gone in the face of the Dark One's opposition, his whispered words, his armies sent.

Balor had braved the elements. He had feasted on wormy roadbread without complaint. And here he was, in a land that was not freezing cold, but instead was turning to spring, and soon would be summer.

In the summer there would not be so much as an icy wind to stop Balor's westward journey.

And west he had turned, amid the Dark One's withering opposition. Every step, it seemed, he took in defiance of his mortal enemy, the enemy of the gods and all goodness and light.

The enemy of the gods and all goodness and light did not want Balor to be king, to receive all that the stone crown he wore represented. And if the enemy of the gods and all goodness and light did not want something, then Balor should pursue it with all his heart.

As he pressed through the woods, as a trickling rain began to pour, amid the spring wood that seemed dead but soon would be alive, Balor did not see elves, but as he crossed westward, he saw rokahn shouting and fleeing from view, on black wolf or by foot. Had the rokahn pillaged the Elf Lands? Had they seized control of it?

Balor feared. But if he gave in to fear, he would not do the opposite of what the Dark One wanted, what therefore the gods wanted — for Balor to be a king, and to have a throne.

Beyond a forest, amid grassland, was a city that had been seized by rokahn. Black flags had been raised upon the walls of a vast city, a city of elven architecture with houses of curved roofs and the forms of belfries and towers — now overrun and pillaged by the rokahn.

The elves had abandoned the Elf Lands. Where had they gone?

Rokahn blew horns as Balor and his undead army approached. The gates of the seized city opened and rokahn came pouring out, rokahn and kehrad and a kind of creature, with blue or green skin, that half resembled rokahn, and half resembled elves.

The blue creatures had staffs, and as they locked eyes with Balor, Balor felt a pestilence in his blood, like they were trying to take control of the blood flowing in his veins. Balor drew up his staff and struck.

He struck with magic, and the blue creatures' staffs began to burst, one after another. Balor was the better mage.

As they stood in stunned silence, Balor gave the command, and the undead army, part vampire and part rokahn, began to charge the rokahn lines, and besiege the city, once elven, which had fallen into the Dark One's hands.

The battle ensued, rokahn against undead, and as soon as a rokahn was struck down, Balor gave him animation and enlisted him into his service. His creatures climbed the walls, and his creatures stormed the gates. His undead wylocks harried the rokahn besieging the town, and as Balor charged into the town alongside his host, he realized this town was the city of Lunadrias, once the bulwark of the elves' eastern frontier, now a rokahn citadel.

It had been a rokahn citadel, but Balor's army was making quick work of them, and with each fallen rokahn, another soldier was enlisted in Balor's service.

~

Balor was at in the midst of Lunadrias, watching his soldiers do their work. With ghostly grace and a fearlessness that was the key marker of the undead, they fought or they died, but they always pressed ahead. Through an avenue lined with starstones, past a Garden of Life with a tree that the rokahn had cut to a stump and burned, Balor pressed, watching as his soldiers reclaimed the town of Lunadrias from the Dark One.

His undead wylocks issued siren calls, as the army grew in size and strength with each fallen rokahn.

Balor, he sensed, was at the threshold of victory, and what would the Dark One send at him now?

He sensed a change in strategy, or so he would guess, as the army now twenty thousand in strength paraded before him, a countless undead host now marshalling before the walls of the cleansed — or was it defiled — Lunadrias?

Lunadrias, guardian of the elves' eastern frontier, had now been captured by Balor. And Balor was closer to kingship than he had ever been.

Now came the counterstrike, Balor guessed, the Dark One sending all his might to stop him from reaching the elven capital.

For Balor knew all too well where the throne he sought was. It lay in the royal city, in the City of Light itself, Danarion.

There, the promise that his crown represented could be fulfilled.

Chapter Thirty-Two: The Gods' Promise

The rokahn were leading Reev, Ajax and Blarer through the walls of an ashen valley. Above head, the sun was hazy and ghostlike, an orange beacon barely distinguishable from the smoky sky.

Ajax was whimpering softly as they were led to their fate. And Reev was fighting guilt, because he knew he had led them to it.

The task he had been given, to drive the armies of the Dark Tower before him, had seemed impossible. He had sought help elsewhere, and in the end, had only led two young men to their doom.

So what was there to be done now, and what hope could there be? He looked about the walls of the ashen valley, and saw shadows stirring, up above the shadows of stunted trees wafting in the wind.

The rokahn had removed their cloaks, and so they were walking about clearly as Telantines, with lightning marks on their necks, and Reev bearing bound around his neck a Telantine coin. They were visible, clearly seen, as the band of rokahn forced them at a breakneck pace toward the Dark Tower.

As Reev uttered prayers, the hopeless situation was met with a feeling of inexplicable hope. The wind gusting and blowing the shadowy stunted trees was fresh and did not seem sent from the Dark Land or its poison air.

What was this wind? It was fresh. It had a hint of coolness. And as Reev pushed on, the feeling of inexplicable hope was bursting within him.

A rokahn fell in front of him. In the panic of the moment, Reev saw an arrow sticking out of his chest.

Rokahn barked orders and scrambled through the valley,

drawing their swords and axes, as the forms of figures appeared above the walls of the valley.

They were Telantines, Reev saw, in the sunlight, some in loin cloths and some in trousers, some baring lightning mark tattoos and others, their Telantine identity clear only because they were among the others. As some Telantines loosed arrows from bows, other Telantines rushed down into the valley heaving swords, and were making quick work of the rokahn.

A Telantine pierced a rokahn straight through, ahead of Reev, and then in one swift motion sliced Reev's binds apart. Reev's hands were now free, and he scrambled into the Telantines' ranks, to safety.

A battle had now consumed the valley, rokahn against Telantine, darkness against light. And as Reev withdrew to the sidelines of the battle, he saw that the Telantines were prevailing, and that the Telantines were more numerous.

There were hundreds of Telantines, armed with swords and cutting the rokahn down.

He heard Blarer shout, "Pandarus!"

And Reev looked up, and he saw, standing above the valley, was a Telantine who seemed the greatest among them. His hair was a dark brown, his eyes keen and full of vigor. At his side was a broadsword forged of steel, and though he was not part of the battle, his presence seemed to direct his underlings, as they made quick work of the rokahn.

A rokahn's head went flying from his body. Another rokahn went down with a cry, pilloried by swords.

And as rokahn fell, and the Telantines cut a path through them, Reev's feeling was relief, washing through him, that the mission had not failed, that there was still hope.

There was still hope, he knew, and he told himself that, and tried not to think further ahead than his rescue. The enormity of his task was great — indeed, beyond words — but for now, he would relish the fact that Pandarus, the Telantine warlord, had rescued Reev, Ajax, and Blarer, from a terrible fate.

"Forward!" shouted Pandarus from his perch up above the valley.

Ajax and Blarer had found their swords, and had drawn them. They now were joining their brethren as the rokahn did battle.

The rokahn could no longer retreat, for Telantines blocked all passage, and on either side of the valley, and up above, they stood in the rokahn's way.

The rokahn's were hooting and howling cries of fear, and locked swords out of desperation, feebly batting what blows of the Telantines' swords they could, as they fell, one after another, to the ashen ground.

Reev uttered prayers of thanksgiving, and began to search the perimeters of the battle. He saw, in a cart the rokahn had been pulling, his sheath, where he could find his sword Doomblade. He rushed to the cart and took the sheath. He drew Doomblade, and it glittered in the dim Dark Land sun.

The relief washing through him seemed complete as the rokahn fell, one after another, as rokahn and Telantines crossed swords, and the rokahn were cut down.

Relief — beautiful relief, and as the Telantines gained the upper hand, and the last of the rokahn fell, none having been allowed to retreat, Reev looked up to Pandarus and saw him bathed in sunlight.

The rokahn dead were scattered through the valley, and the Telantines began to pilfer their swords and axes, and remove their bloodied breastplates and their armor. Nothing, it seemed, was left that could be used for the coming war.

Ajax, Reev recalled, said a "Great War" was coming. What did he mean?

Some Telantines carried weapons, and others loaded them into carts. Then Pandarus began to shout and give orders, and the Telantines made a hasty retreat through the valley under the Dark

Land sun.

Reev, Ajax and Blarer had been rescued from a terrible fate. And Reev had so many questions.

What did Ajax mean when he said a "Great War" was yet to come?

~

They crossed the region which Blarer had called Abollonia, across ash-strewn rock and beside rocky ridges and cliffs. They moved at a breathless pace, with little chance for rest, as they crossed the landscape with an urgency borne of danger.

For Reev knew that the Telantines were badly outnumbered, that though they had killed scores of rokahn, there were only a thousand, by Reev's estimation, total in Pandarus's band.

They moved swiftly, and as the dim sunlight faded to a dark dusk, they had reached a deep valley in which Reev saw countless tents, and fire pits ready to be tended. There were crates full of pilfered supplies, probably taken from rokahn during raids, lying in all corners of the camp. And as Reev and the other Telantines arrived, relief washed through him… relief, and now, thoughts of his mission.

He at last allowed himself to comprehend the enormity of the task he had been assigned.

~

He told Pandarus of the mission he thought had been given by the gods, words uttered by his father as he died.

"I must drive the armies of the Dark Tower before me," Reev said. "Then, I can draw out the Dark One's Hand to defeat him. When the Dark One believes he is under threat, he will make a mistake."

Pandarus's eyes glittered in the light of a campfire, now burning in the pitch-dark night. "Wise words," he said, "and yet a task that would seem impossible. The rokahn and the anguipeds number a million before the Dark Tower, and the spawning pits are active. Their number grows each day, each hour, spilling forth out of the vile pits."

When Pandarus said something was impossible, it seemed to Reev's mind to be impossible indeed. It seemed impossible, but for his father's words that seemed to his mind to be a command not from him, but from above.

Could someone's words be a command from above?

Could Reev, instead, be reading too much into his father's words? Could they be words born of delirium, of a man at death's door?

Ajax and Blarer were beside Reev at the fire. From the crates in the hidden camp, other Telantines were taking road-bread and bits of salted meat, enough victuals to last the night.

He eyed Ajax and remembered his words. He said to Pandarus, "What is this Great War that you were promised?"

"A Great War was promised to all of us," Pandarus said in the flickering firelight. "A slaughter, of rokahn and anguipeds, to drive the Dark One and his minions from the Dark Land, yea, from Varda. The Great War is our final victory, the final victory of the Telantines over the anguipeds."

Reev marveled at his words. And yet, the idea of a Great War seemed impossible now, for they were badly outnumbered, and when Reev explained what he had intended to do, Pandarus indicated it was impossible.

It had seemed impossible to Reev, and now he knew it was. Impossible — and yet he had already done something that another had called impossible. He had done what Spymaster Marius had called the height of folly, charging forth and slaying a jotunn by himself.

Could he take such bravado to the Dark Tower, and drive its armies before him?

"I must drive the armies before the Dark Tower," Reev said. "I really feel it's true."

"Then we should wait," said Pandarus, "because of the gods' promises. The Great War beckons, and each day, more of us arrive from every corner of Varda. They come for the promise, of the raven's feast, and they come more and more as the day approaches. Now, the Sea of Ghosts are calmed by a strange magic. The waters are placid and tranquil, and the way is open to the Dark Land where it had not been before."

Reev stirred in the night, in the light of the campfire, and decided he would give no disagreement. As Telantines arrived, perhaps an army would be formed, an army to drive out the anguipeds and rokahn before the Dark Tower.

But something Pandarus had said troubled Reev. For though more Telantines arrived each day, from all corners of Varda, for the promised Great War, Pandarus had said the spawning pits were active, and the Dark One's forces were growing stronger.

What, then, could Reev do?

He supposed he had to wait after all. He supposed he would have to wait, for he could not venture before the armies of the Dark Tower himself, alone.

Could he?

~

The days pressed on, the days and nights, and as Pandarus said, more Telantines arrived by the day. They came, armed with swords, for the day promised to them, the Great War that would put an end to the anguipeds and their rule over Varda.

Reev knew, the anguipeds had put one of their own on the Imperial throne, that by conspiracy and deceit they had gained control over the most powerful human kingdom in Varda. Reev wondered what had happened to Verrus, the unworthy emperor, who now ruled on the Imperial throne. His edicts had been unjust, and the people had cried out. His rule had been oppressive, and had twisted the Empire into something it had never been before.

The days pressed on, the days and nights. The numbers of the Telantines were growing stronger, and Pandarus's band of raiders was quickly turning into an army. The Sea of Ghosts, with its violent waves, had been stilled, and whether by boat or through mountain passes, the Telantines were arriving for the day promised to them.

The Dark Land, the Dark One and his minions, were under siege, though they were unaware of the siege. Their enemy was gathering behind their walls, behind their gates.

But all Reev could think of was the command from his father, the command that seemed like a word from above. All he could think of was the task that had been placed upon his mind and on his heart, to drive the armies of the Dark Tower before him.

But as the Telantines grew in number, and Pandarus's army was more numerous than ever, the enemy also was gaining strength.

Reev knew that he had to complete the task his father had given him. He knew it in his heart and in his mind. But how could he drive the armies of the Dark Tower before him?

How, even with all the Telantines' might?

Chapter Thirty-Three: Risky

Wrinn was on the front lines, and ahead of him, the massing armies of rokahn and anguipeds had locked shields. They had come again to dislodge the army from the Steaming Gates. With his quarterstaff braced in his hand, Wrinn knew that they would fail.

But did he know? His heart trembled. He wondered what the army, who had failed up to now, had up their sleeves.

He was afraid, he realized, and his knees were trembling.

An anguiped in a bronze mask shouted, "Gibboroth, our father's messor!"

A creature strode out from the ranks of the soldiers, a creature half again as tall as the tallest anguiped. He was cloaked in what appeared to be a breastplate of silver, and he had a jagged sword in a sheath at his side. His face was bright red, his eyes reptilian, and his mouth ended in a beard of tentacles.

Wrinn was horrified at the sight of him, and he wondered what this "messor" was. All he knew, it was one of the Dark One's highest lieutenants, and he was here to make war on the elves, on the forces of light gathered here, who were standing against the darkness.

Gibboroth, the messor, drew his blade, and the anguipeds and rokahn drew their weapons and cheered in turn.

They would dislodge the army in the Steaming Gates, or so they hoped.

But as the armies stirred, and faced each other, there was a figure pushing through the elven ranks wreathed in glittering sunlight. It was the Field Marshal, Sintari.

"Gibboroth, the Dark One's messor," said Sintari, "I challenge you to a duel."

Sintari, Reev saw, was now wielding a sword of *estirion*. It was colored blackish-purple, with streaks of green and blue spots. Wrinn realized, he had seen this sword of *estiron* before, in the hands of another. It had belonged to Velérion, the crown prince, who was now dead. It was called Nagaró, "the Eye of the Serpent."

Gibboroth strode forth, like a puppet on a string, as if he had no choice to do what he had been challenged to do, once he had been summoned.

The Field Marshal, Sintari, brandished Nagaró in his hands as he strode out before the opposing armies to do battle.

Gibboroth in return brandished his jagged sword, and his tentacle beard writhed in the weak Dark Land sun. The armies watched, Field Marshal against messor, champion of darkness against champion of light. And they were an audience now, an audience for a battle of the ages.

"If I win," said Gibboroth, "you will retreat from the Steaming Gates."

"And if I win," said the Field Marshal Sintari, "you will withdraw, and not return."

Gibboroth struck, and Sintari answered with a parry. Sintari struck, and Gibboroth dodged, and then drawing back his head, vomited green acid in Sintari's direction.

Flecks of the acid burned Sintari's forearm, and he wailed in pain in reply. As Gibboroth ducked and wove around, and sped about Sintari's form, Sintari struck, again and again, in vain, as Gibboroth dodged with serpentine grace.

Gibboroth cried, and charged in a frenzy of slashes and stabs, and cut a length of blond hair from Sintari's head. Sintari weaved and dodged, just barely managing to avoid certain death, and the elven army's defeat.

As Wrinn watched, he thought Gibboroth had been weakened somehow, that something had stricken him and removed an ancient strength. He saw, about his red skin, small holes, where Wrinn could envision wires being implanted. He wondered why Gibboroth was not fighting with the strength of the Dark One's lieutenants of old.

Sintari rolled to the ground and struck; Gibboroth parried just barely. Sintari charged forth, and now it was his turn to meet his opponent in a wild frenzy. Sintari struck a mighty blow, *estirion* against steel, and Gibboroth's blade shattered, riven in two.

Sintari slashed and slashed again, opening up a wound from the top of Gibboroth's body to the bottom, and vile green acid spilled forth, the fiendish equivalent of blood. Gibboroth issued a wordless cry of pain, as his body seemed to quiver in view of the wound.

But Gibboroth continued to fight, even as his body disintegrated. His red hands, which Wrinn saw ended in claws, swiped with a merciless fury, swiftly tearing at Sintari, as Sintari withdrew with elven grace.

Gibboroth barreled ahead and laid hold of Sintari by the neck. He picked up Sintari as acid continued to pour from his wound. Sintari dropped Nagaró helplessly.

And from the ranks of the elven armies came a figure in shining armor, galloping forth on an Elvish horse.

Against the rules of the duel, the elvenking came galloping, and heaving his blue *estirion* sword in his hand, severed Gibboroth's head, and the Dark One's messor fell dead to the ground, in two pieces.

The anguiped in the bronze mask who had announced the arrival of the Dark One's messor began to shout. "The rules of the duel have been violated. We will not withdraw!"

"And neither will we!" cried the elvenking.

Sintari was straining to breathe, taking heavy breaths and panting. At last, he gathered up Nagaró, the *estirion* sword he had been given, and summoned up all his strength. He retreated to the elven lines, as the two armies converged, and did battle.

~

The battle, that day, was a stalemate, anguiped and rokahn against elf. Wrinn slew ten rokahn, fighting side by side with his brothers, and he thanked the gods that night when he returned alive again, to his wife Shomré, once called Rosalie.

"I love you," he said to her.

"I love you," she replied.

And the warrior and his wife retreated to bed, on that day, a day of battle in the Dark Land, a part of the light fighting the darkness, the darkness now threatening to spill across the world.

Chapter Thirty-Four: Love

The city of Galiope had changed since Fortunato had left, but the love he had for his bride, and the love she had for him, was unchanging. They had bought a townhome in Middletown and Ambrass had made it her own. She had painted the once-whitewashed walls shades of rose and gold, and she had placed jars full of red roses on the window. Outside, in the city abroad, it was spring, turning to summer. Ambrass was seeming to have a hop in her step as she walked about, as she dusted the curtains and made sure everything was just so.

How beautiful was she, walking about, as Fortunato reclined in his chair beside the unlit fireplace. He realized he had everything all he had ever wanted. The fight against the Dark One had consumed all he had in him, but he had made his contribution, and now he would live, in light and life, with the one he loved, all his days.

He had lost much over the years. Gastreel, his partner in the fight against the Dark One, and his dear friend, was dead. He had suffered wounds he thought he would never recover from, but he had recovered. He had stricken dead Seymus's Six Servants and forged a northward path to Galiope. He had arrived, as his rescuer Setanta had promised, to find his bride waiting for him in the city itself.

Now, they were staking a life for themselves. The townhome, Fortunato had bought with all his earnings, his gains some licit and some illicit, over the years of adventuring and bringing the minions of the Dark One to their end. But Fortunato, though he and his bride were comfortable, wondered if he would eventually find some job around the city of Galiope to stay busy. Ambrass, after all, had not ceased her work in the Dragonpaw Inn.

"How do you like it, love?" Ambrass said as she stood in view of flowers she had placed near the window.

"I love it," Fortunato said. "I love everything. I love you."

And Ambrass strode up to him and pecked him on the cheek.

Fortunato had lost so much, but he had gained everything. He had gained his love, and now she was standing before him, radiant in her beauty and splendor. They had met not far from here, in the Dragonpaw Inn, after he had fallen to a dark iron wound. She had mended him with care and grace, and the rest, he supposed, was history. The rest was history — but history was being written. Their life together was just beginning to unfold. And Fortunato thought there would be surprises along the way. Something seemed poised on the tip of Ambrass's tongue, something it seemed she wished to tease out of him.

"What is it?" Fortunato said. "What do you want to say?"

Ambrass's cunning look turned to a bright warm smile. "Oh, something big, my love," she said. "Something wonderful indeed."

What was wonderful? What was more wonderful than her, standing in the sun's light, in view of the roses, in the home they now shared?

Could there be something more wonderful than her?

Fortunato didn't think so.

"What is it?" Fortunato said. "Tell me."

"Let's go for a walk," Ambrass said.

~

They held hands in the brisk spring air, walking down the avenues, the streets and homes and thoroughfares of Galiope. They walked past Imperial soldiers standing guard, in view of elves and humans walking side by side, conducting their business or hurrying on their on their way.

Ambrass and Fortunato were then on High Street, and they

turned, in view of the light of the bright and kind spring sun, the weather promising to become warm soon, and truly kind.

There were buds on the branches of the trees, growing along the streets, and soon they would be green leaves full and true.

The promise of spring was all about Fortunato and Ambrass… the promise of spring and summer, and Fortunato sensed, the promise of something else.

What was it that Ambrass wished to tell him? What was it, that could not long remain hidden? Would Fortunato have to tease it out of her?

She led him down High Street, pushing through the crowds, and the joy on her face was threatening to spill forth. Something clearly joyous was on her tongue, and it was ready to escape when their feet trod upon the Bridge-O'er-Galios.

"Fortunato, love," Ambrass said, "I am with child."

Fortunato met Ambrass in an embrace, and then he heaved her in his arms, picking her up across the bridge's great breadth. She smiled, and she laughed, and Fortunato tried to be careful, holding her aloft, remembering her words, that a child was now growing inside her, growing more ready to be born.

"Oh, what shall we name her?" Fortunato said.

"Her?" Ambrass said. "I thought it was a him."

It did not matter, boy or girl, the child they would soon have would be a blessing indeed. And Fortunato and Ambrass would be father and mother to a growing child, a child, Fortunato sensed, that would grow up in a world much better than the one he had known, a child who would grow up in a world where the Dark One was defeated.

What would that look like, a world where the Dark One was defeated?

He reflected on the Dark One's defeat as he set Ambrass down, and took her by the hand as he led her home.

Fortunato had done his part in the war against Seymus. But he knew the Dark One's defeat would come from someone else, someone promised to tread him underfoot.

Thoughts of the child swirled about him as he pushed through the doors of the townhome. They would tell Glenda, and Fortunato would send a message to his parents, who had returned to Ríva.

Their child would soon be born.

Would he, or she, grow up in a world where the Dark One was defeated?

Chapter Thirty-Five: The Challenge

Reev, standing beside Ajax and Blarer by the glassy waters of the sea, watched as boats began to appear into the horizon, and Telantines aboard them greeted their brethren with shouts of joy. The numbers had swelled in the weeks since he had joined Pandarus's marauders, and the band of raiders, once a thousand strong, was now building into a true army.

They were arriving by boat, and by mountain pass. Pandarus had dispatched Telantine warriors in every part of the Dark Land to direct the would-be warriors to the region of Abollonia, and Pandarus's camp.

Thus far, the anguipeds had not been able to stop them, nor did they seem entirely aware of what was going on, as the heat of the Dark Land built to a scorching fire, and walking across the ashen earth itself became a dolorous task.

Reev knew that when the army had built to a sufficient extent, Pandarus was willing to try to drive the armies of the Dark Tower before him. But even now, now that five thousand had become ten thousand, ten thousand against a million or more did not seem great odds, even when it was Telantine against anguiped.

The boats reached the shore and Telantines stepped out, garbed in loin cloths. There were about a dozen, and a few were wielding spears, while others had swords.

Here they were, gathering for the Great War they had been promised. But the odds had never seemed so poor, the danger never so great.

~

Back in the camp in Abollonia, in the valley in the ashen earth, they were growing short on room for tents. They were packed in the valley, and the Telantines to Reev's mind seemed without count. So many had arrived, bearing sword and spear, against the Dark One. But the Telantines were so outnumbered as to be counted out, if it were not for the gods' favor.

But how could they possibly defeat an army so vast, Reev wondered, even with all the warriors in the world? To him it seemed, the rokahn were continuously pouring out of their spawning pits, and the survivors of the devastation of Ash-Land — every surviving anguiped — was massing before the Dark Tower.

If the Telantines were defeated, the armies gathering before the Dark Tower would venture forth to dominate the world. And a world dominated by anguipeds was a world without Telantines, a world without hope.

Reev remembered that, one night, and held it to his heart, as campfires started, and Telantines began to cook rice in pots — rice, pilfered from a tranche of food the Telantines had raided.

Rice, Reev thought, would be a nice change from the salted meat and dried jerky, the road-bread baked without taste that the anguipeds fashioned for themselves. Reev hungered for something good.

But he would eat well, and he would drink all the wine in the world, when the Dark One was defeated.

His defeat, though promised, seemed an impossible task.

It seemed impossible, but Reev had slain a jotunn, and he had charged into the fray without thinking. He had charged into the fray without thinking, and in the process rescued his father, who had then died in peace.

He had died in peace… he left him with a command, to drive the armies of the Dark Tower before him, and draw out the Dark One's Hand.

Blarer, sitting across from him on the other side of the fire, had a sparkle in his eye. "Reev Nax," he said, "tell me where you're from, again."

"Norwood," Reev said, "in the Empire."

"Norwood," Blarer said. "I've never heard of it."

There were chuckles among the Telantines gathered around the fire.

"Few have," Reev said. "But it was a good place to hide from the Dark One's minions, until I came of age."

The chuckles and smiles faded, and Blarer now had a serious look on his face. "The Dark One's minions are all about you, now," he said. "Thank the gods the rokahn didn't take you to Mudamir, like they intended."

"Who is Mudamir?" Reev said.

"An anguiped," Blarer said. "That's what he is, technically, but over the decades he's changed. He is the castellan of the Dark Tower, and he bears a scourge in his hand that can eviscerate anything it touches. His armor is so thick hardly any sword can pierce it, and he never leaves the Dark Tower, unless it's to kill Telantines."

"Has he killed any Telantines?" Reev said.

"A few I know of," Blarer said. "My brother, Theodore, fell to his scourge. I can feel him looking down on us now with approval."

"Your brother," Reev said.

"Well," Blarer said, "in a manner of speaking. We're all brothers, all of us Telantines. We're all in this together, and when we die, we'll be together, then, too."

That was one way of putting it.

But Reev felt he had never been happier — at least, in a sense. He was enduring great hardship. But among his fellow Telantines there was scarcely any fear, only a sense of love and intense belonging. The Dark One's whispers had no effect, so close together with his kinsmen.

And though it had been said before, and it had become a saying,

Reev thought it was true, that whatever happened, they would be together forever.

Whatever happened… the Dark One's defeat had never been so far away.

As a Telantine approached and began to distribute bowls of rice, Reev tried not to think about how difficult the task was before him, how impossible the odds — a million warriors before a baleful tower, a million warriors who, man for man, could slay a hardened human soldier. How was it possible? How was it possible for Reev to drive the million before him, even with all the Telantines in the world? Was it impossible?

Reev thought anything was possible with the gods. But would they listen?

The rice filled his stomach. It was the only good food he had had for months.

And yet, being in the presence of his brethren had been worth the cost of the travail.

Here was the final battle.

The final battle had arrived… but where was the Great War that had been promised?

~

Reev awoke in his tent to cries of "We've been spotted!"

And in the light of dawn, there was a frenzy as Telantines swiftly gathered their tents and packed them on their backs. In a frenzy they departed, hurrying from the valley across the ashen earth, and as they walked at a rushed pace, there were whispers Reev heard, "Mudamir…"

The hazy Dark Land sky was shining, and the ten thousand Telantines, it seemed, could not be hidden much longer. Would their swell of increasing numbers at last force the Dark One to act, and send his million-strong army after them?

Reev didn't think so, as he pondered it. Only ten thousand Telantines were gathered thus far. He would send a smaller force to dispatch them.

As they raced through blackened earth, there was the sound of horns blowing, deafening harsh horns that signaled the approach of an army. When Reev looked back, there were the forms of armored anguipeds in black cloaks, and armored anguiped horses they rode astride, galloping in the Telantines' direction.

Pandarus gave a signal, and the Telantines turned about. They drew their sword, and Reev followed them a moment later, swiping Doomblade from its sheath and brandishing it in the hazy Dark Land sun.

There was an anguiped riding at the fore of the horsemen, and Reev knew it was Mudamir.

For he was covered head to toe in iron armor, and in his hand was a massive scourge that Reev thought could tear a horse to pieces in one stroke, covered in cruel barbs and spines.

How many were they? They stretched into the horizon, the anguipeds on horses, but these were not the armies gathered before the Dark Tower. They were not rokahn, but anguipeds, and if they had been a part of the terrifying host, they were not the whole.

Pandarus strode to the front of the Telantines, bearing his sword.

Mudamir hissed, and vile dribble escaped his horse's mouth.

Mudamir, Castellan of the Black Tower, surely had a look of wrath on his face, behind the helmet that was like the mask of a leering phantom.

His armor was so polished and so well maintained, it glittered even in the faint Dark Land sun.

"Mudamir," said Pandarus. "I know, the Dark One who rules on this Dark Land cannot resist a challenge. Nor can his children deny a challenge, when a challenge is issued. I propose a duel, man for man, Telantine against anguiped. If I win, you let us go."

"And if I win," said Mudamir, "you and all Telantines will let us slit your throats."

Reev thought he would resist such an action, if the duel went how Mudamir wanted. After all, he was not the one who made a duel.

"You know us well," said Mudamir, and dismounted, "but you know well you will not overcome me, or the Scourge of Brimstone."

"I will put that to the test," said Pandarus.

He strode forth, as the other Telantines looked on, and looked at Mudamir in his abominable, glistening armor. He strode forth into the open ashen ground, bearing nothing but a sword. He like many other Telantines, was dressed in a loin cloth, with no armor to protect him.

How could he possibly defeat such a champion of Hell?

Reev prayed under his breath as Mudamir and Pandarus began to circle around each other, in the weak Dark Land sun, darkness against light, Castellan of the Dark Tower against the captain of the Telantines.

Pandarus had the advantage of mobility, but Mudamir was wreathed head to toe in iron plates that would not be easily dislodged. And his scourge… his scourge!

Mudamir flicked his scourge and it was like a wave of metal, cascading into the distance, rippling and ending with a blow that Pandarus just barely managed to block, with an artful parry of his sword.

Pandarus charged forth as Mudamir hissed and howled, and as Pandarus pitched back his sword to strike, Mudamir flicked the scourge all over again. There was another ripple, and the scourge's barbs struck Pandarus and tripped him, ripping across his flesh and opening wounds. Pandarus was bleeding as Mudamir pitched the scourge back entirely, and then struck again, but this time, Pandarus was swift, like a killing bolt in the night.

He had tackled Mudamir to the ground, though he was bleeding, and the wounds that the barbs and spines had opened up Reev worried he'd never recover from.

Mudamir had fallen, and his iron armor was bulky. He would not easily return to his feet. But he struck again, mightily, and the scourge did the work he could no longer do, sending Pandarus flying into the distance, onto his back, where more wounds had opened up, and now his entire body was dripping with blood.

Pandarus sped ahead, across the rocky ground, heedless of danger, heedless of death, knowing he now bore not just the hopes of the Telantines, but the Dark One's defeat, on his shoulders.

Mudamir flicked the scourge again, but Pandarus slashed with his sword, and severed three ropes from the scourge in a perfect blow.

He charged to Mudamir and pierced him in a wild frenzy, until his sword found weaknesses in Mudamir's armor, until he had been stabbed ten, twenty, thirty times straight through — and a dolorous blow, severing his head.

Pandarus was like a painted man of the war god, totally red. But he drew breath, and the anguipeds knew the challenge he had made.

Did they respect the challenge? Reev did not know, and perhaps it was just the sight of Pandarus garbed like the war god. They wheeled their anguiped horses around and fled.

Telantines scrambled to Pandarus, and began to clean his blood and his wounds. An hour and two hours, and his wounds were dressed. A day, and he was on his feet, and marching, at the head of the army, toward the shore.

Chapter Thirty-Six: Rosalie's Dream

Shomré was stirring in the tent, writhing about in the night darkness, and Wrinn was beside her, awake as she twisted about and then began to utter words, senseless words he thought first, then something he knew, "Reev…"

He shook her awake, unable to sleep, and she had a look of bottomless terror in her eyes a moment, before she gained control of her emotions. Her ragged breathing turned to heavy breathing, the shallow look of terror in her eyes turned to mild fear. And then she was still.

"I've had a dream," said Shomré, once called Rosalie. "A terrible dream…"

"Tell me about it," Wrinn said, softly, to the woman who had become his wife.

"I saw a throne," Shomré said.

Wrinn peered into his wife's eyes, and placed a hand on hers, so as to calm her.

"A throne made out of skulls," Shomré said. "A man sitting upon it. The man — " She howled a wordless howl of fear. "The man — he is near…"

There was motion outside the tent and Wrinn stormed out of the tent flap, to protect his wife. He did not see a man or throne made out of skulls, but instead the Field Marshal Sintari, speaking softly to a warrior.

Sintari fixed his brilliant green eyes on Wrinn, looking at him questioningly. "Is something the matter?" Sintari said.

"I — " It seemed silly, but the look of panic in his wife's eyes had then stirred panic in him. "I'm sorry… my wife has had a dream."

"Dark dreams are not uncommon in the Dark Land," said Sintari, "for here, there is haunted memory, a memory of grave crimes, crimes of the heart."

"She said she saw a man," Wrinn said. "A man on a throne."

Sintari's eyes sparkled in a moon that didn't seem to be there, amid a sky so dark it seemed not just to suck away all light, but also all hope.

"A man on a throne," Sintari said. "I and Vlesti were discussing…"

The warrior standing beside Sintari had long black hair, and his keen grey eyes also seemed to sparkle in the moon that, to Wrinn's estimation, was absent.

"There is talk of someone having stilled the waters of the Sea of Ghosts," Sintari said, "and yet, the stilling of it is an illusion. There are sinkholes that have opened up, eddies and whirlpools, and now crossing it is even more treacherous, if it were possible, than before."

Wrinn's fear returned, the fear that had started with his wife's panicked mumbling.

"A human man crossed the waters, though," Sintari said. "Not Reev, or a Telantine, but someone else. A man, and with him a hundred others. Someone the anguipeds and the inhabitants of the Dark Tower are calling *Amir Alfajr*."

"Could he be…?" Wrinn started.

Could he be what? What was he saying?

"Who is this man?" Wrinn said.

"Some claimed he is an Imperial," Sintari said. "Others, scouts, swear by his anguiped eyes. He seems to have a dark purpose as he traverses the Dark Land. After all, those of dark purpose thrive here…"

"*Amir Alfajr*," Wrinn repeated. He had heard that title before. An anguiped had uttered it.

"The anguipeds have taken notice of him," Sintari said. "It

seems, they look upon him with favor.

"The elvenking is troubled — but His Majesty wishes to be cautious. He does not know what powers this *Amir Alfajr* has, if he changed the nature of the Sea of Ghosts. Some claim he is bearing Serpentax, the Dark One's own sword."

"*Amir Alfajr*," Wrinn repeated at a whisper, and when he had spoken the words, it seemed an icy hand gripped his heart, turning it to an icicle in his chest.

The tent flap stirred open.

Shomré, once called Rosalie, stepped out, and her beauty in the night banished Wrinn's fear. Then the fear returned, at the thought it was his duty to protect such a beauty from danger.

It was Wrinn's duty to protect Shomré, once called Rosalie, from *Amir Alfajr*.

"Wrinn?" she said. "What's going on? Is everything all right?"

"Just talking about your dream," Wrinn said.

Could that be what they were talking about? After all, she had dreamed of a human man who terrified her.

Amir Alfajr… surely, that was who Shomré had seen.

Shomré sidled up to him and met Wrinn in an embrace. Wrinn kissed her on the forehead.

"It's all right," Wrinn said. "I'll protect you from *Amir Alfajr*…"

He took Shomré by the hands and led her into the tent.

~

They made love, even at a time such as this. Exhausted and winded, Wrinn hoped she'd be able to get some sleep, to dream more pleasant dreams than before, and not send her husband into a panic.

The camp never quite died down, and the elven warriors slept in shifts.

"The Steaming Gates have held strong," said Shomré.

"The elves seem strong," she continued, softly, at a whisper. "The enemy has not dislodged us. We've defeated them. But it cannot be."

"What do you mean?" Wrinn said softly.

"It cannot be," Shomré said, and perhaps she was delirious from fear, from exhaustion. "We've defeated them, but it cannot be. We will be dislodged from the pass. We will be defeated. Because the strength of the elves is spent."

"Oh, come now," Wrinn said. "You're not thinking straight."

"The strength of the elves is spent," Shomré said. "The enemy is stronger than in its first iteration, and we are weaker. That means, Wrinn, they aren't sending the full force of their troops.

"They could destroy us, if they wanted to…

"They have another strategy in mind…"

Chapter Thirty-Seven: Pressing Ahead

Balor had gone westward down the road, in the direction of the throne he wanted, because the master of the Haunted Forest did not want him to achieve it.

He was walking westward as fast as his legs would take him, but at abandoned villages he would pilfer whatever stores of food he could find. The stores of rokahn bread were wormier even than the bread in the vampire lands that had been left out for years.

But all pleasure seemed to be gone from Balor, and all he wanted was the feeling of euphoria that would come with an achieved goal.

So he walked, and he was walking, with a wormy piece of bread in his hand, when he met what seemed like an unstoppable force.

An army twice the size of Balor's was headed straight at him, the blue rokahn he had learned were called kobolds, the regular rokahn and kehrad on black wolves, and so many wylocks they were like a swarm of bats in the night.

"Charge!" Balor commanded his troops, and he wondered if the Dark One would be able to stop his approach into Lamdar, and stop him from seizing the throne.

The throne of Solendir, he recalled — that was what he was after. The throne of Solendir was his life's goal, what he hungered for above all.

If he had the throne of Solendir, he was sure, he would be happy.

His undead hordes, both vampire and rokahn, charged forth with a fearless gait, brandishing swords and spears, on this battlefield somewhere on the nebulous border of Lamdar and Londor.

Their steely undead gait met with the wild frenzy of the Dark One's hordes, as kobold mages tried and failed to work their blood magic on the undead, whose blood in their veins was either gone, or dead.

The rokahn were cutting swathes into the undead horde as Balor kept the rokahn far from him with bursts of force and spears and arcs of necromantic fire. He began to bludgeon them with force, killing them with sudden vigor and then reanimating them in swift succession, creating soldiers faster than the rokahn had cut them down.

He could hear the Dark One whispering, his forceful words in his ear, trying to stop him. But he fueled it, remembering that if the master of the Haunted Forest did not want something, then that something was for his good.

Spears and arcs, bursts of necromantic fire, some withering and some force and sudden reanimation, and the monstrous horde the Dark One had sent, an army that could conquer a nation, was being met with the power of Balor.

The army that could destroy many human kingdoms was buckling before Balor's blows and his sudden reanimation, and the thralls that were being created with each sword stroke and every gout of force sent from his staff.

The rokahn were giving wild cries, and the hoots and howls Balor was coming to realize were not war cries, but cries of desperate fear. Some rokahn were beginning to turn back and flee, knowing if they died, they would join the countless host, the host that Balor had summoned, and that was now growing stronger with each desperate gambit the Dark One made.

The Dark One, desperate… how about that?

~

The rokahn that had not died were scattering into the woods

amid the vast woodland, the nebulous border between Lamdar and Londor, the wild fields once covered in snow but now were blooming. Balor pressed the advantage, seeing that his army had turned from an inestimable host to a sea of undead bodies, now mostly rokahn given unlife. Balor would press ahead, he vowed, as he saw their scattering forms, and the sun was beginning to sink low in the horizon.

But he knew also that the Dark One would not cease trying to halt his westward movements.

The Dark One was desperate to stop Balor from reaching the throne of Solendir and claiming it for himself.

What would Balor do when he had become the elvenking? What would he do when all the armies of the elves were at his beck and call?

He did not know, but it seemed the elven armies were vanished, that all elves were gone from elven towns, and that fortresses and fastnesses had been abandoned to the Dark One and his minions.

The Elf Lands had been abandoned to the Dark One's minions — the Dark One, who was desperate to stop Balor from sitting on Solendir's throne.

Balor pressed ahead, westward down the road, and did not stop his walking even as the sun set over distant hills. He ate his wormy bread and uttered something not unlike a prayer of thanksgiving, pondering all that had gone on, and all that had happened to him since the three hags took him to the Haunted Forest.

He thought they did not want the best for him, but did they? He thought they had manipulated him, but perhaps they were manipulating him to become a weapon against the Dark One. Perhaps, in their manipulation, they had driven him into a task that was for his, and for Varda's good.

At some unearthly hour, as a moon arose, a bright beacon, and the stars were clear to be seen, so far from any city lights, Balor turned and looked at his work. The undead looked at him with dull eyes, their mouths hanging open, their minds full of a hunger they did not fully understand. They would serve him, this countless host, a host that could conquer the world, but also a host that Balor could destroy with a flick of his staff, and remove the animation from their bodies.

Balor could conquer the world, he realized. He could conquer the Elf Lands and beyond.

But all he wanted was to sit upon Solendir's throne.

He wanted to take from the elvenking what was his.

But why?

Why was the Dark One trying to prevent him from taking Solendir's throne?

Chapter Thirty-Eight:
Joy Ride

The Telantines had reached the shore of what had been the Sea of Ghosts, and the death of Mudamir seemed to have startled the one who abided in the Dark Tower.

Reev, in the company of Pandarus for months now, had developed a respect for Pandarus, whom he considered his leader, and would follow him to the furthest ends of Varda.

But he remembered, one burning hot day by the shores of the sea, what had been his father's dying words, what he now considered to be much more — that he should drive the armies of the Dark One before the Dark Tower, so as to draw out his enemy.

Only when the Dark One seemed in imminent peril would his Hand feel urged to act — so had said the Lady of Danyen, confirming there was something more to his father's words.

The Telantine host gathered by the shore of the sea was now fifteen thousand strong, and though the Telantines continued to arrive, padding the numbers of Pandarus's army, the numbers of the Telantines were beginning to slow, the boats navigating the treacherous sea fewer in number.

Would the number of the army stall out at fifteen thousand, when an army a million strong was before the Dark Tower, and that was only a small portion of the Dark One's force?

How then could victory be achieved, Reev wondered, in the heat of the day, as he looked into the glistening waters of the sea.

Perhaps, he would have a word with Pandarus.

He found Pandarus on the perimeter of camp. The sun wreathed his dark brown hair in light, and he was standing in his loin cloth, with his sword at his side.

"Pandarus," Reev said, insistent. "I truly feel I've had a word from the gods, that we must drive the armies before the Dark Tower."

"If I'm not mistaken," said Pandarus, "the word of the gods was that the armies gathered at the Dark Tower were to be driven before *you*."

Reev knew it was true. But he was one man. He needed help. "I need help," Reev said aloud.

"Perhaps," Pandarus said, "but the Dark One has recovered from the defeat of his castellan. A force is on its way to defeat us for good, and I doubt they'll accept a challenge this time."

The Dark One had perhaps learned his lesson, not to accept a challenge by his minions against one much greater than themselves.

"What will we do, then?" Reev said.

"We will flee, or we will fight," Pandarus replied, "with our eyes on victory, as before. With boldness, and courage, and yet with shrewdness and wisdom."

That seemed the Telantine method.

But they were only fifteen thousand against an inestimably vast host.

They began to make their way across the ashen earth, leaving behind the waters of the sea.

What month was it?

It seemed the Dark Land had two seasons, hot and very hot, and whenever there was rain it was tinged with sulfur. Yet amid the poison earth, Reev saw stunted trees nonetheless growing, somehow surviving the elements.

Widespread agriculture, however, was beyond the Dark Land, and now that Ash-Land had been scattered, food was imported for the Dark Land's armies from afar, food extracted at a price.

Reev wondered if the desolate state of the Dark Land and its lack of resources could be turned to the Telantines' advantage.

But what were they, fifteen thousand against a host as numerous as grains of sand in the seashore?

What were they, Reev wondered, and how could they overcome the odds, he wondered, as Pandarus stopped his gait, and the Telantines drew swords amid the ashen ground, and an army had appeared on the horizon.

They were rokahn and anguipeds as before, anguipeds in steel armor with cruel-edged weapons. There were rokahn on black wolves, and kobold mages. But as the limitless host of the Dark One approached, against the fifteen thousand Telantines, Reev saw the Dark One had truly brought all his might to extinguish the Telantines forever.

For in addition to the countless anguipeds and their rokahn thralls, there was the form of something, aloft in the air.

Were it not for Gastreel's history lessons in Norwood, Reev was sure it was a dragon.

Gastreel had said that all dragons were gone from Varda, but the draconic creature was far larger than a silver drake or a white drake. Its massive form was a shadow across the horizon, as it flapped its wings, and began to spew fire.

Its scales were colored black, and its eyes were a hideous green that glowed in the darkness. Even after it stopped breathing its gout of flame, smoke was escaping from its nostrils as it soared through the air, under the weak Dark Land sun.

Yet Pandarus did not wail, nor did the Telantines tremble. A promise carried them forward, a promise they seemed to believe, despite the odds.

The promise of a Great War, waged on the anguipeds.

Pandarus shouted, and drew his sword. He brandished his sword, and the Telantines brandished theirs in reply. Reev, seemingly always a step behind his brethren, drew Doomblade and waved it in the dim Dark Land sun, amid a smoke wreathed sky, and a dreadful foe in the horizon.

The dragon soaring through the sky was the centerpiece of the Dark One's forces, not the countless host arrayed on the ground below. It soared and made a show of spewing fire, a display of dominance intended to terrify, as it circled about the fifteen thousand Telantines, a host outnumbered a countless number to one.

Reev knew that whatever happened to the Telantines, they had the fate of his father, spirited away to bliss. He treasured that in his heart as the dragon circled about the countless host. He had a feeling that whatever happened to them, the victory was already won.

As the dragon circled about, the army of anguipeds were standing back to witness the dragon's coming devastation and not charging. The dragon was such a dreadful foe, they didn't want to get in its way.

The dragon dove, and as its titanic body, a shadow on the horizon, began a descent toward the ground, it opened its jaws — the size of a warship — and spewed out its fiery breath. A jet of fire streaked across the ground as Telantines acted in concert, diving out of the way, and as Reev struck with Doomblade, clipping its tail.

The dragon rose back up toward the sky, not having killed a single Telantine, and the anguipeds in the army beyond were beginning to stir, hoping that the dragon they had brought would do all the work for them.

The dragon was circling about the fifteen thousand Telantines standing in the ashen rock and earth, and its dark shadow was difficult to distinguish amid the dark sky and the sun that did not give much light in the Dark Land.

The Telantines turned with every motion of the dragon, following its outline across the sky, never giving up hope even against hopeless odds, remembering what the gods had promised them — a Great War and a slaughter of the anguipeds.

The dragon made a turn, wheeling its body around, the size of a city, and a Hellish gleam appeared in its green eyes as it descended, again attempting to destroy the last of the Telantines forever.

It opened its jaw, and the fire it now spewed as it made a second descent spilled over across the ground, singeing Ajax's hair across from Reev, as Blarer howled a war cry, and charged — even into the dragon's path. Blarer had leapt upon the dragon's neck, and the last glimpse Reev saw was Blarer astride the dragon's neck, with his sword in his hand. As the dragon rose into the sky, Reev realized Blarer was riding with it, that he was now in the limitless sky, circling above the gathered Telantines.

But the dragon was beginning to roar, now — to wheeze, to whine in pain.

The dragon seemed to be forced in a direction it did not wish to go, as the dragon turned from the Telantines around, then off into the distance.

~

When the dragon made its descent, it was whining in pain, and it was aimed now at the gathered army of anguipeds. He heard a roar of pain, as if Blarer had stabbed the dragon in the neck, and in response the dragon opened his mouth and emptied the fiery contents of his stomach.

Fire poured, spewing the ground, and the anguipeds did not move in concert like the Telantines. Fire erupted, and it scorched the battlefield, killing hundreds and maybe thousands with each second that passed. The anguipeds were scattering, and the Telantines responded, charging in their lighter clothing and their lighter gear.

As a slaughter was had, spreading from one corner of the

battlefield to another, the dragon was continuously screeching in pain, and it became clear that Blarer, riding astride the dragon's neck, was piercing it with his sword.

The dragon had made another turn in the sky, forced by a hostile rider, and it was making yet another descent toward the anguiped army, which was now fleeing. Again the dragon emptied its stomach of fire, and this time all the fire in it was spewed, an inferno killing thousands, turning a countless multitude to dust.

The dragon was dropping from the sky, wounded from Blarer's constant piercings. It skidded and then it crashed, killing scores more anguipeds as it slowed to the ground. A cloud of dust was kicked up as the Telantines charged any anguipeds foolish enough not to flee.

Pandarus was sprinting toward the dead dragon and to the warrior mounted upon its neck.

Its neck was like a pincushion, pierced by so many wounds that it was amazing it had clung to life for so long.

Blarer was radiant, and he allowed the Telantines to swarm about him, giving him plaudits. He wasn't about to stop them from telling him he had saved the day.

The anguipeds had fled. A dragon had been commandeered and then killed.

And Reev, standing in the heat of the Dark Land sun, was happy the Telantines had lived another day.

~

More Telantines arrived that night, and though the arrivals had slowed to a trickle, the death of the dragon and the devastation of the army had surely sent the Dark One's minions into a panic.

Fifteen thousand now, and increasing, and in the dark of the Dark Land night, Reev was filled of a strange kind of gladness.

Still, the odds were against them. Still, the betting man would bet on their defeat. But they had defeated a foe much more numerous and more powerful than themselves, and they had lived to fight another day.

Pandarus gave orders, and they would retreat to a new fastness to fight off the Dark One's minions. Reev wondered if waiting was the best strategy, if they should fight now.

For the armies of the Telantines were not increasing as fast as the Dark One's armies were, and the armies of the Telantines were stalling at around fifteen thousand.

If this was as strong as the Telantines would become, why not strike now?

Days after the death of the dragon and the battle in the ashen fields, as the Telantines encamped in a valley, around springs of water, a Telantine joined them with whitish blond hair, his neck tattooed with lightning marks, carrying a spear in his hands.

His name was Uldrich, and he claimed to be a soothsayer, a speaker of hidden truths. He announced, that night, that the Great War was coming, and it was imminent. Reev gave no disagreement.

But he felt he had heard a command, seemingly from his father but really from above, that he should drive the armies of the Dark Tower before him.

Would Pandarus relent? Would he send his army, now, to drive the armies of the Dark Tower away?

He recalled Pandarus's words.

If I'm not mistaken, the word of the gods was that the armies gathered at the Dark Tower were to be driven before you.

Chapter Thirty-Nine:
In the Fall

It was the late summer. The air was thick and sultry on the townhome porch, and Ambrass had a light in her eyes. Fortunato had a cup of wine his hand, and Ambrass insisted that it was all right for him to drink, though the midwife had told her not to.

Her pregnancy had become noticeable, and it had become a betting game in the city, whether the child of Ambrass would be a boy or a girl. It seemed everyone, rich or poor, young or old, were just living in the wake of Ambrass and Fortunato's wedding, and the joy it seemed to have brought to everyone in the city.

Soon the child would be born, and he and Ambrass would sit out together on the happiness of a summer night, and both of them would have cups of wine in their hands.

The townhome, though, would be full of noise, and Fortunato knew their life would change forever.

He had another child, and he prayed for Alondir silently as Ambrass stirred, trying to get comfortable in the seat of their porch, in the heat of the summer night. He prayed for the child now growing within Ambrass, that the child, whether boy or girl, would be happy and healthy and strong.

He thought of the struggle surely now underway on the other side of the world, as Fortunato's happiness now was complete, as he had hung up his sword forever.

He knew he had done his part, and he knew without his part, the defeat of the Dark One would have been more difficult.

But the Dark One's defeat, he sensed, was sure.

He sensed, the Dark One's defeat was inevitable.

But could he be certain?

Ambrass was stirring, her belly large, the child within her growing with each passing week and day. But the summer night was deep, and the city was calm, and at peace.

Fortunato thought that though the Empire now controlled the city, not much had changed, the same faces wandering about, the same people going about their business. Not much had changed, but for the fact that the tower of the wizards was leaning, and that the wizard order was completely gone.

Gastreel, he recalled, was the one who had dealt the order of wizards the fateful blow. The order of wizards had tried to kill Gastreel. They had tried to destroy one the gods favored, and in turn they had been destroyed themselves.

Wasn't that the way of the world?

He took a deep sip of his wine and eyed his wife, still straining to get comfortable, in the heat of the summer night.

When would the child be born?

"When the leaves began to change color," the midwife had said, like some soothsayer, "the child will be born."

When the leaves begin to change color — that's when Fortunato's life would change forever. It also happened to be the time he loved Gallia best.

The Empire, where he grew up, was possessed of enviable weather all year round, mountain vistas crowned in snow, hot summers and winters that were never more than a bit chilly.

But in Gallia, where had spent most of his adult life, in the autumn, the trees would change from green to fiery reds and fiery yellows, fiery oranges and earthy browns. There would be mist on cold ponds, and good fishing in the streams and in the lakes of the South Weald. There would be apple cider from the recent harvest, and there would be a chill in the air, a perfect time to don a light coat and enjoy the serene beauty.

That was the time, according to the midwife — Fortunato's

favorite time in Gallia — when the child would be born.

That was the time that Fortunato's child would arrive into the world.

Would he arrive, in that time, in a world where the Dark One was defeated?

Fortunato thought that time would arrive a little later, that the battle would have a little ways to go.

For Reev and Wrinn, battling the Dark One in the Dark Land, if they had arrived in one piece, would have to be shrewd, and use all the wisdom they had in their possession.

That was beyond Fortunato now, though.

Now, all he had was a summer night, and his wife — now stirring — in the seat across from him.

When the weather cooled, the child would arrive. The Dark One would not quite be defeated.

But he had an inexplicable feeling that his defeat was sure.

Fortunato gulped down the last of the wine. "Ambrass," he said, "we should get to bed."

His wife stirred in his seat and gave him a bright smile, then stood to her feet.

"When the weather cools," Ambrass said, "our child will arrive."

"When the weather cools," Fortunato said, and strode up to her, and took her hands in his. He kissed his wife on the cheek, and led her into the doors of the townhome.

The heat lingered, even in the night, but soon they would be able to sleep comfortably, with a fire burning in the room nearby.

"When the weather cools," Fortunato said softly, and guided Ambrass toward their bedroom.

He wondered whether the gods would give them a boy, or if they would give them a girl.

He thought of the forests of Gallia on fire, in red and orange colors to dazzle and fill with joy. But the joy of the forest's colors, in the autumn, when the weather cooled, paled in comparison with the joy to come.

He wondered what child the gods would give them.

He wondered, and he wondered if he should join in with the bettors, if it would be a girl or a boy.

Chapter Forty: Rosalie's Wisdom

The Dark One's armies had not appeared before the elves, now, in many weeks.

The elves, encamped around the Steaming Gates, had drawn swords, and were ready to do battle with whatever the Dark One sent their way, but to Wrinn it appeared he was doing damage without sending any of his abominations to strike.

For now, all anyone talked about was whispered rumor, of the human man — who was not Reev — who had crossed the Sea of Ghosts and now was somewhere… no one knew where… within the Dark Land.

The human man who had crossed the Sea of Ghosts, and now was doing something — no one knew what — was called by the anguipeds *Amir Alfajr,* which some elves took as his name but which Wrinn believed sounded like a title.

He and Shomré were trying to take advantage of the stillness that had produced fear and worry, and were venturing beyond the gathered army hand in hand, to the namesake of the Steaming Gates.

The bubbling pools never ceased their bubbling, steaming hot springs that a few elves claimed to bathe in, despite the sulfurous odor. Wrinn was adventurous, but he was mostly concerned with his wife and her constant fretting, her conviction she had seen *Amir Alfajr* beside a throne fashioned from skulls, in a dream.

"I saw him in a dream," said Shomré, once called Rosalie, beside the bubbling hot springs. Wrinn had clasped her hand in his.

"And what do you think?" Wrinn said. "Are you more afraid of *Amir Alfajr,* or are you more trusting in the gods? Don't you think Reev can handle *Amir Alfajr?*"

"Are you saying," said Shomré, "that the one the anguipeds call *Amir Alfajr* is the Dark One's Hand?"

"I don't know what I'm saying," Wrinn replied. "I'm just saying, the light will defeat the darkness. Don't you think so?"

Shomré nodded her head and turned back, looking behind the sulfurous hot springs, to the armies encamped before the pass.

The pass was called narrow, but it was many miles, and elves filled every inch of it, and spilled beyond.

"Do you know what I think, Wrinn?" Shomré said.

"What do you think?" Wrinn answered.

"I think we're asking for trouble, waiting here," Shomré said. "The Dark One has something planned for us, and it's not for our good. We should be attacking, not sitting idle here. If we're idle, he has time to plan. If we attack, he'll have to respond."

"Perhaps, my wife should be planning the war effort and not the elvenking," Wrinn said.

"Do you think so?" Shomré breathed softly.

She did not seem in the mood to be amused.

No, she seemed afraid, and the more Wrinn thought about it, the more he thought she, and all of them, had reason to be afraid.

For weeks, the battle line had not been moved, and though the pass called the Steaming Gates was blocked, and the Dark One could not receive reinforcements from abroad, the news from afar, that a human man the anguipeds called *Amir Alfajr* had arrived from beyond, indicated the Dark One was at work, and he would stop at nothing until the elves were wholly destroyed.

Shomré had a point. She had some wisdom to impart. Perhaps — Wrinn thought — they should bring her wisdom to the elvenking.

~

Alondir, the child of Fortunato and Nenré, having just turned three years old, was waddling about outside the elvenking's tent. At all times, he had a doting audience watching his every step. His blue eyes never failed to steal Wrinn's breath. He had the blueness of his mother's eyes, and the piercingness of his father's eyes. He had his father's hair and his father's powerful presence.

He was always happy, even in the Dark Land, having no care — it seemed — in the world.

But another was moving through the army's encampments as Alondir pranced about, one who did not have Alondir's boundless joy, one who seemed in a grave mood, walking before the gathered warriors.

The elvenking had seen Wrinn and Shomré's approach and was meeting them where they stood.

"Your Majesty," Wrinn said, "a word?"

~

Away from the crowds, Shomré expressed her concerns, but the more she spoke, the clearer it was that her words fell on deaf ears.

The elvenking had a fire of anger in his eyes when Shomré had finished.

"The lack of bloodshed concerns you," said the elvenking. "The lack of the deaths of my people brings to you alarm."

Wrinn wanted to say, "That's not what she was saying," but thought better of contradicting a man who held both their lives in his hand.

"Well, I disagree," the elvenking said. "I will be glad, every moment the Dark One has not fixed his wrath upon us, every day that goes by without one of my people having fallen. We have expended much to get here.

"Me — it seems — most of all."

He spoke of Velérion and Nenré, his children, now dead.

And Wrinn knew the elvenking had lost much, and Wrinn thought, perhaps, the time for giving such a man advice was over.

"Every day a wife or a child has not had to experience what I have is a blessing," the elvenking said. "And we will do our duty and stand guard, and do no more. I will not be grieved that elves are not dying, Shomré."

He turned in a furor and departed.

Shomré had a look of hurt. Then, she eyed the elvenking distrustingly.

"Don't worry," Wrinn said. "You tried to help. And besides, I love you."

He met Shomré in an embrace and kissed her on the cheek.

But as the elvenking departed and entered his tent through the tent flap, Wrinn was looking at him in distrust.

But for the smaller creature standing in the tent, prancing about, Wrinn had only boundless respect and inestimable love.

Alondir, he recalled, was the first in line to the elvenking's throne.

Chapter Forty-One: Uldrich's Gift

The Telantines had moved about the Dark Land as the months progressed, never staying in one place for long. They were besieging the leader of the Dark Land, the one who abided in the Dark Tower, who aspired to rule from his Dark Throne.

The Telantines had moved so swiftly, the anguipeds had not been able to catch them, but Reev knew it was a losing strategy, for the numbers of the Telantines arriving had dwindled to nothing, and they would never be a force of much more than twenty thousand men. The Great War they had been promised would either come or it would not come.

That, to Reev, seemed the state of things, one night as the twenty-thousand Telantines set up camp in the northern perimeter of Abollonia.

They were not far, Reev thought, from the Dark City.

Reev wondered if they should raid the Dark City, and plunder it.

Reev wondered if that would draw out the Dark One's Hand from his hiding place, and lead him into a battle.

But Reev supposed he already had a command.

He already had a command, he thought, as the Telantines milled about their tents, never with a sword far from their grip.

What month was it? Indeed, what year?

Reev had lost track of time.

He had lost track of time, but he had not forgotten why he had come here in the first place. He had come here to crush Seymus under his foot.

And yet, he had arrived in the Dark Land, and he still did not know how.

He had only a hint of how — to draw the Dark One's Hand from his hiding place, by driving the armies of the Dark Tower before him.

He thought of approaching the Telantines' leader, Pandarus.

But he had already heard from Pandarus his advice, and he didn't think the leader of the Telantines, besieging the Dark Land, was willing to hear an argument. He would not send twenty-thousand men against a million, gathered before the Dark Tower and the Dark One who abided there.

But stirring in the dim light of camp, in the campfires that could never quite burn through the Dark Land's darkness, a figure was approaching.

Reev recognized him as Uldrich, the man who had joined the Telantines months ago, who claimed to be a soothsayer.

Despite the Dark Land's darkness, there seemed to be a brilliant light in his eyes. "I have a word from the gods," said Uldrich.

That was a bold statement, something Reev would never dare say.

"You were told to drive the armies of the Dark One before you, in view of the Dark Tower," Uldrich said. "I will explain it to you, more fully.

"For you may, with the aid of the twenty-thousand Telantines, drive the armies of the Dark Tower before you. But then the Great War promised will be a skirmish and not a slaughter. The task ahead of you will then be more difficult, and the victory not so sweet.

"However, if you drive the armies of the Dark Tower before you, by yourself, then the Great War promised will be a slaughter indeed, and the victory will be complete."

It was a difficult word. Driving the armies of the Dark One, in the Dark Tower, before him, alone, seemed impossible. But weren't impossible things what Telantines were meant to strive after?

Weren't impossible things meant to be his goal?

And didn't he want to make his brethren's joy complete? He

didn't want to disappoint them, did he?

He wanted the Great War promised to them to be all it could be.

"Another word," said Uldrich. " 'Remember, remember, the fall of Qadirra, and how it happened in the first place. ' "

Reev watched as Uldrich vanished into the night.

He watched as Uldrich vanished into the night darkness, and the task laid upon him seemed clear, to drive the armies of the Dark One before him — by himself — without any aid. The task seemed monumental, far more impossible than defeating a jotunn alone was.

But didn't he want to give his brethren his all? Didn't he want the Great War to be all it could be?

He found Pandarus standing beside Blarer, near the fire. He said to him, "Leader, I'm going to the Dark Tower, to drive the armies before me, by myself. I feel that the gods want me to find a way, though it seems impossible…"

There was respect in Pandarus's eyes then, and it did not seem he wished to disagree, or to stop Reev from a task that would appear the height of recklessness.

"If that is what you feel you should do," Pandarus say, "then you go with my, and our, blessing."

Reev nodded.

He found his pack, and filled it with road-bread, and his waterskins with water. He departed into the night, then, uttering prayers under his breath.

The journey to the Dark Tower would be long, and how he would drive an army of a million before him was still beyond his ability to grasp.

~

As the days progressed, he slept in canyons and in mountain valleys, making his way mile by mile across the hot days and warm nights. He slept in places where he was concealed, and he saw that the patrols of anguipeds were growing in number, and the rokahn were becoming more numerous.

And as he slept and crept carefully across the landscape, he dwelled not just on the bulk of what Uldrich said, but also what seemed to be incidental.

He had said to remember the fall of Qadirra, and how it had happened.

For long before he reached the Dark Land, he had ventured to a city doomed. He had helped engineer its doom by freeing a Telantine weapon from its holding place, a mighty weapon called Heaven's Spear that had destroyed Qadirra and apparently streaked across the sky, thousands of miles, before destroying Ash-Land not far from here.

He recalled, and tried to reminisce, all that had happened that led up to the fall of Qadirra and its imminent destruction.

The words of Uldrich, though he was a soothsayer, remained inscrutable to him.

What did Qadirra have to do with driving the armies of the Dark Tower before Reev?

~

The days progressed, and at times Reev would hide, and at times he would press ahead, with the movements of the troops now filling the Dark Land, more numerous than ever.

He fought terror at the sight of platoons of anguipeds in armor walking by, or at the sight of the countless host of rokahn he would have to face — and drive before him, by himself.

Yet he traveled carefully, and remained out of sight, taking every step with caution, so that he would not be seen.

It helped that the Dark Land was so dark, and let in precious little light, that even in daylight, seeing was not as easy as in the world abroad.

And it helped that Reev knew what awaited him if he somehow failed, that if he was stricken dead like his father, his fate would be good.

It helped, but he did not wish to fail, and he would do everything in his power to achieve the victory for his brethren. Each step was careful as he pushed through the landscape, following a road that wound eastward through the Dark Land.

One night the dim lights of the Dark City appeared in the horizon, and at the thought of its denizens he drew in a cold breath of air, fearful that somehow the denizens would take note of him, and seize him.

He uttered a prayer that somehow they that inhabited the Dark City would turn away from their ways and flee the Dark Land, before the slaughter that would soon overtake it — or so he had hoped — would swallow them in the aftermath.

He had passed the Dark City, and the Dark Tower was at the door.

He refilled his waterskin in a spring of water, overlooking a rocky cliff. And he said a prayer, for speed to his feet, for wisdom of his actions, as he found himself in a forest of stunted trees, and a scenery of rocky cliffs and dried-up pools and lakebeds.

He was in a wilderness, but he thought he knew the way. He had been down the nearby road once before.

In the wilderness, surrounded by stunted trees, he was near the Dark Tower, but the armies and the anguipeds did not seem to inhabit the forest. Indeed, growing green things and life seemed anathema to them, and they avoided it. They seemed to like better the ashen wastes, the blowing dust and the poor, hot air that characterized the Dark Land.

He pushed through the stunted trees, and he thought he was at the threshold of his goal.

Days, or was it weeks, after he had left the Telantines temporarily behind, and the forest of stunted trees became a cliff — a valley he knew all too well, the fire of camps, a multitude so vast he swallowed a breath of panic… and a towering form of darkest darkness amid the darkness, the promise of the Dark Tower, in the middle of the night.

But there was light, Reev saw, out of the corner of his eye. In the middle of this deep darkness, there was bright light to be found.

It was the form of one he knew, a warrior of light herself wreathed in light.

But the Lady of Danyen was changed. She wore a white gown, as before, that radiated light wherever she stepped. But as she looked at Reev, teasingly, and her green eyes sparkled, he saw that she was covering her hair with a veil, and that the white gown was different from before.

Reev strained to think of what all this meant, and how the Lady of Danyen was attired differently from before.

The white gown she wore was changed — and the veil.

She was in the attire of a woman ready to be wed.

"Why — ?" Reev started.

But the Lady of Danyen walked up to him in her gown and her veil, and pressed her finger to his lips.

"I am dressed as a bride," said the Lady of Danyen, "for I am about to be married."

Reev had so many questions, so many questions he thought that the Lady of Danyen would not be willing to answer. He had so many questions, like how she could be married, when she was an apparition, the ghost of a woman who now was long dead.

"I — " Reev started.

But the Lady of Danyen shook her head, and her veil seemed to fall slightly lose, threatening to bare her burnt gold hair.

"I will hear no argument," said the Lady of Danyen. "I am a bride, and I am about to be married."

She was gone then, and Reev was alone, alone as a dim dawn arose over the Dark Land, and he could see the massing forms around the Dark Tower. A million, or was it two million, now gathered to fight on behalf of the Dark One?

A million, or two million was it, stretching into the horizon?

A word from his father, and a correcting word from a soothsayer, had driven Reev to this fate. It was his task, not just to drive these countless multitudes before him, but to do it by himself.

It seemed impossible, and it seemed so impossible that a Telantine could not do it. And he did not know where to begin, how to drive these countless throngs before him — how to do it, indeed?

And yet, he had made up his mind, to try… to give it his all.

He was not alone.

He had the Lady of Danyen.

He had the memory of his father and his father's fate.

And he had Uldrich's words, ones he thought held the key.

Remember, remember, the fall of Qadirra, and how it happened in the first place.

Chapter Forty-Two:
The Birth

It was a sunlit day not long after All Hallows when Ambrass gave birth to twins.

They were a boy and a girl, the girl with hazel eyes and the boy with eyes of blue.

The midwife's eyes sparkled in the lights of their townhome. "What shall you name them?"

Fortunato looked to his bride. After all, it was she who had been through so much.

The midwife held up the girl to Ambrass.

"Gemini," she said.

She set Gemini to Ambrass's breast and held up the boy.

"Dandari," said Fortunato, "because he will see the world made new."

~

The midwife left them and they spent the day together, Ambrass, Fortunato, Gemini and Dandari. They had spent months preparing for a boy or a girl's arrival, but not both. And so the next day Fortunato purchased another crib, and another set of toys.

Ambrass and Fortunato, Gemini and Dandari would spend the rest of their lives together. The two infants would spend the next year exploring their world, which consisted of the townhome. They would learn to talk — perhaps, to dream. And Fortunato and Ambrass would guide them every step of the way.

As Fortunato held Dandari that night, and comforted him as he cried, beside the fire, he considered all that had gone on, all that had led him to this happy point. He recalled, the dark iron wound he suffered, that no one thought he would recover from.

He recovered from that wound, he thought, because he was a Telantine. And that meant that Gemini and Dandari were Telantines too.

Ambrass had a look of exhaustion, that night, sitting beside the fire, but also supreme joy. For Fortunato thought her joy seemed complete in this moment, sitting beside the fire in the townhome with their two children.

Fortunato wondered how the bettors in Galiope would react to being thwarted. For everyone who had bet that a boy had would be born had been correct, and everyone who had bet a girl would be born had been correct, too. So how would the coin hat had been wagered on be distributed?

Fortunato chuckled softly at the thought as he clutched Dandari to his chest, as Dandari hiccupped and then whined softly, and then seemed to be slowing down, ceasing the writhing of his arms and legs. Would he soon sleep?

Fortunato knew that he and Ambrass would not be getting a lot of sleep in the days or the months ahead.

He wondered what sort of world Dandari and Gemini would grow up in, if it would be better than the world that Fortunato knew. Fortunato supposed it all depended on the outcome of the war underway right now, whether the Dark One would be defeated, or the forces of light extinguished.

In the light of the fire, Fortunato tried not to dwell on a bad outcome. But he knew it was out of his hands now.

Others were now fighting this war, and he had hung up his sword forever. He would have to fight other battles now, and he would have to pick them, when Dandari or Gemini resisted eating a certain food or disobeyed their mother or father.

Fortunato would try to train Dandari and Gemini well, so they could grow up to be the best people they could be.

Fortunato hoped the long odds would be realized, that the Dark

One really would suffer a defeat. But he knew the Dark One's armies were vast and countless, and even now they were sweeping across the lands of the Elf Lands and the lands of the Dweorg. The armies of the Dark One threatened to unmake everything Fortunato and Ambrass had known.

Fortunato would cling to hope, though, as he clutched Dandari and patted him on his back, as he rocked him in the light and the relative warmth of the fire. He would cling to hope and a promise from the gods that seemed impossible, that the Prince of the Dawn would crush the Dark One underfoot.

Reev and Wrinn, a world away, were engaged in that struggle now. If they had died, Fortunato thought he would somehow know. In such a situation, he'd think the rokahn and kobolds would break past the Imperial frontier and lay waste to Galiope. In such a situation, he thought, the world would have already fallen by now.

But the world had not already fallen.

Across from him, in the light of the fire, Ambrass was beginning to nod off with a joyful smile locked on her face, as Gemini cooed and stirred slightly.

Fortunato could not afford to worry, and he would not. Tomorrow, they'd buy more toys. All the earnings Fortunato had made over the years, gained over decades of fighting the Dark One, would be spent on Gemini and Dandari, and any future children they had.

Future children… but two were enough to think about, for now.

He prayed quietly that Dandari would grow up in a better world than the one he had known. He prayed Gemini would learn to walk and talk in a world where the light had defeated the darkness, where the Dark One had been crushed underfoot and his armies demolished.

But reports of the wider world had inspired doubt, wars in every part of the world and encroaching on the Imperial frontier, kingdoms destroyed by rokahn pouring in from the north and the south, armies of monsters unseen in more than a thousand years, laying waste to the glittering thrones of elvenkind.

The odds seemed impossible to everyone around Fortunato. But Fortunato had found a northward way to Galiope, and he had found his bride. Fortunato had done seemingly impossible things, because he was a Telantine.

Reev was a Telantine, Fortunato knew.

The defeat of the Dark One was not impossible.

The defeat of the Dark One had been promised.

Chapter Forty-Three: Words of Prophecy

Balor had at last crossed into Lamdar, after facing countless skirmishes. He could see in the distance countless tells, mounds built up from the building and rebuilding of towns up from generations.

He could see in the far distance vineyards that were now overgrown and wheat fields now covered with tangled weeds. Lamdar had been abandoned.

The Dark One had greatly slowed Balor down.

He had marched in opposition to him, and every mile, every town, had been a battle of rokahn versus undead. His army was now countless, as numerous as grains of sand on a seashore. The undead rokahn and undead vampires had formed a vast host, and yet through sheer force of numbers, and sending all the gathered armies available to him, the Dark One had made a journey of what had been months to the better part of a year.

Now, though, he was at the threshold. He could see the green grass threatening to turn brown, and he could feel a cold breeze blowing — the distant form of snowcapped peaks, standing at a great distance from himself, now standing alone.

He was at the border, and he had fought for every mile he had traversed. Every step he had taken had been in opposition to the Dark One.

And the day had arrived, when he would achieve his goal, and the Dark One had not stopped him.

He took a step across the border, what he thought was Lamdar proper.

And then he saw, he was not alone.

A vast host was riding toward him, men in black armor and

steel swords.

But as they drew near, Balor saw they were not men, but creatures that were sort of like elves, but for their green complexion and that their yellow eyes that hinted of a reptilian ancestry. They were bearing scimitars, and they were countless, stretching into the horizon.

Balor uttered silent curses, that he would have to battle here — even at the threshold of the throne.

The Dark One had made every day of travel cost Balor a week, and every month three months. Here he was — at the threshold of his goal — and why would it surprise him that the Dark One would throw everything he had at him, every power he had at his arsenal?

They were thousands, they were tens of thousands… they were more than tens of thousands, and they were armed well.

The Dark One was trying so mightily to stop Balor, but he did not know why.

As the green-faced warriors cut swathes into Balor's army, as some of them were pierced by the swords and spears of the shambling undead, and fell dead, Balor found he could not give their dead bodies reanimation, that they were immune to the powers of necromancy.

For the first time, Balor was afraid, at the thought that this new army the Dark One sent was the one that could, at last, stop him in his tracks — perhaps kill him.

But he focused on the green-faced warriors himself, and one by one, blasted them with balls of necromantic fire and severed their heads with discs of necromantic energy. He was whittling them down, but as the sun grew lower in the sky, here at the threshold of Lamdar, he saw he was losing ground, that the green-faced warriors were cutting deep into his ranks, and that Balor was helpless, because he could not turn the dead against them.

He was helpless, he thought, and though scores of the green-faced warriors were dead, Balor realized he was stepping back and retreating, and as the day was late, he saw that half of his undead army had been cut down by a force much smaller than itself.

But as the sunlight waned, the sunlight began to glitter on something in the distance.

The sunlight was glittering on armor, and it was not the dark grayish-black armor of the green-faced warriors. It was armor that was bright and polished, like silver.

There were scores of riders on Elvish horses, dressed on armor with their beasts dressed in barding. They were wielding lances, the Elvish knights, and for a moment Balor was afraid, that the doom had surely at last come for his undead host — green-faced warriors joined with Elvish knights.

But the Elvish knights were riding toward the green-faced warriors, and as they struck, devastating the green faced warriors with their lances and bowling into their lines, Balor saw it was not the undead they were focused on, but Balor's enemy.

How was this — the elves, whom he had aspired to take the throne from — were on his side?

The green-faced warriors were hissing curses as they fell to the lance, and then to the drawn sword, as the Elvish knights made quick work of them — already weakened by the battling of untold numbers of undead.

Spear against scimitar, and sword against scimitar, Elvish knight against abominable green warrior, and the elves were prevailing over Balor's enemy. But Balor was mystified, that the elves wished to help the one who wanted Solendir's throne.

Sun was setting, and the green riders had fled, or were dead.

Balor's undead army had been halved.

The Elvish knights, who had inexplicably helped Balor, were stirring on their horses. They were not striking at Balor's undead army. One of them pulled off his helmet, baring a head of long brown hair and bright blue eyes.

"The Deedal Prince of Lamdar, Anandari, regent of Lamdar in

the elvenking's absence and caretaker of the throne of Solendir, bids Balor welcome," announced the Elvish knight.

His blue eyes sparkled in the soft sunlight, in this land that, at the cusp of winter, had weather that was kind.

"Your arrival has been long foretold," the Elvish knight continued. "Indeed, it has been commanded. We will not stop the gods' command, and your arrival is welcome, Balor.

"We did not know a host of the dead would accompany you. But whether you are accompanied by the dead or by the living, the Deedal Prince bids you welcome."

Chapter Forty-Four:
A Memory of Fire

The armies stirred, and Reev was waiting for his chance. There were more than a million gathered before the Dark Tower, now, countless hordes stretching into the distance, surrounding the Tower before continuing into the limitless horizon.

Reev, waiting for his chance, still had no idea how to drive the armies from the Dark Tower, how he could possibly drive them before him, by himself.

But he was growing more daring, and he was getting closer to the edge of the armies, and day and night, hiding behind trees or behind crates or barrels, he was observing them.

There were rokahn, he knew, and there were also certain tribes of humans. There were kobolds and kobold mages. But the leaders of them all, the commanders, the generals and the seneschals, were anguipeds. The anguipeds were the leaders of the Dark One's armies, the topmost officials of every division and battalion.

Reev thought the armies, gathered, were waiting for a command from the master of the Dark Tower.

He had a sense, one he wasn't sure where it came from, that the Dark One was waiting for what he expected, the defeat of the Telantines, before he gave the order for the armies to disembark.

He was waiting to send this countless throng before the kingdoms of humanity, where he had already devastated the kingdoms of the elves and was currently locked in a brutal struggle with the dwarfs.

Reev felt a responsibility at the thought, the thought he was charged with making sure it did not happen, that this army spilling forth did not venture forth to slay everyone he loved and everyone he knew.

The Dark One had kept his strongest force for humans, the beings he hated above all, the ones he most wished to destroy.

And Reev, somehow, was charged with driving this countless throng before him.

He had a command, and he had a clue.

Remember, remember, the fall of Qadirra, and how it happened in the first place.

How had it happened in the first place? He had pressed an indentation in the desert sands, and the city had erupted into fire, a blazing inferno.

But before that, he had purified two shrines. The shrines had freed the hindrances that prevented Heaven's Spear from erupting and laying waste the city that the Dark One loved.

He had purified two shrines, but he didn't think purifying a shrine would have anything to do with driving the armies gathered at the Dark Tower before him.

Or did it?

He watched as the rokahn and the tribes of wicked humans paraded before the Dark Tower, and anguipeds rode between and before them, lording over them.

He watched, from a hiding place behind a crate, and then a hiding place closer to the Dark Tower, amid a stand of stunted trees, concealed in foliage.

The midday sun was weak in the sky, but the day was warm, sweltering, and uncomfortable.

He felt a sense of something rising in the crowd, some anticipation written on their faces, as they looked about, to each other, and then to the Dark Tower.

Reev, standing a hundred yards away, could see the Dark Tower and its dark symmetry. As he fixed his eyes where the rokahn had turned about and were staring, he saw that carved into the Dark Tower was a rostrum, and that someone was walking out of the Dark Tower.

Reev shuddered at the thought that the Dark Tower was a tower indeed, not just a monument, and that people truly dwelled within it. He couldn't fathom the twisted mind of a person that lived in the Dark Tower.

The rostrum was clearly visible to everyone in the Dark Tower, for miles around — indeed, every rokahn, kobold, anguiped and human thrall could see the rostrum clearly, and the one now walking to the edge of the rostrum to speak.

The speaker at the rostrum had a mask with eye holes and the mask ended in barbs and spikes.

He heard scattered mumbling amid the wicked humans, a name or a title, "the Dark Docent."

And the Docent began to speak at the rostrum, first in an ululating tongue that caused Reev to shiver, what he recognized as Doomsday. Then he began to speak in the guttural tongue of the rokahn.

He was holding a thick black book.

The Docent began to speak then in the Imperial tongue, for the humans gathered before the Dark Tower.

"Today's conquests," said the Docent. "The fortress of Grabad in Molkoro falls this day, the first of Anthanos. The fortress of Cathbad in the land of the Dweorg has been besieged. The towns of Nardur have been seized, and occupied by a great force of our troops."

The Docent departed, disappearing into the darkness of the tower, and what Reev noticed most of all was that the rostrum could be seen by every soldier of the million gathered before the Dark Tower.

The rostrum was clearly visible, being so high up, for miles around.

A rokahn stirred and looked in Reev's direction. Reev swallowed a panicked breath. He waited, and then he hurried away, far from the enemies' lines, and pondered all he had seen.

~

Remember, remember, the fall of Qadirra, and how it happened in the first place.

In the first place, Reev remembered, there were two shrines that hindered the power of Heaven's Spear, the Telantine weapon that had destroyed Qadirra.

There had been two shrines, Reev recalled, that had to be purified before Qadirra was destroyed. He had purified the first one after his friend, Ivan Xandrast, had opened the door with his magical artifact, the Skeleton Key. But the second shrine, the Shrine of Hyperborean Hindrance, had been a much more difficult affair.

Purifying that shrine had taken siege and craftiness and cunning. It had taken alacrity and skill.

What else had it taken?

Reev remembered, it had not been easy, and the southron mercenaries that the Agent of the Oculus had hired had been fodder for the anguipeds. The southron mercenaries had been no match for the anguiped warriors with the splint mail and their curved swords of a wicked sheen.

The southron mercenaries had proven to be no match.

But the shrine, Reev remembered, had been purified, because Heaven's Spear had been launched, the city destroyed.

He recalled, he had help.

For as in the Dark Land, there had been surviving Telantines who had come to his aid near the ruins of Qadirra. The surviving Telantines had in the end given him aid, and had helped purify the shrine.

What had driven the anguiped armies away?

As Reev pieced it together in his head, a puzzle swirling about him, he recalled the rostrum that the millions gathered before the Dark Tower could easily see, for miles around. Anything placed in the rostrum could be seen by the armies gathered before the Dark Tower.

And what had driven the anguipeds away, near the ruins of Qadirra, had been something that had elicited a memory, an ancestral memory buried deep within their minds.

The sight of a Telantine beacon had terrified them and sent them scrambling away from the shrine they had been protecting.

Could a Telantine beacon terrify the million? Was the ancestral memory, the sight of it, so strong?

Reev knew, if he placed a Telantine beacon in the rostrum, it would be seen by the armies gathered there.

He was in the woods. He had a sword. He could chop trees, and though he did not have nails, he thought the bark of a sapling would be able to tie the wood into the shape of a Telantine beacon.

He would scale the Dark Tower. He would place it in the rostrum. With flint and tinder, he would set it alight. And then he hoped the anguipeds and rokahn gathered before the Dark Tower would remember the Telantine beacon, and what it meant.

~

He chopped wood from the forest, and carved bark from saplings. He took the wood, and began to fashion it into the Telantine beacon's shape. It wasn't perfect, but it formed a crude shape of what he remembered, a poor but relatively clear rendition of what the Telantine had fashioned near the city of Qadirra far away.

He waited until dusk, and then he waited until night.

Cloaked in darkness, armed with the Telantine beacon, he saw the million gathered before the Dark Tower were sleeping or not sleeping, but that they had entered into their restful period. It was as good a time as any for Reev to try what he thought was his best hope for success.

He found himself stepping between the rokahn, trying to avoid the light of torches and lanterns, and the deep darkness of the Dark Land cloaked him, preventing the rokahn from seeing him.

As he stepped through the ranks of the armies, trying to remain in the shadows, he was making progress, getting closer to the Dark Tower, under the light of a moon that was cloaked in ashen clouds and a darkness it could hardly pierce.

He was at the wall then, facing the rostrum. He searched for handholds. He laid his hand upon a brick, and tried to pull himself up with one hand as he held the Telantine beacon for another.

There was something — the snarl of the rokahn.

A wave of uttered curses.

Rokahn began to shout, and as Reev turned, he saw he had been spotted.

And standing in the midst of the deep darkness were eyes he thought he recognized, not eyes he thought he feared.

There was a toxic fume of something, a ghastly smell. And Reev blacked out.

~

He awoke in the forest, to the light of a lantern, to the sight of Agent Secunda.

Secunda, an agent of the Oculus, he had last seen near the ruins of Qadirra and the city that had been destroyed. Indeed, she had been intimately involved in the purifying of the shrine that had loosed Heaven's Spear.

Agent Secunda was grumbling as Reev stirred awake, and he could see that his Telantine beacon, within the reach of his arms, had fallen apart — bound, as it had been, by the weak bark of saplings.

"The forgetfulness powder I had to use cost the Oculus a fortune," Agent Secunda said. "You had better be more careful, Reev. There's a place for bravery, but not for recklessness."

Reev stirred, on the ground, thankful that Agent Secunda had rescued him, but smarting at her words.

"You call that a Telantine beacon," Agent Secunda was grumbling. "It scarcely looks like a tangle of wood."

Reev sat up. "Will you help me, Agent Secunda?"

He recalled, the last time he had seen Agent Secunda, she had not been in a good state. A magic bracelet had taken control of her. Spymaster Marius had said that she had been in "detoxification," but apparently, Agent Secunda had recovered.

"Of course I will help you," Agent Secunda said. "It's the Oculus's job, their sworn task to bring about the Dark One's doom. Of course I will help you.

"I'll have us fashion a true Telantine beacon. And we'll wait for the perfect moment, not the second best or the third best moment. We'll give it our all."

Reev was glad to have her help. And he supposed, there was a place for charging into the fray, but the Telantine beacon he had assembled, without proper nails, hardly resembled anything than a tangle of wooden logs.

A proper Telantine beacon was required — oil to light it, not flint and tinder and a prayer. A saw, and wood, and nails, to make it as it should have been.

Reev would have to give his best, not his second best.

And it was good to have help. It was good, when fighting the Dark One, not to fight him alone.

Chapter Forty-Five: Light Against Dark

For the first time in months, trumpets blew in the elven camp, trumpets that Wrinn recognized as calling warriors to battle. Shomré had a panicked look, sitting beside the campfire, glancing from her steaming pot of crawfish gathered from the Sea of Ghosts — a panicked look, as if it was the last time she would ever see her husband.

Perhaps, it was. And Wrinn had a terrible feeling. So as Shomré set her pot aside and stood up, he met her in an embrace and kissed her on the lips.

"I love you, Shomré," he said, and ran his hand through her locks of bright gold hair.

"I love you, Wrinn," said Shomré, once called Rosalie.

And he felt a pang at his heart that he could be saying goodbye forever.

For he knew the Dark One's armies were far stronger than the elves, and that they had been leaving them alone with intent. Had they decided, at last, to abandon whatever dark strategy they had engineered, whatever caused them to leave the elven army, at the Steaming Gates, alone?

He shuddered at the thought of the elves' doom arriving after so long.

He had been so long in the Dark Land, he forgot what the sunlight looked outside it. He had forgotten what it looked like, the bright blue sky and the feel of a gentle breeze that was not a hot wind of poor air, with the scent of ash.

He had forgotten, but as he peered into Shomré's eyes, he had a feeling he would see that bright blue sky and feel that gentle breeze again.

He had a feeling — that day would come soon.

For now, it was just a feeling. But he prayed it would be more than a feeling.

Uttering a prayer, as he embraced Shomré, he asked that it be true.

He turned and walked through the elven camps, as elves around him ran with swords drawn — a last battle, Wrinn wondered? The final stand, against the Dark One's armies?

~

They were met, on the front line, by creatures of Hell. Beyond the ashen landscape were what appeared to be fires, but Wrinn saw that cracks were opening up the earth of the Dark Land far away, that the Dark Land, called *Naron Da*, was converging into Hell. The lines between Hell and the mortal world were beginning to blur, as the creatures of Hell strode forth — towering giants of creatures with red skin and red tentacle beards, demons in the flesh, armed with barbed spears and spine-edged swords, come to destroy the elves once and for all.

After a stinging defeat in the First Shadow War, they hoped to end all the elves' hopes in the Last Shadow War. Here, the fate of the elves had been decided.

He saw, the Dark One had not bothered to send any but these demons with tentacle beards, and that there were about a dozen standing on the fire-pocked ground, ready to deal a devastating blow to the elves from which they could not recover.

The Dark One assayed to ensure they would not recover. But the elves were the Light's firstborn. The elves had remained strong.

Alongside the Telantines, they had brought all their force of arms, all their strength, to bear against the Dark One and his armies. The elves, fighting alongside the Telantines, were doing battle with the creatures of darkness.

And the dark day, it seemed had arrived.

The elvenking was galloping forth to the front lines, on his Elvish horse. He had brandished his blue *estirion* sword, and there seemed to be despair in his brown eyes as the horse reared up on his hind legs.

"What is this?" the elvenking said. "Creatures of darkest Hell… minions of the Dark One. We shall not waver, we shall not break."

But the elvenking's voice was wavering.

He seemed stricken, aghast at the sight of these red humanoids, walking now in view of mortal men.

Unlike Gibboroth, their antecessor, they did not seem weakened, or stirred to life or flesh by the power of another. There were no pock marks in their flesh where wires had been placed.

No, the border between Hell and the mortal world was weakening, and *Naron Da* was beginning to take after this master, as the Dark One was preparing to enter the mortal world, as the struggles of elves and men over the millennia had tried to prevent.

Yet though the elvenking was radiant with despair, other elves were not so.

The Field Marshal, Sintari, was on a horse of his own, and his eyes were full of confidence and light, amid this dark place. He had brandished the sword he had taken from the Crown Prince Velérion, the blackish-purple *estirion* blade called Nagaró.

Where the elvenking had caused Wrinn's heart to tremble, the confidence and light in Sintari as he galloped forth, and began to speak, filled Wrinn with hope. "Creatures of darkest Hell… minions of the Dark One. Your defeat is sure. It has already happened."

The red humanoids with the tentacle beards regarded Sintari, and their hideous reptilian eyes seemed to dilate at the sight of him.

There was a champion of light, or two. There was one possessed of confidence, and one weak.

Wrinn feared what would happen when the demons charged

with their barbed spears and their spine-covered swords.

He knew, the final battle was at hand, light against the darkness, the Dark One's defeat or the slavery of mortalkind, in a darkness to consume the world.

Wrinn would fight for the cause of Light. He was one of the champions of Light gathered here, to do battle. And he resolved he would give his life to the cause, if necessary. Shomré, and so many others, were counting on him. He could not let Shomré or anyone else down.

Light… against the darkness. And Wrinn had cast his lot in with the cause of Light, forever.

One of the red demons strode forth. Wrinn saw that, in addition to the barbed spear he was holding, he was carrying a whip. He struck with the whip, and the whip hooked the legs of an elven warrior at the front lines. He flicked with the whip, and the elven warrior came flying toward him, before he impaled the elven warrior on a spear.

The elvenking uttered a wordless wail, and then charged weakly ahead. He had not given a true signal, but after a moment's hesitation, the elven armies took it as a command, and charged.

The elven armies had drawn swords and spears, as they began to pillory the red demons with blows of the sword and spear. Wrinn watched as the bodies of elves flew into the air, cast aloft by fell blows of the red demons.

Would Wrinn's heart tremble? Would he be faint?

He remembered Shomré, but then he remembered the cause of Light itself. He had to brave for the sake of them both.

He rushed ahead, charging through the front lines, as one of the red demons slashed with his sword and sent a dozen elves flying away with one stroke. Wrinn rushed up to one of the red demons, close enough to see the yellow of his reptilian eyes; he struck with his quarterstaff and felt the wood bounce off the red demon's hide. He slashed with his longknife and cut a wound, sizzling green acid blood, before the red demon took notice of him and struck with his spine-covered sword.

Wrinn had sheathed his longknife in the same motion he brought up his quarterstaff to block.

Spine-covered sword met quarterstaff fashioned from the fair forests of Doncalion. The fair forests of Doncalion, which the gods had created, held firm against the abominable sword, and Wrinn went flying backward, striking the ground with his quarterstaff — a length of red yew — in his hand.

The red demons were slaying scores with each stroke of their swords and spears, and their whips drew back any elf who showed any sign of fear, who fled. Elves were flying through the air as the blows met them with infernal force, amid cracks opened up in the distance, and flame.

There was a toxic fume in the air as Wrinn stood to his feet, bruised and battered but still breathing. He had been injured, and he wondered if he had broken something, but he would not give up until all of him was expended.

He charged forth at the red demon as its reptilian eyes locked with him. Heedless of the danger and the sword that could send him flying and kill him in one stroke, Wrinn met him in a flurry of blows fit for a master of *dó kentas*, the elven martial art that he had been trained in, the Way of the Staff.

He bludgeoned the red demon with his quarterstaff and speared him in the head. He alternated between longknife and quarterstaff as he pilloried his foe with slashes and blunt strikes, until the demon had fallen back, and a slashing of the longknife severed three tentacles from the red demon's beard in one stroke.

The red demon roared in pain, a roar to terrify and despair, but which filled Wrinn with hope, for it showed the enemy they faced was not invincible.

The red demon struck with his sword, and again Wrinn went flying, bruised and battered and something more, but still he drew breath, still he had the breath in him, and the strength in him, to fight.

He had risen to his feet, and the number of the elves dead was countless.

But the Field Marshal, Sintari, struck a dolorous blow with his *estirion* sword, Nagaró. One of the red demon's heads was severed — and yet, the red demon with the severed head continued fighting. Another slash of the sword, and Sintari made an artful dodge, avoiding the blow of the sword that could lay him waste. Sintari struck the red demon's arm, severing it, and the sword fell from his grip. Sintari gave a cry, then pierced the red demon's heart. The red demon erupted into flame, and a shockwave rippled through the battlefield, knocking many elven warriors dead.

The red demons were beginning to explode and fall to the ground, one after another, as the elves proved there was still strength in the Light's firstborn yet.

But as Wrinn looked back, he saw the numbers of the elves had been halved, and that the elvenking was galloping away and fleeing, weeping softly.

Wrinn knew there was still strength in the Light's firstborn, but the elvenking seemed taken with despair at the sight of so many elves dead.

~

The red demons destroyed, Wrinn returned to his camp that night, and he had survived. His wife Shomré was waiting for him with a stew of crawfish caught from the Sea of Ghosts.

A victory had won, but it had come at a great cost. So many elves had died, Wrinn worried there wouldn't be much of a force left, to fight whatever the Dark One sent.

But as he ate the stew of crawfish, with his wife at his side, he had a feeling that the Dark One's defeat was imminent. Though so many had died, he had an unshakeable feeling that Reev Nax was still alive, that the crushing of the Dark One underfoot was imminent.

He could not shake that inexplicable feeling of hope, even having seen the elvenking fleeing and weeping. He could not shake that feeling, even in the wake of so many elves dead.

He took a bite of the crawfish stew.

"To the dawn," he said, and Shomré's blue eyes glistened.

"To the dawn," Shomré said.

Wrinn, despite the situation, felt the dawn was coming — indeed, that the promised dawn was imminent.

For he knew, despite so many elven dead, that there was strength in elves, and in Telantines, yet.

Chapter Forty-Six: Endings and Beginnings

It was a day in Anthanos when a familiar face arrived in Godsgate.

The main gate of Galiope was open, and when Fortunato, fetching some food for the night's dinner, in a farmers market in Cathedral District, saw that familiar face, he was filled wih gladness.

It was Ivan Xandrast, the former warlock, having apparently made the journey from the unfathomably distant part of the world, where Fortunato had last seen him.

Why was Fortunato so glad? He pondered why, as he purchased a bushel of lettuce and carrots from a vendor.

He thought that he perhaps shouldn't be so glad to see Ivan Xandrast. After all, Ivan Xandrast — who was called Xan by those who loved him — had caused the Sage's party to split up when Reev needed them most. Xan had accused Fortunato of being the Dark One's Hand, and in anger and fury, Fortunato had ventured off into the desert.

Out of outrage, he had abandoned the quest. The audacity of Xan's accusation had caused Fortunato, faithful to the quest up until that point, to abandon the journey to *Naron Da*.

Why, then, was he glad, to see Xan arrive, dark-haired and dark-eyed, still wearing a kirtle — a kirtle, now soiled?

Perhaps, he was simply glad that Xan had survived, that for all his flaws, he had made his way through a world spiraling out of control, where rokahn and kobolds laid cities waste, and an unworthy emperor was on the throne. He was glad to see Xan, and he realized, he had forgiven Xan for what he had said in the spur of the moment. He had forgiven Xan for the dark accusation that had caused Fortunato to abandon his quest.

Fortunato had abandoned the quest, and found another purpose — a purpose, to be united with his love Ambrass. It was that purpose, Ambrass, that had led him to this farmers market in Godsgate. Tonight's dinner needed to be cooked.

Fortunato set the bushel of lettuce and carrots aside and strode into High Street to meet Xan, where he was. Xan stopped, fearful at the sight of Fortunato.

But Fortunato said, "I forgive you, Xan," and they met in a light embrace.

Xan seemed taken aback, and then he said, "I'm sorry, Fortunato." He departed down High Street, as Fortunato looked on, as Fortunato gathered up the bushel of lettuce and carrots, and then made his way back to the townhome where his wife Ambrass was waiting.

~

Dandari was stirring, and Ambrass had set Gemini down onto the ground in her playpen. Gemini was flapping her arms about, in view of the toys that Fortunato had bought for her.

Ambrass seemed exhausted. But Fortunato knew she was loving every moment of motherhood.

Fortunato set the bushel of carrots and lettuce in the kitchen.

Ambrass was planning to cook a beef stew tonight. Fortunato couldn't cook for the life of him.

But Ambrass seemed tired, and what's more, the sight of Xan walking about had stirred something in him.

He returned to the living room, and saw his bride hovering above Dandari, dangling some toy above his head. "Ambrass," said Fortunato, "I think you need a break."

Ambrass looked at him with exhaustion her eyes, exhaustion and, seemingly, a sense she knew that he was right, that she was tired and she needed someone else to cook dinner tonight.

Someone else needed to cook dinner, but the dinner had to be good.

"I can't cook for the life of me," Fortunato said, "but I think we both know someone who can."

Someone who could — and when Fortunato made the suggestion, his wife Ambrass knew just what he meant.

~

He watched his bride as she donned her fur coat and then wrapped the babies tightly in swaddling clothes. Fortunato took Gemini, and Ambrass took Dandari, and together they opened the door of the townhome, and strode into the darkening night.

They were hungry, and they were tired, and a better hand would cook dinner. They would have dinner, and they would have good company, in a place where a good dinner and good company could always be found, the place that Fortunato and Ambrass loved, besides their townhome, most of all in Galiope.

It was the place they had met for the first time, the place where the story of their love had begun. It was a place that Fortunato thought Gemini and Dandari, when they were older, would get to know as well as their parents.

The Dragonpaw Inn was piloted by a steady hand, one who knew her way around a kitchen, and also a cellar. Glenda had a recipe book that was the envy of Galiope, and she knew just the exact measurements and the right portions to put together a meal that would fill Ambrass and Fortunato's stomachs this night for just a penny or two.

The other thing Fortunato liked about the Dragonpaw Inn was the company he invariably ran into when he made his way there. There was no way of telling what faces would greet him when he walked through the Dragonpaw Inn's doors.

As they walked through the brisk Anthanos air, Fortunato saw that the trees of the city had mostly shorn their leaves, that it was about winter. Dandari and Gemini would see their first Gallian snows, and their parents would be there to guide them every step of the way.

Gemini was babbling, wrapped up in cloths, kept warm by the cloths and by her father's embrace, as Ambrass strode ahead, making her way through Galiope's dark streets, toward the Dragonpaw Inn they both knew and loved.

~

Lights were shining in the window, and there was the sound of clinking cups and laughter, echoing through City Square. Whatever happened in the wider world, the Dragonpaw Inn was a place of happiness and light. It was a shelter, where the cares of the wider world stopped at the door, and could go no further.

They stepped through that door, the four of them, the door they loved, and when they stepped through, they were not disappointed.

~

In a booth were Anthanlas and some men, Fortunato thought, he had seen in a different guise, as bandits of the Lune Valley. In another booth was Rose, sipping a cup of wine. In another booth was Ivan Xandrast with a cup of tall ale, a light in his eyes that Fortunato had never seen before, a light that Fortunato thought would endure, forever.

On a stage, Dolley Wulfrun was crooning out a tune.

And standing behind her desk, as always, was Glenda.

Glenda's eyes brightened with delight at the sight of Fortunato and Ambrass and their children, and she strode up and made some wordless sound of joy. "Oh, Dandari and Gemini have come to see their godmother," she added, as the sound of clinking cups and chatter, the din of mirth and joy, swirled about them.

Glenda approached them and squeezed Gemini's hand and then Dandari's arm. "A dinner, at once," she said.

Ambrass and Fortunato sat down at a booth, and they were served a fairy morel stew. The stew was salted and spiced to the perfection that Ambrass and Fortunato had come to expect, and each bite was delight.

Ambrass had a cup of wine, and she delighted in it — the taste of it rolling down her tongue, what had been forbidden to her not so long ago, before the children had been born. Glenda had brought out a cradle, and the babies happily cooed and twisted their limbs about as their parents ate.

The sound of joy, the din of mirth, the clinking cups and idle chatter, threatened to intoxicate Fortunato, and then he let it intoxicate him. He looked about to happy faces in the light of the Dragonpaw Inn.

Here — their story, the story of Ambrass and Fortunato began.

And here — it seemed — their story would end. It would end when they were old and gray.

Fortunato's eyes looked about and tried to spy the room where he had been taken, after he had suffered a dark iron wound. Ambrass had cared for him so diligently, and though she had resisted his advances at first, Fortunato thought they both knew they were destined to be together.

And now they were man and wife, with two children, amid the din of joy and mirth, the clinking of cups. The delectable broth of the fairy morel stew filled Fortunato's stomach as he looked upon his bride. Ambrass's eyes sparkled in the light of the Dragonpaw Inn.

~

Ambrass looked into her husband's eyes, her husband, whom she would love and cherish forever. She looked about, trying to spy the room where they had first met, where she had taken care of Fortunato — wounded by dark iron — like a baby, like one of the blessed creatures now twisting in the cradle beside booth.

She peered into her husband's eyes and saw, in those eyes, her own soul. She beheld her husband, and knew she had found the man she had been destined to spend the rest of her life with. She smiled and touched his hand. She peered at his hand, and then to his eyes, and then looked about her, to the scene of joy and mirth spilling forth, the clinking of cups, the sound of chatter.

Glenda walked by, and refilled Ambrass's glass of wine. Ambrass thanked her, and looked about her, and then back into her husband's eyes.

Here, their story had begun, and here, their story would end. It would end when they were old and gray.

And as Ambrass stirred in her booth, and eyed Dandari and Gemini, she looked to the front door, and saw a figure walking through.

She had red hair, the woman, and she was dressed up in fine clothes, in a red gown, as if for a date.

She walked through the Dragonpaw Inn's main hall.

Ambrass realized it was Ramona's servant girl, Amée.

Amée seemed to see what she was looking for, and then she sat down at a booth, where Ivan Xandrast was waiting for her.

Joy, mirth, the sound of chatter and clinking cups.

She peered into her husband Fortunato's eyes again, and saw both their souls.

It was here their story had begun, and it was here it would end.

It would end when they were old and gray.

Chapter Forty-Seven: Solendir's Throne

The Deedal Prince had led Balor across Lamdar. The trees of Lamdar were beginning to shed their leaves, at long last, and a chill was beginning to spread over the bounteous land, as the Elvish knights on horses and Balor's undead army traversed the landscape.

The fields Balor had seen, at first, were untended, wheat fields overgrown with weeds or lying fallow — a sign that the elves had abandoned their lands, though why they had abandoned them, Balor could only guess. But as they approached the capital, and the form of a peak crowned with snow appeared on the horizon, Balor saw that certain plots of wheat, and certain vineyards, were still in operation, feeding the small army that had remained behind in Lamdar, the small force pledged to hand the throne of Solendir to Balor.

At last, there was a wood, and the Deedal Prince announced that they had reached the borderlines of the city. The Deedal Prince announced that Balor should say a prayer, and Balor complied, and something like a prayer escaped his lips.

Then, through the woods, at the host of a shambling army of undead, Balor found himself at the white walls of a great city. The great city was vast, Balor saw, but it had been abandoned.

"Why has it been abandoned?" Balor at last said to the Deedal Prince, riding ahead of him.

The Deedal Prince turned around, and his long brown hair glistened in the sunlight. "It has been abandoned," the Deedal Prince said, "because every elf is now a warrior, fighting the Dark One. They are in the Dark Land, waging war on their ancient foe."

Every elf was a warrior, it seemed to Balor, except the ones pledged to hand him Solendir's throne.

They passed through forest-lined streets in view of monuments and towers, crossing homes that no longer had people living in them, which Balor, the Deedal Prince, the Elvish knights, and a countless host of undead now passed by. Balor looked about as he walked, and thought that the city of Danarion, the capital of the elves, was a ghost town now fit for the ghostly host that walked the streets.

Balor felt a chill wind blow from the snow-capped mountain that was in view of the city itself, as he made his way down a thoroughfare, pushing past the forested parts of the city in view of the clouds and the sunlight.

The undead behind him began to moan in ghostly tones as the city opened up before Balor and there were monuments, and the palace, on a hill, which he had set in his heart to desire. He had craved the throne of Solendir, because the master of the Haunted Forest had opposed it.

Now, with a petrified crown of stone resting on his head, his desire, which the master of the Haunted Forest had sent all his strength to stop, was at the door.

It was at the door, and he could hear the master of the Haunted Forest's accusatory whispers, and feel his opposition, as he strode ahead, heedless of all the forces that had tried to stop him. He had not heeded such forces before, and he certainly would not now.

There was a garden fair and white, with bushes and trees that seemed metallic, of silver, as they reached the doors of the palace and the Deedal Prince at last dismounted for his horse and beckoned Balor, to enter.

The Elvish knights alike dismounted, but they departed, as Balor, the Deedal Prince, and his countless host of shambling undead entered through the great doors of the palace.

~

The palace was empty, bereft of people, but amid its halls were objects of gold and silver, paintings surely worth the price of many kingdoms, statuaries and porcelain dishes on display. There were carpets lining a tile floor, and as Balor followed the Deedal Prince through the palace's winding corridors, he marveled at the great luxury now abandoned. Now, all there was before Balor were remnants of a life lived in luxury and power, here at the capital of the Elven World, Danarion.

Balor tried to set his marveling aside as the Deedal Prince led him through more corridors, past a vista of the garden, past a banqueting hall where elves of old surely feasted in luxury, up a set of stairs, through rooms lined with purple curtains or curtains of blue.

And Balor struggled to catch his breath, as the Deedal Prince pushed through another door, at the palace's highest level.

~

The throne room of Solendir was a vast chamber with a vaulted ceiling, dominating a wing of the elven palace. The room was painted blue and red, and even in the elvenking's absence, there were lanterns burning in alcoves to make the throne room as bright as day.

The Throne of Solendir was a throne worthy of the elvenking's splendor, crafted out of gold, festooned with ruby and emerald and lapis lazuli, sapphire and pearl and carnelian. The throne dominated one side of the vast chamber, and its seat was imprinted in platinum with the form of the Solardi, the sun and tree symbol of the people of light and life. From the gold and platinum throne were gold spires, radiating in a sunray around the vast throne.

And Balor, though his heart felt cold from all he had witnessed, the death and destruction he had faced, all the opposition of the Dark One that had been sent to stop him from reaching his goal, felt stunned by the sight of the Throne of Solendir.

His heart was warmed, but behind him were wordless moans, and as he approached his goal, what he felt the gods and his own heart wished him to do, he realized that by his presence he was changing the throne room. For as he took his first steps toward Solendir's throne, about him the forms of silver ghosts were swirling, the aftereffects of his necromancy.

The Deedal Prince had stridden before the Throne of Solendir. He was waiting for Balor to do what was prophesied.

The Deedal Prince began to speak. "Balor," he said, "it was your forefather that uttered the words, that his offspring would sit upon the Throne of Solendir, and reign over the kingdom of his enemy. But you should know, your people, the vampires, have chosen Light. The curse of your people has lifted, and they shall live in the light of the dawn forever. When the dawn arrives, the vampires shall abide in its light. And so shall you, Balor. What are you waiting for?"

Balor did not know what he was waiting for. Perhaps, he did not know how to act, how to feel, in the face of his life's purpose at last being accomplished.

The Deedal Prince was looking at him as he lingered.

How could the words of a vampire be a prophecy? How could the words of his ancestor, Gilden, be true?

Then he realized the master of the Haunted Forest was still at work, still trying some desperate effort to somehow prevent Balor from realizing his goal.

The master of the Haunted Forest was using to deceit to stop him from reaching the goal the gods had placed upon his heart.

He took the steps toward the glittering stone of the Throne of

Solendir, in view of lanterns placed in alcoves.

He felt the opposition of the master of the Haunted Forest erupt in wails as he turned, and as Balor sat on Solendir's throne.

229

Chapter Forty-Eight:
A Worthy King

Trumpets blew, and Wrinn brandished his quarterstaff.

At the front lines of the elves gathered at the Steaming Gates, an army had arrived, stretching into the horizon.

Anguipeds and rokahn soldiers — red demons — a countless host stretched from one end of the horizon to another.

But they were standing far off, as an anguiped on a horse strode forth.

The anguiped, Wrinn saw, was wearing a bronze mask.

"I summon the elvenking," the anguiped uttered in a crude dialect of Elvish.

~

As the elvenking galloped forth at the anguipeds' call, the elven lines stirred. They were waiting for something — it seemed, something terrible.

And when the elvenking had arrived on his horse, his eyes once bright were radiant with despair.

They were radiant with despair, but the elvenking seemed to be hiding something from his people — something, on the edge of his tongue.

For when the anguiped in the iron mask, on his anguiped horse, met the elvenking's gaze, they were parading something behind him, a tent hoisted on poles — something, it seemed, the elvenking recognized.

"Your Majesty," said the anguiped in the mask, "as our missives have told you, the House of the Tannin has almost been rebuilt, and *Amir Alfajr* awaits for his ascendancy.

"As I said to you in your missives, we know you and your people have been through much. But if *Amir Alfajr* had already come, would your people not be destroyed and weakened? No, *Amir Alfajr* has come, and your people will reign as they had.

"You have been through so much, the death of your two children. *Amir Alfajr* bids you come to the House of the Tannin, as it rebuilt."

Wrinn was mystified by the anguiped's words, but where Wrinn was mystified, verging on disgusted, there appeared a dark gleam in the elvenking's eyes.

"The gods have taken from me Velérion and Nenré," said the elvenking. "*Amir Alfajr* would do no such thing. I will go to the House of the Tannin in service of *Amir Alfajr,* and I bid my people come with me."

The elvenking galloped forth beyond the front lines, toward the lines of the enemy.

He turned in the light of the sun, and his eyes radiated betrayal, as no other elf stirred. "Will my people not follow me, into the arms of *Amir Alfajr?* Will my people not see their fortunes restored… fortunes, it is clear, that were destroyed by the Telantines?"

In the light of the sun, it seemed the elvenking's skin was turning a greenish hue.

A few elves began to join him, to the elvenking's certain doom. A few, and then many — and the elven armies, once shattered, were divided into camps, between the Dark One's deception, and the ones who had held firm.

Wrinn held firm, and looked upon the elvenking and the other traitors with disgust, as he turned back and saw — as the traitor elves departed with the Dark One's forces — the Field Marshal Sintari remain behind, with the true elves.

The traitor elves were marching into the distance with the Dark One's forces.

But there was an inexplicable gladness in the Field Marshal

Sintari's eyes. He was saying, "Alondir, king!"

~

"Where's *nonni*?" said Alondir in the midst of camp, as the elves who had remain true circled about him.

"Where's *nonni*?" said Alondir, with a confused look in his eyes.

But Sintari said, "Your *nonni* is gone. But you, dear child, are now the King of the Elves, and in the dawn you shall reign…"

Alondir seemed to understand, for a delighted look in his eyes appeared.

And Wrinn thought, after all this time, that the elves had a worthy king.

~

The true elves, the remnant who had been left behind, steeled themselves and vowed to remain firm. They practiced war drills in view of Alondir, vowing to battle to the end, until the Dark One's final defeat. When Reev Nax and the Telantines crushed the Dark One underfoot, the true elves would crush him underfoot, too.

And Alondir was king.

Chapter Forty-Nine:
Fire and Blood

Reev had waited until night.

In the afternoon, he and Agent Secunda had chopped down trees and sawed the wood, and nailed the wood, into the shape of a perfect Telantine beacon. They had doused it with oil, and Agent Secunda had given him something better than flint and tinder, an invention of the Oculus — a small stick that could erupt into flame when it struck a surface. She had given him a set of pitons to climb the surface of the Dark Tower, and then she had set him on his task.

The Dark Tower stretched before Reev, a dark monument against a dark sky. With the Telantine beacon strapped to his back, Reev carefully made his way through the rokahn ranks, cloaked — again — in the darkness that had concealed him before, but where his task had not met with success.

He thought he heard a rokahn growl — but then Reev turned back and saw the rokahn was growling at something else. He thought he heard an anguiped shout, but he ignored it, and pressed on, and he was not followed.

He took his pitons and hammered them into the surface of the tower as he climbed, steadily, toward the rostrum.

He was at the height of the tower when he set the Telantine beacon in its place. He could see the million gathered before the breadth of the tower, and even in the pitch darkness of the Dark Land night, the sight of the vast host threatened to steal Reev's breath.

But his breath was not stolen. The Telantine beacon, now, was in the dark. But soon it would not be.

Reev struck the fire stick against the stone and it burst into a small flame. He touched the Telantine beacon with the flaming stick, and watched it erupt in flame on the rostrum of the Dark Tower.

The Telantine beacon blazed in the night.

And Reev saw the fire of the beacon in the anguipeds' and the rokahn's eyes.

When the fire appeared in their eyes, they seemed to remember something, deep within their bodies — an ancestral memory to terrify. They began to gibber, and then they began to scream.

They began to scream, and then they began to run.

They were fleeing, the million gathered before the Dark Tower, in every direction, dispersing in every direction throughout the Dark Land.

Reev saw, so high from the rostrum, a band of Telantines moving in from the south, some holding torches and some bearing swords.

The Telantines took notice of the million anguipeds and rokahn, fleeing every direction. They brandished their swords, and then they charged, and the Great War had begun.

Interlude:
The Glorious Empire

Sergio Baris

A tidal wave of truth had spilled through the Empire, from Imperial Square to every town square throughout Anthania, to Gad and to Eloesus, and even to the depths of Khazidea.

The Empire had been captured by a hostile non-human species, and the outraged citizens of the Empire had drawn their swords, and been compelled to act.

Sergio had torn off his Imperial half cape and set aside his breastplate. He had deserted from the Imperial Army when he heard the news, that a hostile non-human species, the anguipeds, had put one of their own on the throne.

When Verrus had given orders that everyone of Telantine descent be killed, the Telantines all seemed to evade their fate by mishap or by accident, or by the help of Imperial citizens. And now, Sergio Baris was following a man of Telantine descent down the Path of Tidus toward Imperial City.

His name was Miles Gloriosus, and he was called the Glorious Emperor, and he was declaring the Glorious Empire.

As Sergio followed, at the head of the train, composed partially of citizens and partially of deserted soldiers, he could not help but note they had not been stopped in all this time. They had carved a path down the Path of Tidus, and no legion had come to intervene.

It became clear, as they passed down the Path of Tidus to Imperial City, that the Imperial Army — having learned the truth — was refusing to stop Miles Gloriosus, that they were refusing to intervene in the coup, that they were no longer defending Verrus, the unworthy emperor who sat on the throne.

~

From Imperial Square, to the palace, Sergio Baris marched, and the gates of the palace were open to him. The Imperial Guard, what remained of them, met Miles Gloriosus before the Grand Porch where — Sergio saw with disgust — the statues of Claudio and Numa had been beheaded by Verrus.

But the Imperial Council, which had hated Verrus from the inception, was filtering in through the hallways and corridors, men of distinction and rank, their heads crowned in white or gray. Their bodies were covered in white tunics, with purple sashes, and as they eyed Miles Gloriosus, a rebel, Sergio Baris did not know what to expect, whether they would seize him and condemn him to death for treason, or whether they would give in to what the people demanded, the mending of a captured empire and a captured throne, or whether they would do what the arcane laws of the Empire said had to be — the oppression of an interloper, and the deaths of the Telantines.

The Speaker of the Council seemed a mouse of a man, but when he beheld Miles Gloriosus in the light of the Grand Porch, something more than timidity came to him.

Miles Gloriosus was standing in the light of the sun, before the beheaded statues. His tufts of brown hair raised generously above his head. His eyes were gray and keen. Though it was against the law for a man who was not emperor to wear purple, at Sergio Baris's insistence he was wearing a purple tunic, knowing full well what it represented.

The Speaker of the Council eyed Miles Gloriosus from top to bottom, and then side to side. As his timidity washed away, he began to speak. "So this," he said, "is who the people demand to be their emperor."

"The people," said Sergio Baris, "and all justice, and all our ancestors in Heaven."

The Speaker of the Council smiled quaintly. "You know we do not like Verrus," he said, "and in fact — you should know — the unworthy emperor has now disappeared, and lost contact with the Imperial Council. He is absent. Perhaps, he has chosen his fate.

"I know the laws and regulations of the Empire are against this, but can we truly thwart the will of the Imperial people, when their will is so clear?"

~

Sergio Baris watched in the council chambers as a round of votes and motions were underway. He knew what they were doing technically contravened the law, but the Imperial Council had the power of the people behind them.

Miles Gloriosus stood in the light of the Council House's dome as the votes took place, as Sergio Baris stood by and watched, hoping that what he wanted was possible, that the captured Empire and captured emperor would be replaced with an Empire and an emperor as it should be.

Verrus, the unworthy emperor, had made so many evil decrees, against the good of the people, that Sergio Baris felt his crimes cried out for justice.

And the thirty faces of the Imperial Council, as they took their votes with aplomb, seemed to agree. After all, they had not resisted Miles Gloriosus and those who surrounded him bursting into the Imperial Palace.

Nor, Sergio Baris realized, had the Imperial Army.

The rounds of voting was ended, the austere looks on the Imperial Council's faces were seeming to give way to humanity warmth.

"By a vote of twenty-nine to one," said the Speaker of the Council, "the Imperial Council recognizes the ascension of Miles

Gloriosus as emperor."

And so it had occurred, the triumph of the people over the anguipeds, the proclamation of the Glorious Empire and the Glorious Emperor — a Telantine.

Chapter Fifty:
The Great War

The Great War began, and it began with slaughter.

Reev watched as the Telantines charged into the forms of the rokahn and anguipeds, as their fleeing forms sprinted or rode away in every direction from the Dark Tower.

The Telantines were charging them with their swords, and as Reev descended from the Dark Tower, and joined his brethren, and drew Doomblade, he saw the anguipeds and rokahn falling by the score, cut down by the Telantines' blades, as the Telantines cut a path through them.

Reev joined them, piercing an anguiped in an iron mask straight through, and then cutting rokahn down in a barreling charge, piercing a kobold mage and slicing another kobold mage's staff in two.

The scene of the Dark Tower was unfolding pandemonium as Telantines burst through the anguiped and rokahn lines, some garbed in trousers and others in loin cloths, but all carried forward by the boost in morale that had come with the scattering of the anguipeds and rokahn before the tower.

As Reev cut through the line, a rokahn — a kobold — two anguipeds in one stroke, he saw the bright face of Blarer cutting a bloody path through the Dark One's ranks with his sword, until the blood gathered before the Dark Tower was dripping onto Reev's shoes.

Such a slaughter — such a massacre, and yet, Reev recalled the reason for why he had been told to drive the rokahn before the Dark Tower. It was to finally put an end to his enemy, the Dark One's Hand, and crush his master underfoot.

~

As the Telantines cut down the anguipeds and rokahn as they fled, they too were beginning to spread out in every direction, hunting down their enemies wherever they showed their face. Reev joined in with Blarer as they fought together, side by side, as the panic in the anguipeds from the beacon joined to the panic at the sight of their compatriots fleeing.

They were fodder for the Great War that the Telantines had been promised, and as Reev cut a path through the Dark One's armies, it was difficult — amid the bloodshed — to recall just why he had been commanded to do this, why he had been told to give his fellow Telantines what they wanted.

A day later, and the Great War continued. Reev had hardly slept, and had found shelter under some rock beside Blarer, as other Telantines had fought into the day, never ceasing the task they believed they have given, the battle they believed had been promised to them.

Reev and Blarer had tried to catch their breath, and as they stood amid scenes of slaughter and bloodshed, others joined them — Pandarus, with the light of the sun in his face, and Ajax.

The sun was beginning to peek through the Dark Land's darkness, as Pandarus thanked Reev quietly for making the Great War all it could be.

They drew swords together, that morning, and together did battle, hunting down the fleeing forms of rokahn and anguipeds as they fled.

They had drawn swords together, and they battled together, and the number they slew was without count, until before the Dark Tower was the scene of a massacre.

The forms of dragons, taking flight, soared overhead, but as Reev watched, what appeared to be ghosts were blinking into sight, seizing control of the dragons as they flew, and piercing them with ghostly swords.

Here was the Telantines' victory, the Great War that had been promised to end in great victory.

They battled together, Pandarus, Blarer, Ajax and Reev, for a day, and then two days. They formed a patrol for a week, and at the end of the week, the sun in the Dark Land was like the sun in the wider world, a bright and shining day — a new day, and the Light had even spread here.

One night as they battled a host of red demons, as the demons burst into flame one after the another, to the pillorying of Pandarus's sword, there appeared in the dim light of the moon what appeared to Reev's mind to be shining forms, the glittering ghostly forms of soldiers dressed in mail hauberks and bearing swords of a strange make, led by a king wearing a crown. The ghosts, too, were joining the Great War that the Telantines had been promised, cutting swathes through the Dark One's armies as the Dark One's armies continued to disperse.

That night Pandarus, explained the anguipeds' dire situation. "An army of elves is guarding the only way out," Pandarus said. "They're preventing escape. And the Sea of Ghosts is still, but it only seems calm. Whirlpools and eddies have appeared that most any boat cannot navigate."

"And the mountain passes?" Reev said.

"I thought you would know," Pandarus said, "the dwarf king you named is preventing any of the Dark One's forces from leaving."

Reev smiled at the thought, of the king of the dwarfs, Arn Steelforge, living up to what a king of the dwarfs should do.

He smiled at the thought, and then, with Pandarus and Blarer, with Ajax as well, brandished his sword, and continued to battle the shifting forms of the Dark One's army.

And he smiled at the thought of his beloved friend Wrinn, still standing guard at the only pass out of the Dark Land, at the thought of the elves standing side by side with the Telantines, for the final victory.

As he did battle with the anguipeds and the rokahn, they seemed to have lost heart, as the Great War consumed all of the Dark Land, and the Telantines cut them down.

~

The next day seemed more brilliant than any before it, and the anguipeds and the rokahn cowered in the light of the bright sun, the sun that had never been brighter in the Dark Land.

But perhaps, when the Dark Land had not been dark, it had been that bright.

As the anguipeds and rokahn winced in the light of the sun, and red demons swarmed about they and the Telantines, trying to recover in the wake of their disaster, Reev and the other Telantines continued to cut a path through their forces.

Under the bright sunlight, which had not been so bright in the Dark Land for thousands of years, the designs of the Dark One did not seem to have so much effect, nor were they terrifying.

Reev watched as Blarer drew his sword and did battle with a red demon, as Telantine sword locked with a barbed sword that red demons carried. He watched as Blarer disarmed the red demon and slashed him, and he watched as the red demon exploded in the light of the sun, sending a ripple through the rokahn and anguiped ranks, as Reev tripped and almost fell.

More dragons had arrived, and through the ranks of the charging Telantines there were beginning to appear the forms of massive worms piercing out of the dirt, and the Telantines did battle with these — what Reev thought were called pit worms — as Reev saw the Telantines had reinforcements.

For from the sky, brilliant ghostly bursts of light were descending, and when they descended, there were impacts of ghostly white fire. Reev wondered if they were the ghosts of weapons like Heaven's Spear, or if they were weapons formed from memory. Yet whether they were formed of spirit or from light itself, they were destroying scores of rokahn and anguiped with each volley, and the fearful minions of the Dark One were fleeing from their sight — fleeing from the ghostly weapons, exploding, into the paths of Telantines armed with swords.

The enemies of the Telantines now lay dead for miles around the Dark Tower, and the devastation, one morning — weeks after it began — Reev at last took stock of. He surveyed the craters in the ground from Telantine weapons, the indentations where red demons had burst into flame, and he thought all the designs of the Dark One had failed, but for the mission he had come to the Dark Land to complete, the crushing of the Dark One underfoot.

The driving of the armies before the Dark Tower, it was said, would draw the Dark One's Hand from his hiding place. But Reev wondered if all this slaughter and devastation had driven him away, if the words of his father Simeon and the Lady of Danyen had been incorrect.

"Come on!" he heard Blarer shout in the distance. "The Great War continues."

~

That night, they continued to fight, in the ash-covered valley, now far from the Dark Tower. As the Telantines did battle with the fleeing forms of anguipeds and rokahn, Reev saw that his work at the Dark Tower's rostrum was being copied.

For now ghostly forms of Telantines were appearing on

hillsides, and Telantine beacons formed of ghostly material were beginning to burn in the night. Each night, the ghosts of Telantines and their beacons were appearing, driving the anguipeds into the living Telantines' swords, and furthering the cause of the Great War.

Days had now passed, perhaps weeks, and Reev had not forgotten what he had come here to do. But what he had come here to do still seemed beyond his reach… the crushing of the Dark One underfoot.

One night, in the light of the Telantine beacons, he approached Pandarus.

Pandarus, now, had slaughtered scores in the midst of this Great War.

"I was told," Reev said, "by my father, and by my mentor and guide, that if I drove the armies of the Dark Tower before me, it would cause the Dark One's Hand to show his face."

Pandarus's eyes gleamed in the light of the ghostly Telantine beacons, which now were lit unceasingly, each night, on every hilltop, in the midst of the Great War.

"Don't worry," Pandarus said. "Don't think so much. Just do what duty calls us to do. We must finish this Great War."

But as Pandarus turned and charged into the ranks of the Dark One's minions, shouting words of war and fury, Reev realized he had a lonely task, one for which he carried the burden. The Telantines were in the midst of their Great War, but it was he who would have to crush the Dark One underfoot. And it was he who would have to learn how.

~

To every corner of the Dark Land the Telantines had dispersed, but Reev, Blarer, Pandarus and Ajax stuck together. They formed a cadre of warriors, battling the Dark One's minions side by side, cutting down red demons, rokahn and anguipeds alike, whether it was day or night, morning or afternoon.

The Telantine spirits joined them during both day and night, fighting side by side with their living brethren. And Reev, as the days progressed to weeks, wondered if a month had passed since the Great War began.

Reev thought of Gastreel, now in Heaven. He thought of Fortunato and Ambrass, far away. He wondered what had happened to Bala. And he uttered a prayer one night, for them all, as he and his cadre of warriors gathered.

They had found, in the course of battle, an anguiped camp stocked with food. They had not taken the time to rest, and now they were trying to catch their breath.

In the distance, Reev could see bright Telantine beacons, and anguipeds fleeing from them.

He had tried to catch his breath. He had prayed.

And though Pandarus had not offered any advice, Reev's task that still seemed beyond his reach was heavy on his heart, the crushing of the Dark One underfoot. But the Dark One's Hand had not shown his face. Where was he?

And who was he?

The road-bread was stale, but it filled Reev's stomach. The water from the water keg had a bitter Dark Land taste, but when Reev passed over the Dark Land's creeks and streams, he thought their poison was beginning to clear.

Indeed, as the Telantines slew the Dark One's minions, the Dark One's grip over the Dark Land seemed to be fading. And Reev had an inkling, a thought, that the Dark Land had not always been under Seymus's control.

When had it become under Seymus's control, and when had the Dark Land been filled with darkness?

The darkness was clearing, and Reev could see the stars and the moon brightly shining, almost as bright as they did in the world beyond. He thought that Ambrass and Fortunato, Wrinn and Bala, Glenda — innkeeper at the Dragonpaw — were also seeing these stars and moon, and at the connection to people so far away from danger, there was a light in his heart, a light that the Dark One and the Dark Land, and his Dark Tower, could not take away.

"We've won," Reev said.

"No," Pandarus said, "there is work to be done. The Dark One must be defeated."

The Dark One, defeated — that, Reev remembered, was his task, to crush the enemy of the Telantines underfoot.

But he thought that the Telantines, and the elves, would crush him underfoot as well.

The method still escaped him. Still, what his father and his mentor had said would happen had not occurred. He had not heard anything, whether whisper or rumor, that the Dark One's Hand had been stirred from his hiding place.

He knew the Great War continued.

~

The next day, Reev was like a wild man, cutting swathes into the rokahn and the anguipeds as Pandarus, Blarer and Ajax fought at his flanks. Amid the tumult, he heard a loud cry, as an anguiped charged him on his horse. But Pandarus moved in front of him, cutting down the anguiped horse and sending the rider harshly to the ground.

Reev stood stunned, as the battlefield swirled about him, as the earth began to quake, and then a cloud of rock and dirt burst in an explosion from the ground.

A pit worm now faced Reev, a pit worm with a body segmented and ridged, its maw covered in barbs and spines, threatening to swallow him whole. Reev dove out of the way as the pit worm struck at him. He slashed with Doomblade and the *estirion* cut a bleeding wound into its iron-hard purple skin.

Pandarus rushed ahead and slashed at the pit worm's lips, and Reev feared it would swallow him whole, as from the heavens one of the ghostly Telantine flames soared down and exploded, rending the pit worm to scattered bits of fleshy debris.

The ingenuity of the Telantines endured, even here, all these millennia later. It had reappeared, now, for the Great War, the Great War that now raged from one corner of the Dark Land to another.

But when the Telantines had cleansed the Dark Land, could it still be called the Dark Land?

Reev did not think so.

In view of the crater and the pit worm that had exploded, Reev charged into the anguiped lines, buoyed by the appearance of the ghostly Telantine weapon and a feeling of invincibility he knew was incorrect.

He watched as Pandarus bowled through the anguiped and rokahn lines, cutting down a red demon to an explosion of flame, as Blarer did battle with an anguiped swordsman, as Ajax mounted a dragon and commandeered it, forcing it by sword-blow to empty its reserves of fire.

Weeks had now passed, Reev realized, maybe months. And the Dark One's Hand had not stirred from his hiding place. He had not, as his father and his mentor said, been stirred to act.

There was no sign of him anywhere.

But Reev had a feeling, despite all that had occurred, despite the fact his goal remained out of reach, that the word from his father and his mentor the Lady of Danyen would not fail, that the Dark One's Hand would show himself, as the Great War raged.

But as of now, none of the Telantine warriors had said anything about the Dark One's Hand.

They did, however, begin to talk about a Dark Throne.

In the moonlight, as Telantine beacons burned in the distance, and gave light to a makeshift camp, a Telantine whose name, Reev learned, was Hus, began to speak.

"There is a throne, fashioned out of skulls," Hus said, "south of the Dark Tower. It was there the Dark One thought he would reign, once his victory arrived."

But instead of a victory, a Great War had consumed the Dark Land, and the armies of the Dark Tower had scattered.

In the light of the moon, under the stars, in view of the beacon, Reev pondered what Hus had told him, the Dark Throne south of the Dark Tower.

He pondered what he had been told, and questioned it. Would the Dark One's Hand, if he was still alive, be near the Dark Throne?

Where else would he go?

But still, the Dark One's Hand had not revealed himself. Still, he had not been driven out of hiding. And Reev thought, when he had been driven out of hiding, the Telantines now waging their Great War against the Dark Land would know.

Still, Reev believed the word from his father was something more, that the words his mentor confirmed were true. He believed that, having driven the armies before the Dark Tower, Reev's enemy would show his face.

Then, somehow or some way, he would crush Seymus under his feet.

Chapter Fifty-One:
Slaughter

The light of a new day arrived in the Dark Land, and the Dark Land's light no longer seemed so dark. It was a new day, as the Great War continued to spill from one corner of the Dark Land to another, a land surrounded by mountains and a narrow sea.

Reev took stock, in the light of the new day, of what had occurred. Behind the Telantines' lines, moving ever southward and eastward, were so many bodies as could not be counted. Birds of prey constantly circled about in the sky, and Reev winced at the thought of vultures having their feast.

The scale of the Great War staggered Reev as he looked back, but he knew the Great War was not yet won, that the battle lines were continuing to spread forth, and the Dark One's might had not yet been squelched.

~

With his brothers Pandarus, Blarer and Ajax, Reev continued to do battle. That day, was it weeks, or was it months later, the Dark One emptied his dark dungeons.

Creatures were striding forth, gray hided beasts with red eyes and many horns, creatures that at first Reev regarded with fear, before Pandarus charged ahead, and began to strike.

He slashed the edges of their massive heads, as the Telantines dispersed nimbly, refusing to remain in the path of the beasts, for now it was their turn to slaughter, not the anguipeds and the Dark One.

With the cutting of their skin, and the opening of the wounds, the beasts ground their hooves to a halt, and then slid motionless to the dry dusty ground.

As the beasts slid motionless, Pandarus mounted one on the back and then beckoned. Ajax and Blarer followed on their own, and then Reev mounted behind Blarer.

The Dark One's dungeons, emptied, were then turned against him, on this day, who knew what month, in the thick of the Great War.

The ranks of the anguipeds and rokahn, already fearful, broke and ran, but they were not fast enough to outrun the beasts that Pandarus had commandeered. The monsters bucked with their horns, impaling anguiped and rokahn alike, as more dead joined to the countless behind the Telantines' ranks, the Telantines' ranks now moving more swiftly than ever.

Reev saw the beasts from the Dark One's dungeons had failed to do anything but aid the great war, for other Telantines had followed Pandarus's lead, and having wounded the gray-hided beasts, had mounted them and charged ahead — astride them. They bucked with their horns, and they had trampled the anguipeds underfoot, as something appeared in the distance — the glittering waters of the sea.

Reev saw, then, that the Telantine had slain everything in a direction southward, countless miles from the Dark Tower, to the Dark Land's border. Where then was the Dark Throne that the Telantine, Hus, had spoken of?

Pandarus seemed to have a look of regret on his face. "The Great War is coming to a close," Pandarus said. "I wished it could have lasted forever."

As he sat astride the gray-hided beast, he took his sword, and placed it exactingly at its neck. He shoved the length of steel into it, and the gray-hided beast uttered a pained whine, then slumped to the ground.

The Telantines followed, one after another, as their mounts, which they had commandeered from the Dark One's dungeon, were no longer of use.

As Blarer, riding ahead of Reev, followed, piercing the mount exactingly in the neck, Reev hopped off the monstrous creature, and again took stock of the devastation the Great War had left.

They had come to the Dark Land's borders, the sea now still but filled with eddies. And in the light of the sun, which was so bright as to hurt Reev's eyes, could no longer be called dark.

Well, Reev supposed, he could only say that about the sky. For his task still had not been completed, the crushing of the Dark One underfoot, and Seymus's final defeat.

But the Great War, having swept across the Dark Land, from the Dark Tower to the sea, hundreds of miles away, was coming to a close. The Telantines had their final victory over the anguipeds, and now — what remained?

Reev thought, the final piece of the puzzle, the defeat of the Dark One himself, and his Hand.

But how could that be achieved?

How could that be achieved, Reev wondered, even in light of the fathomless rokahn dead, the countless bodies stretching from one end of the Dark Land to another?

How, he wondered, in the light of the sun, in the light of the sun, now bright — as bright as any sky, anywhere else, in Varda?

He wondered if in the wake of the Great War, the Dark Land would not just be as bright as elsewhere in Varda, but also that it would bloom. He wondered if the rains would come, and flowers and grass would grow. He wondered if, in the years to come farmland could be planted... farmland plotted by Telantines?

In the wake of the Great War, anything seemed possible. Anything seem possible — but how could his father's word be fulfilled, and the words of his mentor? The Dark One's Hand, it seemed, had not yet been drawn out from his place of hiding.

Or had he, somehow?

Had he, and had Reev missed his opportunity to crush the Dark

One underfoot? Would the gods allow that to occur?

Pandarus, Blarer, Ajax and the gathered Telantine hosts had ventured north into the wake of the Great War's devastation, and began mercy killings of those anguipeds and rokahn who clung to life. Reev wondered if he had missed his opportunity, or if his father's words had been less meaningful than he thought.

Was it possible, they were just words from his dying father and nothing more? Could the Dark One's Hand have fled him entirely, and escaped the fate he deserved?

No, Reev did not think it was possible. But he did think that he had accompanied Pandarus, Blarer and Ajax in the midst of the Great War, and the Great War that had swallowed the Dark Land had come to a close. The anguipeds had been utterly defeated, and their rule had been ended over Varda.

Now, it was time for Reev to find the Dark One's Hand — to venture forth unquestioningly, and crush Seymus under his feet.

He watched as the Telantines strode out far afield, far into the horizon, carrying out killings of mercy in the light of a bright sun. He tried to catch his breath. He knew what he had to do, but he wasn't sure where he should go.

And so he waited, and breathed, and drank from his waterskin. He ate some road-bread from his pouch, and amid the devastation of the Great War, he stood still.

In the late afternoon, Pandarus returned from his mercy killings. He wiped the blood off his sword in the grass, and then sheathed it. He eyed Reev. "It seems, friend, you have a mission that none of the rest of us can follow you to," Pandarus said. "One that falls on our shoulders collectively, but you particularly. The crushing of the Dark One underfoot."

"I don't know how to do it," Reev said. "The prophecies said I would do it. That I would know how."

"And do you know?" Pandarus said.

"I know," Reev said, "that I must face the Dark One's Hand."

Pandarus stirred in the light of the bright sun, amid a vista of the devastation left by the Great War. The devastation stretched, hundreds of miles, into the distance, well beyond Reev's horizon.

"You must face the Dark One's Hand," Pandarus said. "I do have a bit of rumor I will share with you.

"There is a man who crossed the sea last year, around the time you arrived. He seems human, but my men who've seen him claim he has the eyes of an anguiped. The anguipeds have gathered around him, calling him by a title, *Amir Alfajr*. Last I heard, he has been lingering in the region near the Throne of Skulls."

"The Throne of Skulls," Reev said. "That's where I must go. Do you know the way?"

Pandarus peered eastward, and then he pointed east. "The Throne of Skulls is in view of this sea. It's east of where we stand. If you follow the sea, you'll find it, if you press on."

Reev nodded. Reev didn't think he'd be able to miss a Throne of Skulls, unless the Dark One's throne was small.

"*Amir Alfajr*," Reev repeated, and he shuddered.

Amir Alfajr, the human with anguiped eyes, could be the Dark One's Hand. The Dark One's Hand would linger near the Throne of Skulls.

"In fact," said Pandarus, "I believe, in the wake of the Great War, that everyone who's survived, of the Dark One's court, has taken shelter there, in view of the Dark One's Throne… where the Dark One wished to reign, in the flesh."

Reev nodded.

He realized the task he had would be lonely. But he would remember Pandarus, and Ajax, and Blarer. He would treasure their friendship all their days. And perhaps, if the dawn ever came, like he hoped, he would have their friendship forever.

~

He left Blarer, Ajax, and Pandarus behind after giving them a heartfelt goodbye. He crossed eastward along the once-violent, but now glasslike Sea of Ghosts. He remembered when he had first witnessed it, how violent the waves had been, sure to capsize any boat. Now, it was tranquil, but its tranquility was deceptive. Pandarus had told him that eddies and whirlpools now sucked in any unlucky enough to try its tranquility.

Pandarus — he would remember and treasure his friendship, forever.

Chapter Fifty-Two:
A Word from a Hero

Eastward Reev pressed, along the glasslike Sea of Ghosts, and the death and devastation of the Great War was everywhere he walked, stretching into the distance. The Telantines had cut down all the rokahn and anguipeds in the Dark Land, and Telantine spirits had joined in. But there was a strength left, it seemed, in the Dark One's forces, ready to make a counterattack. That force, and all of the Dark One's forces, were gathered at the Throne of Skulls.

Reev feared failure. He feared letting the Telantines down. He feared — and as he pressed on, eastward, he began to get a terrible sinking feeling, that the most dangerous task was yet ahead, even in the wake of the Telantines' victory in the Great War.

~

As he walked along the glasslike Sea of Ghosts, he thought on all that had transpired. When his journey had begun, he had not known much. He had not known what was to befall him, or what his true identity was. He had not known he was a Telantine, or that Telantis had ever existed, or that the Telantines yet endured. He did not know of the victory that had been promised to the Telantines.

He had not known much, living in the town of Norwood in the Empire, and his mentor Gastreel had not told him everything he knew. But Reev now knew things, he thought, Gastreel had never learned, Gastreel the Green Wizard — his mentor and friend.

His mentor had died in the Elf Lands, what seemed now long ago. He had died defending Reev, as he had lived taking care of Reev — attempting to mold him into a warrior against the Dark One.

And now, Gastreel was gone. Gastreel, Fortunato, Wrinn — all his companions — were gone from him, and the greatest task, yet ahead, had been placed upon him. For he did not know how he would crush the Dark One underfoot, how he could crush a being immaterial. He only knew that he had to charge ahead, to fight against whatever odds faced him, and he knew that the gods would guide his every step.

But he stopped before the shores of the sea. He felt a tremor. He felt something — stirring in the air.

He saw up ahead, light appearing in the light of the sun, bright light, a figure approaching, walking at an eager step. As the light shone on a white raiment, Reev's trembling heart ceased, as he knew it was an ally. He could feel the warmth, the light, washing over him.

And he saw, it was not the Lady of Danyen.

It was not a woman, but a man, and though his hair in his life perhaps had been dark, wreathed in light it was a shining white. On his neck were lightning mark tattoos. He had a calm, confident gait. It was a Telantine man, a Telantine spirit come to guide Reev.

He and other ghosts had waged war on the Dark Land. Reev had seen them doing battle with the rokahn and anguipeds. And now one approached, one with a calm, confident gait, a kind gaze to set Reev at ease.

"You would not think, Reev," said the man, "in the wake of the Great War, that the enemy would be feeling confident. But they are. They are gathered at the Dark Throne — the leaders of Seymus's council, the chief of them Ur-Nachash. Before the Dark Throne they have built an abomination called the House of the Tannin, and they think the Dark One's victory is certain.

"Ur-Nachash is guiding the Dark One's Hand, Verrus, to his fate, though Verrus does not realize it. They believe, once the Dark One takes physical form, that his rule over Varda will ensue. That's where you come in."

The appearance of the Telantine ghost, wreathed in light, put Reev's heart at ease where his words did not. And Reev realized, he'd like to bask in the ghost's light forever.

"When you see Ur-Nachash's plans come to fruition, you can't back down. You can't be afraid. You have to charge, and trust that the gods will give you the strength."

Reev nodded in view of the Telantine ghost. Did a ghost understand a nod?

"The other Telantines have done their part during the Great War," the ghost said. "Now, it's time you do yours."

The ghost seemed to shine brighter than ever before, and then dissipate into the light of the sun.

~

The ghost's words were inscrutable, unfathomable. But Reev thought, when he reached the Throne of Skulls, they might make better sense. He would try to remember them in the fight ahead.

He remembered his words — that when the moment arose, he couldn't be afraid. He had to charge, into the night.

~

As Reev pushed on, day after day, in view of the death and devastation left by the Great War, he continued to ponder the Telantine ghost's words, and under his breath, he would pray. He would pray — for strength… for guidance. He prayed, to not back down as the Telantine ghost said. He prayed he would know just the moment to charge, that he would know just when to not back down, and the moment where he would not flinch and sprint forward into impossible odds.

He recalled all the Telantines that had gone on before him — men like the ghost who had spoken to him a word of wisdom, men like his father, women like his mother, and all those who went before.

He could feel them from up above, cheering him on, guiding his every step — as he faced the task, and the seemingly insurmountable odds ahead.

The odds — they still seemed insurmountable, even in view of the devastation of the Great War, the countless dead rokahn that stretched from one end of the Dark Land to the other. The Great War, and the Telantines' victory, had not dissuaded Seymus and his council that their rule over Varda was imminent. And he wondered why they were so confident, as he walked along the Sea of Ghosts, fighting his trembling heart, waiting at any moment for the Throne of Skulls to appear in the horizon.

In view of all that had gone on, in the light of the sun — in the light of the gods — he prayed, not knowing what would happen, not knowing what would unfold. For he knew the enemy he faced was fierce, and he knew they were certain their master soon would rule. But Reev knew something else, the word of the prophecies... the Telantines' victory, the Dark One crushed underfoot.

He did not know how, but he knew he would crush the Dark One under his feet — he knew he would, and so would all Telantines.

As he continued eastward, day after day, along the shores of the sea, the trembling in his heart was matched with hope, and then the trembling ceased. He knew he was venturing into enemy territory. He knew the enemy wanted nothing less than his destruction and the ruin of the Telantines. He knew — but he knew other things, too.

He thought of Gastreel and uttered a prayer. He thought of Fortunato... of Ambrass, too. And he thought of Wrinn, still standing guard, as far as he knew, in the Steaming Gates, preventing the anguipeds and the rokahn from escaping the Dark Land. But the rokahn and the anguipeds were gone, dead in the wake of the

Great War.

The Great War, which had spilled from one end of the Dark Land to another, had destroyed the last of anguiped power.

The Great War had devastated the Dark One and all his minions, all save the ones gathered now at the Throne of Skulls, and Reev's greatest enemy, the Dark One's Hand… Verrus Ultimo.

Chapter Fifty-Three:
The Darkest Hour

Albos 31, 1158 Y.E.

Reev had continued to press eastward along the sea. He'd grown tired, but then he would drink. His step would falter, and then he would have a little road-bread to eat, and he'd remember all the Telantines that had gone before him.

Hope fought against fear, and hope was winning, as he walked across the Dark Land in pursuit of his destiny.

When he reached a part of the Dark Land where the devastation of the Great War was no longer in view, where the corpses of rokahn and anguipeds were no more to be seen, he knew he had come behind enemy lines, nearby indeed his enemy, the Dark One's Hand, and Seymus's council.

He dreaded the fearful moment he'd stare his enemy face to face. But then he thought, the gods were with him. He had nothing to fear.

He had nothing to fear, but his heart trembled when the ground began to ascend, and the Throne of Skulls appeared in the horizon.

~

The Throne of Skulls was massive, a towering monument to death, and each part of it was fashioned from skull and bones. It cast a long shadow over the Dark Land, and it did not stand alone.

There was a large building beneath it, built of cinderblock, what Reev guessed was the House of the Tannin that the Telantine ghost said was an abomination. And seeing its fearful symmetry, like the

Dark Tower itself, Reev agreed.

Dark shapes were moving about around the Throne of Skulls and the House of the Tannin, figures both humanoid and anguiped, some in dark robes but all ambling about, as if they were up to no good.

Reev, remembering the words of the ghost, shed all fear and timidity and crept ahead, so as to hear what the figures moving about the Throne of Skulls and the House of the Tannin were saying.

He found a hiding place behind a rock, as he saw the figures amble about and then assemble before one who seemed the greatest of them all.

The greatest of them all was a full-blooded anguiped with green skin and jagged pointed ears. His green skin, despite its greenness, was pale and seemed sallow. A head of white hair fell from his head, and in his yellow eyes, in the pupils, Reev thought he saw a dark chasm.

Gathered about the greatest of them all — whom Reev assumed was Ur-Nachash — were a motley assortment of men and women, whom Reev guessed was Seymus's council.

And Reev saw, to his horror, that gathered amid the crowd was the elvenking, whose skin appeared to be turning green in the sunlight, who had removed his crown, perhaps out of deference to Seymus's council.

"The House of the Tannin is rebuilt," said Ur-Nachash, "and the Tannin will certainly abide there. They will restore our fortunes, and though the Telantines have slaughtered so many, the Tannin will hear us, and grant us our victory."

As the council spoke among itself, another figure was walking beside the House of the Tannin. When Reev saw Verrus, not as the emperor but as he was, walking at the front of what appeared to be a host of Imperial soldiers, it took all the warnings of the Telantine ghost and all the memories of the Telantines who had gone before him not to give into terror.

His flame red hair flared in the light of the Dark Land sun, his bright blue eyes had a sickly pallor, and where the pupils of Ur-Nachash's eyes were like a deep chasm, the pupils of Verrus were the abyss.

Reev knew Verrus now as the Dark One's Hand, his deputy in the mortal world, and he struggled not to be afraid, in view of him. He tried to stay his trembling heart, as Verrus the Dark One's Hand approached, and Seymus's council looked back.

"The House of the Tannin is rebuilt," Ur-Nachash said, again, "and the Tannin will guide us to victory."

"I will guide you to victory," said Verrus. "Do you not trust in me?"

Ur-Nachash had turned, and was staring into Verrus's eyes, a deep chasm against the abyss. And Reev felt frightened, even witnessing that exchange of glances, of two such dark eyes facing each other.

"It is the Tannin who will defeat the Telantines," said Ur-Nachash.

"It is I," Verrus said. "The glory will be mine."

"Like father, like son," said Ur-Nachash. "If it shall be so — go sit on your father's throne."

Verrus looked about, hesitating, cautious.

What Ur-Nachash had wanted him to do all along, was something Verrus seemed to fear. But he had spoken what he truly wanted, that the glory be his, that the victory over the Telantines, which anguipeds thought the "Tannin" had promised, would belong to him and no one else.

Verrus eyed Ur-Nachash, and the changed elvenking. He looked to the men behind him, and then gazed fearfully to the Throne of Skulls.

"I shall sit there," Verrus said, "and the glory shall not belong to the Tannin. It shall be mine — and I shall reign, and no one else."

"So it shall be," Ur-Nachash said, "if you sit on your father's throne."

Verrus gulped and turned fearfully to the Throne of Skulls. He was an ant before it, striding up its steps made of tibias and femurs, crushed skulls and whole skulls.

He stopped halfway up the steps, as if he were fearful of what he was doing, as if he knew what he was doing would end him somehow — and yet, Reev sensed, he would allow no one to take credit for what he believed was the coming Telantine defeat.

He turned back, and the steps he took now were slower, as the changed elvenking looked transfixed, and a wicked, knowing smile appeared on Ur-Nachash's face.

Seymus's council, like the one they served, were deceptive, and it seemed what they were leading Verrus to do was not for his good, but for his ultimate end.

Verrus stopped again, and looked back, as if some part of him sensed this, as if he knew, deep down, what he was doing was his doom. He paused, and the air was perfectly still, and as Reev watched Verrus approach the seat of the throne, he looked up at the Dark Land sun and feared it would turn dark again.

Verrus turned, in view of Seymus's council, and stood before the seat.

Reev remembered the Telantine ghost's words, and thought, hiding before a rock was no place for a Telantine. He would not hide from his enemies. He would face them, in the open.

He strode out from his hiding place, and Seymus's council drew their swords, as Ur-Nachash howled, "Verrus! Sit down on the throne, or he will kill us all, and the cause will be lost forever."

Perhaps it was Reev in his loin cloth and his necklace, his neck tattooed with lightning marks — the startling fear that caused Verrus to fall onto the seat of the throne.

But when he had sat on the throne, Verrus began to change and transform, as his skin turned green, and then to be covered in scales.

When Verrus began to take lumbering strides down the steps, Ur-Nachash's face was one of exultation, and Verrus had a tail, and wings.

Seymus was standing before Reev.

What was Seymus, against a Telantine?

He drew his sword with no fear in his heart. Seymus brandished Serpentax.

Reev charged Seymus, standing on the Throne of Skulls, as Seymus's council fled from Reev like frightened beasts.

Chapter Fifty-Four: Deus Ex Machina

Reev had struck at Seymus, and then he was in a new place.

He did not know what place he was in, but he could see the stars above, and he could see, about him, was a landscape of white rocks. He could see what looked like a tube made of metal, and standing there a man in armor, and beside him a flag, colored red, white and blue.

He did not know what the flag was, or what nation it represented, but as the man in armor took steps, and seemed to float, Reev knew two things, that he was on the moon, and that the man on the moon was a Telantine.

He turned in his vision, and saw green and blue, a vast surface in the light of the moon.

~

The visions were changing, spinning about him, and with each turn of the vision, Reev felt he was growing disoriented. He could see about him a bright sun, and before him was a large rock in a pit, peppered by what looked like Telantine coins, on the rock numbers he saw by one sight, and understood by another, the numbers 1620.

~

The visions shifted again, visions Reev did not understand, but was perceiving.

And he saw he was in the back of a cart, and the cart was

moving up along what appeared to be a track. There was a train of carts moving up the track, and he saw up ahead Fortunato, and behind him Ambrass. Fortunato was holding in his hand an egg-shaped ball made of leather, and as he threw it to Ambrass, she caught it in her hands.

"Stop it, Danny!" Ambrass said to Fortunato, and as Fortunato stirred in his seat, and laughed, he said to her, "Well, you caught it, Amber."

He saw that Fortunato's hair was cut short on the sides, that his shirt was spotted, green and brown and yellow. He had seen them by a new sight, and he had understood their speech by a new vision, amid this world of fun, but was it worlds?

The cart made a breathless descent, plummeting down the track to Fortunato — or was it Daniel's? — delighted cries.

And as he had understood them by a different speech, and as he had seen them by a new sight, he read the feelings of their heart.

He sensed that Daniel had been sent to war, and was beginning to question who had sent him there and why?

He had seen them by a new sight, and understood them by another hearing.

And then they were gone.

~

He was in the crook of a building beside a plot of pavement. He could see objects of metal in the pavement, and he could see in the crook of the building a fire was burning, and that young men and young women were gathered around it. They were laughing and singing songs as one young man strummed a tune on a stringed instrument, as he saw from a keg apple cider being poured, and the song rising up into the evening.

Oh, Reev thought, seeing by a different sight, and perceiving by a different understanding — how blessed were the Telantines, and how blessed was what would become Telantis, before the evil plans of the Sons of Nachash were revealed, and the struggle began.

For he understood, by a different perception, and saw by a different sight, that though Daniel and the man on the moon were Telantines, that at the time of the vision, Telantis was yet to be born. For the flag, of white and red and blue, was not theirs.

~

And Reev was back in Varda. The sun was gone, but a new light had appeared over the hills, a new and glorious dawn, a dawn that would never end.

And at his feet was a serpent, its neck snapped under the sole of his feet. And in view of the light, as it pressed westward, others were coming with its glorious light, and in the wake of the glorious light was a brilliant door.

"Gastreel!" he cried to the one he saw coming.

"Skreek! Neek!" he said to the ones walking through the door.

THE END

Epilogue

In the light of the dawn, the Telantines ruled over Varda.

Under the command of Miles Gloriosus and his successors, the Telantine Empire reigned for more than a thousand years over its possessions. The Empire reigned in peace and justice, under the glory of the Telantines, and its emperors reigned in an unbroken sequence, following the edicts of an advisory Imperial Council. The Empire reigned, and all rebellions ceased, in light of a glorious dawn.

The dawn of the gods, reigning over Varda, brought an end to the rule of Seymus and the anguipeds forever. The gods reigned, and sorrow and grief was no more.

Ambrass and Fortunato had four more children and lived in Galiope, in marital bliss, all their days. Their six children kept them busy, and they would make frequent trips to the Dragonpaw whenever they needed assistance from Glenda.

Balor did not reign over Lamdar, as was assumed, but under the direction of Alondir, King of the Elves, his reign was transferred to the kingdom of the vampires, Nardur, in the far north of Varda. There, the vampires regathered after Seymus's final defeat and the restoration of the Dark Land.

King Alondir of Ríva reigned over the elves in a reborn kingdom of the elves, under the suzerainty of the Emperor of the Telantines, Miles Gloriosus and his successors. His aunt Annenwé proved an able advisor all the days of his reign, although she never lost her love for poetry. Neither she nor her brother Avernathi had joined the elvenking's rebellion, and they lived in peace and joy all their days. Indeed, Avernathi in his time became chief priest.

Cobalt and Asté returned to the land of the elves and spent the remainder of their years frolicking in Lamdar's pastures and drinking from its rivers and streams.

King Alondir, when he came of age, married a human woman from Miles Gloriosus's reborn Empire. And he did not forget the betrayal of the elvenking and his followers.

The elvenking was destroyed with the arrival of the gods' dawn, and so too were his immediate conspirators. Of the elven armies who came to fight the Dark One, about two-thirds remained faithful, and a third joined the elvenking in his rebellion. Among those who were unfaithful and survived, King Alondir's regent punished to a man, executing them in the Dark Land before the ruined Throne of Skulls.

King Alondir's reign over the elves was marked by occasional visits from his father, Fortunato of Ríva, and his wife Ambrass Saida. King Alondir witnessed a minor rebirth of the elves' fortunes, and Danarion under his reign grew greatly in size and in his time, approached the borderlines of the city.

Of the elves who had betrayed the cause of Light, and joined the heresy of the Tannin, almost none of the vampires joined in. Nor did the elves' treaty allies join the heresy of the Tannin, but welcomed the dawn with their whole hearts, and eventually made their way back to their homeland in the eastern parts of Varda, the Kingdom of the Viegs. There, Theudo and his sword-thanes ruled all their days. Rokahn and creatures of darkness, jotunns, who once haunted the mountains in the west of the land of the Viegs vanished with the coming of the dawn, and in Theudo's reign, the harvests never failed to produce their fruit. The wheat crop arrived for the Viegs by the cart, and was never found wanting.

As the vampires returned to Nardur, their homeland, they found they had not lost their curse of bloodthirst, but according to the practices of the righteous vampires before them, they abided by the laws of Dandrinnas, drinking the blood of cows and certain animals, and in the light of the dawn, there were no violators to be found.

Balor, ruling as king of the vampires, reigned from a rebuilt Black Castle and a new Druenel-Hai which expanded with each year, and which never had to endure the pestilence of the Haunted Forest nearby. All signs of the former worship of Seymus, the altars built to sacrifice to him, were demolished, and the curse and all knowledge of the cause of their bloodthirst was eventually forgotten. As the villages and cities of the vampires grew in size, and the population swelled, Balor proved himself an able administrator, in addition to a powerful mage. His abilities as a mage came in handy, however, and his undead servants he used as laborers, as cities expanded and new cities were founded, as prosperity and peace spread from Nardur to far beyond.

Ramona Nax was wed to Nicollo Maiodore all her days. She abided in Sunstone Manor in Gallia, and there hosted innumerable parties and soirees for the Gallian nobility, whose positions of privilege had endured in the wake of the Imperial invasion and did not stop in the reign of Emperor Miles Gloriosus. Indeed, their good fortunes expanded with Galiope, as Galiope grew in size and drew in new citizens from all over the Northern World, as it gained admiration for the part it played in the Last Shadow War.

Ramona Nax's son, Ash, departed in the wake of the dawn, to Imperial City, as he had planned. He was educated, first in Imperial City and then in the east, in the subjects of rhetoric and grammar. An orator in the east taught him well the art of public speaking, and by the time he had reached manhood, he had formed a goal of becoming an Imperial councilor. Position by position, rung by rung, he moved up the ranks from government post to government post. He became well versed in the world of Imperial politics, and was noted for his speaking ability and his eye for public administration by Miles Gloriosus. At the age of thirty-two, he achieved his life goal of becoming an Imperial councilor, and served on the Imperial Council all his days. He married a woman of Imperial descent and had four children. Ramona Nax was a frequent visitor to Imperial

City and Ash Nax's mansion in Imperial City in her later years. She had a habit of claiming that his skill at politics and his crafty political acumen came from her.

The Telantines who had endured since the time of the First Shadow War, or otherwise were awakened to their identity in later years, and participated in the Great War that had been promised to them, forged a kingdom in the Dark Land that grew in size and in population with each passing year. In the restored Dark Land, they plotted fields and grew cities, and their kingdom eventually rivaled the strength of the Telantine emperor ruling from far away.

Pandarus eventually became king of the Telantine Kingdom, which expanded in every direction, up to the border with the Kingdom of the Dwarfs, ruled by Arn Steelforge. And King Arn Steelforge also ruled well, in the Dwarf Kingdom that grew in population with each year and decade, with a peace forged with the ogres on their northern border. In the later years of his reign, Arn signed a peace treaty and a treaty of cooperation with King Pandarus, signed by his seneschal Blarer. Though signs of competition had emerged, all competition and any conflict was immediately ended by the signing of the treaty.

Speaking of Arn Steelforge and the dwarfs, a denizen of their kingdom, Fee Gohn, was joined with his brethren the stone giants in the light of the dawn. When the dawn arrived in Kardir, the spirits of Fee Gohn's wife Ula Nohn and his children returned to their stone bodies. After a few years of confusion, Fee Gohn, his family and the other stone giants reunited in the Dwarf Lands, where they belonged.

But wherever one lived in Varda, whether it was under a king like Alondir or an emperor like Miles Gloriosus, it seemed a Telantine reigned.

What happened to Wrinn? Wrinn and his wife traveled to the land of Lamdar, under the reign of King Alondir, and had a house in the city of Danarion and a cottage in the woods, in view of Mount

Daró. There, they spent all their days, though his wife eventually stopped using the name Shomré and called herself Rosalie. They had ten children. They lived happily ever after — it might sound cliché, but they really did.

Where was Reev in all this time? Well, Reev. That was a bit harder to tell. For the dawn had arrived, and what followed were centuries of prosperity. In actuality, Reev seemed to have vanished, but in truth, he had not. The slaying of Seymus seemed to have killed him, but with the coming of the dawn he had been spirited away to where his ancestors were, in the presence of the gods. He was in Heaven until such time as the distinction between Varda in the light of the dawn and the reign of the gods was to be lost.

When peace and justice were at their height, and prosperity had met its fullness, when the Empire had reigned a thousand years, and the Kingdom of the Telantines in the restored Dark Land was at the height of its strength, when the people of Varda endured days of no strife and all joy, the gods made a triumphant return.

Then, Reev came with them, Reev, Gastreel, Skreek and Neek, Reev's ancestors and all who had passed away in the light of the dawn. All distinction, then, was lost, between Varda in the light of the dawn and the gods' reign. And as all death and grief was then gone, and Seymus had been cast underfoot, and eventually was forgotten, the gods saw fit to institute the completion of the Telantines' hopes.

And the Telantines reigned, under the gods, forever.

Glossary

Times and Dates

Vardic Calendar	Julian Calendar Equivalent
Albos	January
Kaldsil	February
Primrane	March
Tidusca	April
Brenua	May
Aurelios	June
Odens	July
Sextil	August
Harona	September
Brightleaf	October
Anthanos	November
Candlebright	December

Elven phrases

Dra'datsi: "Out-born," an elf born outside the Elven World.

Velati sonoren: "The Prince of the Dawn."

Nonni: "Grandpappy"

Foreign phrases

Qizim: An anguiped.

Mugush-folk: A non-anguiped.

Abollonia: A region of the Dark Land, a center of industry for the Dark One's minions.

Anguiped: A hostile non-human species.

Ash-wing: An undead creature, created spontaneously under certain conditions by a dead anguiped.

Ash-Land: A region north of the Dark Land.

Black wolves: Large, intelligent wolves of the Dragonteeth. They are often captured and forced into the service of rokahn. They are one of the three divisions of great wolves, along with white wolves and brown wolves.

Brown wolves: Large, intelligent wolves who now live among the Viegs. They are noted for their intelligence and great loyalty.

Bane powder: A toxic substance that causes disorientation and confusion, invented by the Oculus.

Cathay: A kingdom in the far east of Varda. It is ruled by a monarch called the Dragon Emperor.

Cathedral District: A large district of Galiope just north of the main gate, Godsgate. It is home to the city's churches and cathedrals.

Cauli: A kingdom in the far east of Varda, under the sphere of influence of Cathay.

Danarion: The capital city of the elves.

Danda: Heaven, the domain of the gods and the gods' followers.

Dark One, the: A name for Seymus, the enemy of the gods, the king of the Abollaren or demons.

Desert of Sinn: A desert west of Cathay.

Dragon: The last of the dragons were believed to have flown west to a lost land beyond the sea. In the past ten years, they began to return to the Dark Land.

Dragon Emperor: The monarch of Cathay. Some consider him the western emperor's eastern counterpart.

Doomblade: One of the original estirion blades, first called Pelladrimas ("Flame of Fire") and wielded by the elven warrior prince Camlon in the First Shadow War. Through many names and owners it eventually made its way into the hands of the human Simeon Nax.

Doomsday: The language of Shadow. Though when spoken, it sounds like formless whispers, the one it is directed towards can always understand it.

Dragonpaw Inn, the: A large inn of Galiope, owned and run by the half-elf Glenda.

Elves: Long-lived beings whose kingdoms and settlements lie in the north of the world. They are divided into several tribes, including the Lamen, the Umen, the Lonen, and the Nurnen. In recent years, the Lamen kingdom lost a war to the Kingdom of Zarubain and untold thousands of elves were brought into forced servitude.

Elvish knight: An elven warrior trained in the art of equestrianship and the wielding of a lance and a sword. They ride on Elvish horses.

Empire, the: A vast state composed of seven provinces, ruled by an emperor and an Imperial Council. It is considered the foremost military power in the world.

Estirion: "Star-iron" is the hardest and sharpest metal known to man. The means of the making of star-iron swords are lost to history; they were said to be forged by Danthelon, the so-called "Wonder-Smith." Only twenty are known to exist; they are considered priceless.

Federati: An elite fighting force of the Empire, tasked with special operations and expeditionary warfare. Originally composed of barbarians, now it is composed of only the finest of the fine soldiers.

Galiope: A large city of the Northern World, called by those that love it the Queen of the North.

Gallia: A region east of Zarubain and west of Kardir, a place of mixed forest and farmland. Its greatest city is Galiope.

Gypsies: A wandering folk who traditionally roamed the world in colorful wagons. In recent years, they were welcomed by the Gallian government and allowed to settle in Galiope.

Imperial: To those outside the Empire, a citizen of the Empire. To those within the Empire, a man or woman originating in the coastal provinces associated with its founding.

Jotunn: A powerful giant directly under the control of the Dark One.

Kanenthas: An elven mage who was said to have battled a host of demons by himself, during the time of the First Shadow War.

Kehrad: The most intelligent species of rokahn, they are thinner built than the other breeds, with angular facial features and often red or green skin. They often become leaders of rokahn war-bands by force of will; however, their smaller size makes them easy targets.

Kheroe: A region in the southwestern corner of the Empire. It is west across the desert from the region of Khazidea and considered to be its counterpart.

Lamdar: The elven heartland, home to the elvenking and the Lamen Elves.

Londor: The easternmost elven kingdom.

Lonen Elves: A tribe of elves known for their atheistic beliefs and their advanced technology in war. They are often black-haired and pale in complexion.

Longknife: A single-edged, sharp knife native to elven metallurgy, used for slashing or piercing.

Market District: A large district of Galiope, north of Middletown, known for its shops, mansions and financial institutions.

Messor: *Sense 1* — The official in charge of the harvest on a manorial estate. *Sense 2* — The Dark One's lieutenant, in charge of the managing of souls imprisoned in the Dark Land.

Middletown: A district in Galiope just north of the River Galios. It is home to many shops and market squares.

Maelstrom, the: A vast whirlpool in the Eastern Ocean. It is the terror of ships across Varda.

Necromancer: A sorcerer with power over death and withering.

Norwood: A small village in the region of Noricum in the Empire, in the province of Gad.

Oculus, the: A secret organization of spies that has operated since before the Empire's founding.

Rokahn: Humanoid creatures known to dwell in the Dragonhorns, considered creatures of shadow. When their population swells, they will often raid the lowlands for food. Breeds include kehrad, toltar, and the standard species simply known as rokahn.

Solgaressi: An elven warrior who lived in the first years of the current era. At a time that rokahn armies were besieging the Elven World, he distinguished himself as a general and a warrior.

Unlife: The magical energy of necromancy when it grants reanimation to a corpse.

Vampire: In Elvish, *druen*—a tribe of elves cursed in ancient times with a thirst for blood.

Viegs: A tribe of humans who swore an ancient treaty of alliance with the elves. They live in the far eastern part of the world, near the Dweorg.

Wildblades: Elven warriors of the Umen tribe who are said to work themselves into controlled rages. They are trained to be ambidextrous and wield scimitars in both hands.

Wizard's staff: An implement of magic that wizards use. Without it, their skill at magic weaving is weakened. The first task a wizard who has achieved full rank undertakes is the fashioning of a staff. They are constructed of crystal and certain types of wood.

APPENDIX 9: A BIOGRAPHY OF VERRUS

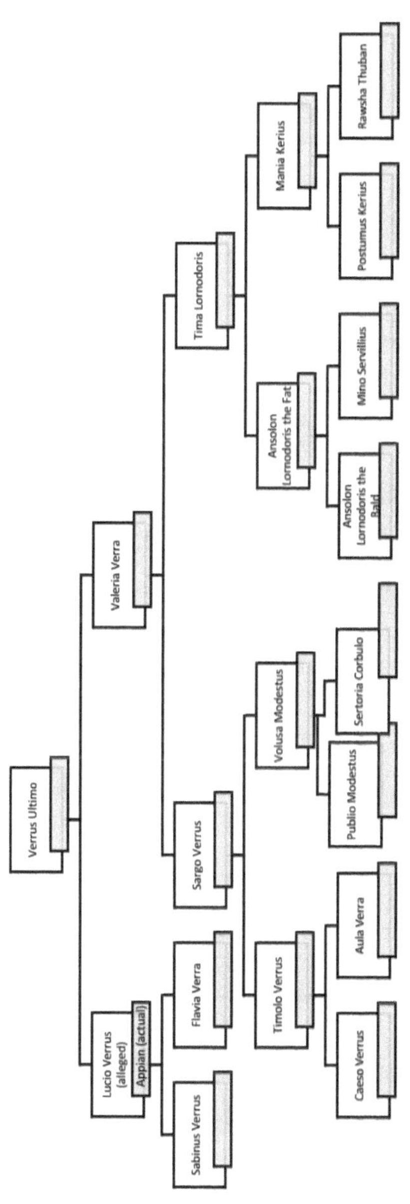

Verrus Ultimo was born in the provinces to Valeria Verra and (ostensibly) Lucio Verrus. His mother, Valeria Verra, was a member of the Empire's uppermost elite, of the August class and of the best pedigree. Verrus Ultimo was born in Thénai, Eloesus Province, and so nicknamed because he was born on the last day of the year — the thirty-first of Candlebright. His ostensible father, Lucio Verrus, was a banker, the Dux of the Venerable Brotherhood of Moneychangers, old by the time he was born.

In truth, during her wedding week, in Imperial City, Valeria Verra had an indiscretion with Appian, Governor of Khazidea and husband of Astarthe. She had hoped that Appian's famous political acumen would be instilled in her firstborn son. Thusly, Verrus Ultimo was conceived.

As a baby, Verrus Ultimo was often left alone and neglected. This treatment continued throughout his childhood.

When Verrus Ultimo was a toddler, Valeria Verra and Lucio Verrus divorced. Valeria Verra soon took up with a legate and Verrus Ultimo and his mother became accustomed to travel in military camps. In the northern campaign against Zarubain, they both came close to war. But fearing the violence, Valeria Verra took her child and they departed. She eventually met and married Marcus Bannius, an Imperial Councilor, moving back to Imperial City, but they divorced when Verrus Ultimo was 13 amid mutual accusations of infidelity.

Valeria Verra and Verrus Ultimo eventually settled in the town of Nichaeus, Valeria Verra having married an elderly housing magnate, Bartis Malchus, whom Verrus Ultimo grew to hate. Valeria Verra has aspired since the time of Verrus Ultimo's birth to have him put on the White Throne and ascend to the emperorship. She hopes to wield power through him.

Verrus Ultimo is a kitharode, and from ages 18 to 25 studied the instrument in the Academies of Eloesus. He is interested in politics but his greatest desire is to be a famed kitharode. He considers the opportunity to play at the New Year's party of Khandaraeus a way to show off his skills, but his mother has other plans.

Verrus has red hair, bright cerulean eyes, and a tall and bulky physique. Verra has dark hair and dark eyes, and at middle age, is stunningly beautiful. Unknown to others, they are members of the anguiped species, by matrilineal descent through her great-grandmother, Rawsha Thuban.

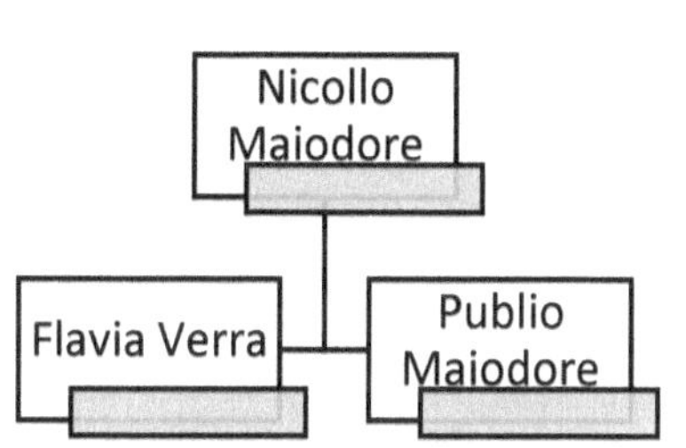

Nicollo Maiodore is a distant ostensible relation to Verrus Ultimo. As his ostensible uncle, Nicollo Maiodore has heard of Verrus but they never met.

About the Author

Cursed at birth with a wild imagination, Andrew Cooper spent his youth dreaming of worlds more exciting than Earth.

He is a graduate of the Odyssey Writing Workshop. His stories have appeared in Morpheus Tales, Fear and Trembling, Residential Aliens and Mindflights, among others.

He is also a graduate of the Creative Writing program at Western Michigan University.

Visit **www.aj-cooper.com** to sign up for the newsletter and stay up-to-date on new releases.

Find him on **x/Twitter** @ajcooperwriter.